Pirates of the Caribbean

From the Magic Kingdom to the Movies

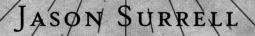

Jason Surrell

Forewords by

Martin A. Sklar and Tom Fitzgerald

A Welcome Book

Disney Editions
New York

This book is for X Atencio, Harriet Burns, Alice Davis, and Blaine Gibson: artists, Imagineers, friends.

And for Ted Elliott and Terry Rossio, whose ghost story made us believe all over again.

The author would also like to thank the following for their contributions to this book: X Atencio, Harriet Burns, Alice Davis, Blaine Gibson, and Dick Nunis; at Disney Editions: Wendy Lefkon and Jody Revenson; at Jerry Bruckheimer Films: KristiAnne Reed; at the Walt Disney Photo Library: Andrea Recendez; at The Walt Disney Archives: Dave Smith and Robert Tieman; at *Pirates of the Caribbean* II & III: Orlando Bloom, Jerry Bruckheimer, Johnny Depp, Ted Elliott, Keira Knightley, Terry Rossio, Geoffrey Rush, Michael Singer, and Gore Verbinski; at Walt Disney Imagineering: Tony Baxter, Patrick Brennan, Denise Brown, Alex Caruthers, Anne Clark, Tom Fitzgerald, Chris Goosman, Bruce Gordon, Jason Grandt, Barbara Hastings, Eric Jacobson, Gary Landrum, Kathy Mangum, Bernie Mosher, Diane Scoglio, Marty Sklar, David Stern, Don Winton, and Alex Wright; at the Walt Disney Studios: Christine Cadena, Dick Cook, Nina Jacobson, and Brigham Taylor. Special thanks for their contributions go to: Lindsay Frick, Jack E. Janzen, Leon J. Janzen, Chris Leps, Kevin Vincent, and Rick West.

The book's producers would also like to thank the following for their assistance: Jess Allen, Stacy Cheregotis, Anne D'Arras, Masayo Enomoto, Julie Enzer, David Fisher, Greg Gujda, Jonathan Heely, Mike Jusko, Chaz McEwan, Betsy Mercer, Mary Mullen, Tracey Ramos, Ed Storin, and Muriel Tebid.

Also by Jason Surrell: *The Haunted Mansion: From the Magic Kingdom to the Movies*, *The Art of the Haunted Mansion*, *Screenplay by Disney*, contributor to *The Imagineering Way* and *The Imagineering Workout*.

Produced by Welcome Enterprises, Inc.
6 West 18th Street, New York, NY 10011.
www.welcomebooks.com

Designed by H. Clark Wakabayashi

PAGE 1: Concept art by Marc Davis. **PAGE 2:** *Rogues' Gallery, Famous Pirates of the Spanish Main* (detail). Concept painting by Bruce Bushman depicting real-life pirates, including the infamous Edward Teach, better known as "Blackbeard," and, in the rear, the two best-known female pirates, Anne Bonny and Mary Read. **THIS SPREAD:** *Buccaneers, Taking a Prize* (detail). Concept painting by Bruce Bushman of a shipboard battle.

For information address:
Disney Editions
114 Fifth Avenue, New York, NY 10011-5690.

Editorial Director: Wendy Lefkon
Senior Editor: Jody Revenson

Library of Congress Cataloging-in-Publication Data:
Surrell, Jason.
Pirates of the Caribbean: from the Magic Kingdom to the movies/by Jason Surrell; forewords by Martin A. Sklar and Tom Fitzgerald.
p. cm.
ISBN 0-7868-5630-0
1. Pirates of the Caribbean (Amusement ride) 2. Pirates of the Caribbean (Motion picture) I. Title.
GV1859.S87 2005
791'.06'8--dc22
2005045554

Printed in Singapore
FIRST EDITION 10 9 8 7 6 5 4 3 2

Contents

Forewords

Dress Rehearsal for One

Pirates of the Caribbean opened at Disneyland in 1967 and became an instant classic. But it's a picture memory from sometime early in 1966, inside a basic warehouse building at WED Enterprises (now Walt Disney Imagineering), that still resonates most strongly with me.

The 1964–1965 New York World's Fair was history; the four Disney shows had conquered the East Coast with Disneyland-style storytelling. Walt Disney had been unofficially crowned "King of the Fair" (*Look* magazine ran the headline: "Walt Disney—GIANT at the Fair"). In typical Disney fashion, Walt had already moved on. "I don't do sequels," he often said. But the lessons from the Fair, and especially from a theater that spun round and round, and a little boat ride called "*it's a small world*," would forever change the world of Disney theme park attractions.

The Carousel of Progress, a Disney show for General Electric, brought human figures created through Disney's Audio-Animatronics system so close to audiences they could almost reach out and shake their hands. Remarkably, these "actors" could deliver the same lines and perform the same actions every four minutes throughout the day!

In "*it's a small world*," thanks to a river of water carrying a seemingly endless procession of 15-passenger boats, more than 3,000 guests per hour could ride through and view up close "the children of the world," singing and dancing minute after minute and hour after hour. And the title song, by Richard M. Sherman and Robert B. Sherman, became the very first "hit" ever to be launched by a theme park attraction.

All of these new "tools" in the Disney creative kit came together as the Imagineers began developing the *new* Pirates adventure. I say "new" because, before the World's Fair changed the course of Disney park history, "Pirates" was being developed as a walk-through attraction. That idea came to an abrupt end with the success—and the lessons—of the World's Fair shows.

That brings us to the warehouse one afternoon in 1965. Design director Dick Irvine had marshaled all the Imagineers to turn Marc Davis's brilliant sketches and Claude Coats's imaginative scenic design of the Auction Scene into a full-size mock-up, complete with Blaine Gibson's sculpted figures, Yale Gracey's special effects, Alice Davis's costumes, Wathel Rogers's and Bill Justice's animation of Roger Broggie's Audio-Animatronics figures, and X Atencio's dialogue and "Yo Ho" song.

John Hench had supervised the building of a wooden "boat," with wooden benches for seating. Rolling across the warehouse floor on wheels, like a tram vehicle, it could be pushed through the scene, at just the right speed to simulate the two feet per second the bateaux would later float along the pirate "river." Everything was in place for a moment never to be seen by the public . . . but forever to be remembered by the dozen or so Imagineers who witnessed it. It was a dress rehearsal for an audience of one: Walter Elias Disney.

And Walt loved it. The man who was seldom demonstrative with his praise in meetings said so, in so many words—he loved it!

Why does this moment stand out as such a vivid memory? Because the man who was so effusive in his enthusiasm for the "prototype scene" in Pirates of the Caribbean would not live to see the real thing completed. Walt passed away in December 1966, a few months before Pirates opened in Disneyland.

Now so many of those talented Imagineers have joined him in that great galaxy in the sky. Surely Walt must know that millions of guests have thrilled to Pirates of the Caribbean in four Disney parks around the world, and millions more have seen the motion picture it inspired.

And the warehouse? It's still there in Glendale, California, where the Walt Disney Imagineers are still conjuring up new magic, because Walt taught us the Disney tradition: you are only as good as your *next* creation. We may look back, but it's only to remember our roots and the lessons of the legendary masters of Walt Disney Imagineering.

—Martin A. Sklar
Vice Chairman and Principal Creative Executive
Walt Disney Imagineering

A Pirate's Life for Me!

Growing up in New York, my introduction to "a pirate's life" was a souvenir map of Disneyland that my father brought home from a business trip to California. It was several years before the attraction would open, but an orange X marked the spot where Pirates of the Caribbean would soon transport Disneyland guests through a swashbuckling adventure. Next came an episode of *The Wonderful World of Color*, where Walt Disney gave a behind-the-scenes preview of the designs and story line for the attraction. Then, in 1967, my father brought back another business-trip souvenir, a vinyl record album of the "story and song" of the now-opened attraction.

By now, you're probably wondering what kind of father would visit Disneyland without bringing the family along! Well, two years later, we finally got that vacation to Southern California, and I was able to experience the Pirates of the Caribbean for real.

You might think the reality of the attraction would have fallen short of the buildup from all those years of waiting. Not a chance! Pirates of the Caribbean was as mind-blowing to me back then as it is today . . . and as it has been for the millions of guests of all ages who've enjoyed this spectacular adventure over the years.

So, what can you say about a show that has been packing them in for decades? What can you say about an attraction that inspired the biggest live-action hit in the history of Walt Disney Pictures and two sequels in production as I write this? All I can say is, that's the magic of Pirates of the Caribbean. It's the magic of Walt Disney and the magic of the Imagineers who created this attraction, and who continue to tell this classic tale around the world.

Why has Pirates of the Caribbean endured? Is it the lovable cast of characters created by Marc Davis and brought to life by Blaine Gibson's sculpture and the magic of Audio-Animatronics? The rich and beautiful costumes of Alice Davis? The immersive settings designed by Claude Coats? The witty script and song penned by writer X Atencio, or the musical underscore of George Bruns? The special effects of Yale Gracey? It is, of course, all of these, and more.

Pirates of the Caribbean represents a milestone in immersive Disney storytelling. Walt and his Imagineers had learned much from their decades of storytelling on the silver screen, Disneyland's first decade of three-dimensional storytelling, and the challenges and breakthroughs discovered while entertaining the masses of the 1964–1965 New York World's Fair. Those lessons enabled Walt and his team to create an adventure of unparalleled scope and artistry that would become (and remain) the "crown jewel" of Disney theme park experiences.

Now, thanks to producer Jerry Bruckheimer, director Gore Verbinski, actors Johnny Depp and Geoffrey Rush, and screenwriters Terry Elliott and Terry Rossio, a new generation around the world is being introduced to the adventures of the Pirates of the Caribbean, and the legacy lives on!

In turn, these films are inspiring a new generation of Imagineers to explore how the new characters and adventures might come to life within our Pirates of the Caribbean attractions. And why not? It turns out that dead men do tell tales, and those tales are as entertaining and enduring as the attraction that inspired them almost forty years ago. "And that be the real treasure!"

—Tom Fitzgerald
Executive Vice President & Senior Creative Executive
Walt Disney Imagineering

Martin A. Sklar (left) and Tom Fitzgerald.

Introduction

DEAD MEN tell no tales . . . until now, that is. For almost forty years the pirates have stuck to their script, but after appearing in E-Ticket attractions at four Disney theme parks around the world and starring in a blockbuster hit film (with the promise of more of both to come), the wildest crew that ever sacked the Spanish Main is ready for their own unique brand of Hollywood tell-all.

Few shows have had the "legs" that Pirates does, sea or otherwise. Only a small number of films and theatrical shows are as beloved and as relevant forty years after their initial release. Pirates of the Caribbean is the quintessential Disney-themed show. It is a triumph for both the group and the process of Walt Disney Imagineering, seamlessly melding storytelling and technology to immerse the audience in an elaborate virtual reality decades before either the concept or the term was in vogue. It is a lavish showcase for the art of Audio-Animatronics, bringing the stars of the show to three-dimensional life in that reality as never before. It is "narrated" by one of the most memorable and hum-worthy songs in Disney history.

One of the hallmarks of Disney storytelling has always been a startling attention to detail, and Pirates of the Caribbean is the premier example of that Imagineering design principle. The experience is sumptuous and simply too vast and complex to take in on one voyage. The audience sees, hears, smells, or feels something new every time they ride on the attraction and that keeps them coming back again and again.

Walt Disney Imagineering, both the practice and the practitioners, was born of the film industry, and Pirates of the Caribbean itself was inspired in part by such legendary Hollywood epics as *Captain Blood* and Disney's own *Treasure Island*. So it should come as no surprise that this timeless theme park adventure would prove just as worthy of cinematic adaptation as any classic novel, Broadway musical, TV show, or even comic book. *Pirates of the Caribbean: The Curse of the Black Pearl*, soon to be joined by two sequels to make a swashbuckling adventure trilogy, may have been perceived by critics as an exercise in corporate synergy in the adaptation of an "amusement park ride." But the colorful characters, atmospheric environments, and daredevil situations were rich source material for an old-school Hollywood swashbuckler with a twenty-first-century edge and sensibility. Using the Disneyland original as a jumping-off point, producer Jerry Bruckheimer, director Gore Verbinski, and screenwriters Ted Elliott and Terry Rossio, with Johnny Depp behind the captain's wheel, produced the third-biggest hit of 2003, launching a film franchise, and creating a cultural touchstone in the process. They also won millions of *new* Pirates of the Caribbean fans around the globe, helping guarantee the continued success and relevance of the attraction for generations to come.

This is the story of Pirates of the Caribbean's forty-year voyage from the Magic Kingdom to the movies and back again, and a celebration of the "rascals, scoundrels, villains, and knaves" who sacked the Spanish Main, both onstage and off, on-screen and off. And, like the attractions and films themselves, it's quite a ride, an E-Ticket adventure that you won't soon forget.

So . . . ye comes seeking adventure and salty old pirates, aye? Sure, ye've come to the proper place. But keep a weather eye open, mates, and hold on tight . . . with both hands if you please. There be squalls ahead. And Davy Jones waiting for them what don't obey . . .

OPPOSITE: Marc Davis concept sketch (1965) of the Auctioneer, one of the most popular characters in the attraction.

Course Heading

Disneyland
and the Magic Kingdoms

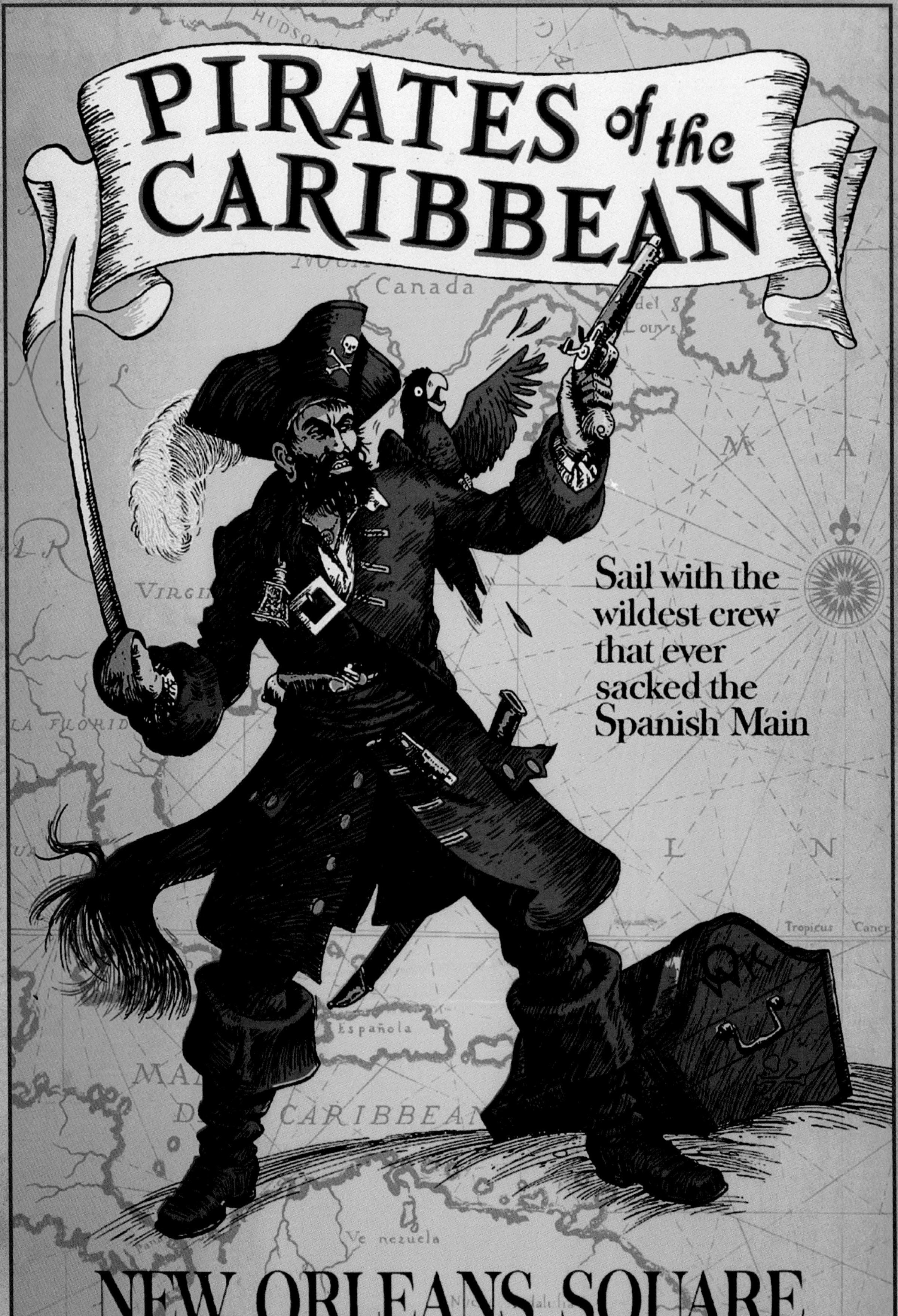
PIRATES of the CARIBBEAN
Canada
Sail with the wildest crew that ever sacked the Spanish Main
Española
CARIBBEAN
Venezuela
NEW ORLEANS SQUARE
© WALT DISNEY PRODUCTIONS

Charting a Course for Adventure

The Busiest Place on Earth

WALT DISNEY would forever refer to Opening Day at Disneyland as "Black Sunday." Projected attendance of 10,000 swelled to over 30,000 due to a counterfeit-ticket scheme. Many of the innovative, complex ride systems broke down, and a gas leak closed Fantasyland for much of the day. The Rivers of America crept across the decks of the *Mark Twain* as hordes of guests overran the riverboat's capacity. The Park ran out of food and drinks almost as quickly as its guests ran out of patience. Only one thing was certain: this Magic Kingdom on 160 acres of former orange grove in Anaheim had come a long way from the eleven-acre "Mickey Mouse Park" Walt had initially planned to build across from his Burbank studio.

Walt took Disneyland's disastrous premiere in stride. Like "Steamboat Willie," *Snow White and the Seven Dwarfs*, and *Fantasia* before it, Disneyland was something completely new and original, and he recognized this, enduring the slings and arrows of critics with good humor as he pushed to make his latest and grandest dream a reality. Attractions went down because no one had ever tried to transport people in flying pirate ships suspended from an overhead track before, or attempted to run a consistent show over and over again by employing a cast of mechanical—but sometimes just as stubborn—jungle animals.

Early on in Disneyland's planning, Walt realized that conventional architects and conventional thinking were not going to cut it—he knew he was going to need a full-time staff of creative artists and designers from his movie studio to make his dream a reality. And so, on December 16, 1952, Walt founded Walt Disney, Incorporated—quickly renamed WED Enterprises (for Walter Elias Disney; the group was renamed once again, as Walt Disney Imagineering, in 1986)—to design and build Disneyland. "We're always exploring and experimenting," Walt said of WED. "We call it Imagineering, the blending of creative imagination with technical know-how."

Among WED's earliest recruits were art director Ken Anderson, who had made significant contributions to the Silly Symphonies *The Goddess of Spring* and *Three Orphan Kittens* as well as *Snow White and the Seven Dwarfs*; and production designer Harper Goff, a veteran of such classic films as *Captain Blood*, *The Adventures of Robin Hood*, and *Casablanca*. Ken had been working with Walt on Mickey Mouse Park since 1948, and both men on other precursors to Disneyland since 1951, a full year before the formal inception of WED.

In 1953, former 20th Century Fox art directors Marvin Davis, Richard Irvine, Bill Martin, and Herb Ryman joined Ken and Harper at WED to collaborate and expand on the design and planning of Disneyland. They were followed in 1954 by another Fox art department expatriate, Sam McKim, and John Hench, a versatile creative talent who had first signed on with the Disney studio as a story sketch artist on *Fantasia* in 1939.

Walt saw the Park as a unique opportunity to tell stories in three dimensions instead of two. These first Imagineers all came from the motion picture industry, and they applied the art and craft of filmmaking to the emerging concept of the theme park, looking to Disney's animated and live-action features as source material and storyboarding the new rides and attractions as they would a motion picture. Walt even "performed" the rides from start to finish, just as he used to act out the plots of cartoon shorts and features for his artists. A new art form was born.

While a calamity-fraught opening day may have deprived Disneyland of the title "overnight success," the Park nevertheless proved to be an unqualified victory as Walt and his theme park pioneers worked out all the bugs. In the first seven weeks, more than a million people passed through the turnstiles, exceeding attendance projections by 50 percent, and

OPPOSITE: Pirates of the Caribbean attraction poster, designed by Marc Davis. **PAGES 10-11:** Marc Davis concept painting depicting a densely populated tavern scene in an early walk-through version of the attraction.

spending 30 percent more money than expected while they were there. Unlike many of Walt's earlier, risky experiments in unproven forms of entertainment (with the obvious exception of *Snow White*), Disneyland was an artistic and commercial triumph. And that could mean only one thing: Disneyland would have to grow rapidly to meet an already overwhelming demand.

First Additions

Walt made additions and enhancements to his Magic Kingdom almost immediately, addressing the Park's vital capacity issues as well as his own ongoing creative concerns and perpetual desire to "plus," or add to, the guest experience. Any expansion projects had to be carefully considered to ensure that they would enhance the Disneyland experience without taking away from what was already there. "When we add a new element to this system, we have to consider very carefully what the facility is and what it will do to round out a guest's day," Imagineering Legend John Hench said in a 1984 episode of *Disney Family Album*. "It's got to be a new experience, but it's got to fit in harmoniously with the others that are here."

Walt embarked on the most ambitious expansion of Disneyland in 1959, when he commissioned three major attractions for the east side of the park. The majestic Matterhorn rose from a previously unoccupied wooded area along the Fantasyland-Tomorrowland border and its roller-coaster-style bobsled run was Disneyland's first bona fide thrill ride. The perpetually underdeveloped Tomorrowland also received a much-needed infusion of life with two new additions featuring innovative ride systems: the Submarine Voyage and the Disneyland-Alweg Monorail System. The Imagineers were more than living up to their name, employing—and in many cases creating—cutting-edge technology to tell all the unique, experiential stories Walt was envisioning for his audience.

Westward Ho!

Even though Disneyland's east side was the focus of Walt's attention in 1959, he never lost sight of his kingdom's "westward expansion," which meant new attractions for Adventureland and Frontierland. In addition to Tom Sawyer Island and the *Columbia*, Walt continued his foray into the wild frontier with an authentic Indian Village and the Rainbow Caverns Mine Train, a railroad ride through rocky desert landscapes and a network of caves filled with colorful waterfalls.

One of his nagging concerns was a patch of unspoiled wilderness at the bend in the Rivers of America. At the time, the southwest corner of

OPPOSITE: Sam McKim concept sketch of a New Orleans–themed subset of Frontierland slated for the barren land at that bend in the Rivers of America, an area that would go on to become a "land" unto itself, New Orleans Square. **BELOW:** Rare 1954 Herb Ryman concept sketch of a sinister buccaneer underworld, first proposed for a New Orleans–themed subset of Adventureland, or, as it is labeled in the sketch below, "True Life Land" (derived from Walt Disney's series of True-Life Adventure films). The sketch indicates that Walt Disney's interest in some kind of pirate experience for Disneyland pre-dates the opening of the Park.

Frontierland was occupied by Magnolia Park, a quiet, restful spot filled with shade trees, park benches, and a quaint bandstand. The park was located between Frontierland and Adventureland, providing a smooth transition between the two geographically and thematically diverse areas. Walt planned to use Magnolia Park and the surrounding river-bend site for the proposed expansion.

At one point, Walt assigned John Hench and WED art director Bill Martin to work with Tommy Walker, Disneyland's first director of entertainment, to develop the area, which he wanted to be reminiscent of New Orleans' French Quarter, with a collection of shops, "dining under the stars," and a bandstand featuring live music. In an ominous hint of adventures to come, a beached pirate ship, with treasure chests overflowing with gold and jewels and loot scattered around the remnants of a sea battle, lent a distinct pirate overlay to the area. In fact, one of the first renderings of just such a New Orleans–themed area (then envisioned as a subset of Adventureland, or "True Life Land," as it is labeled on the drawing) pre-dates the opening of the Park with Herb Ryman's 1954 concept sketch depicting a "Pirate Shack" and "Bluebeard's Den." But nothing came of those early creative endeavors.

Walt later spoke to his vision for that prime piece of riverfront real estate: "Disneyland has always had a big river and a Mississippi sternwheeler. It seemed appropriate to create a new attraction at the bend of the river. And so, New Orleans Square came into being—a New Orleans of a century ago when she was the Gay Paree of the American frontier. . . . From the lacy iron grillwork of its balconies to the sound of a Dixieland jazz band and the sight of the majestic riverboat *Mark Twain* steaming 'round the bend at the foot of Royal Street, New Orleans Square recalls her namesake, the fabled 'Queen of the Delta,' as it was a century ago when cotton was king and the steamboat ruled the Mississippi."

The Old South had always had a major design influence on that side of Frontierland. Elegant, wrought-iron balconies graced the second floor of Aunt Jemima's Kitchen (later known as the River Belle Terrace, Walt's favorite restaurant). The Swift Chicken Plantation Restaurant, which sat further west on the banks of the Rivers of America, was housed in a plantation-style mansion and served another hallmark of the region—fried chicken.

The planning of New Orleans Square began in earnest in 1957, when Sam McKim created the first general view of the entire area. Walt revealed his

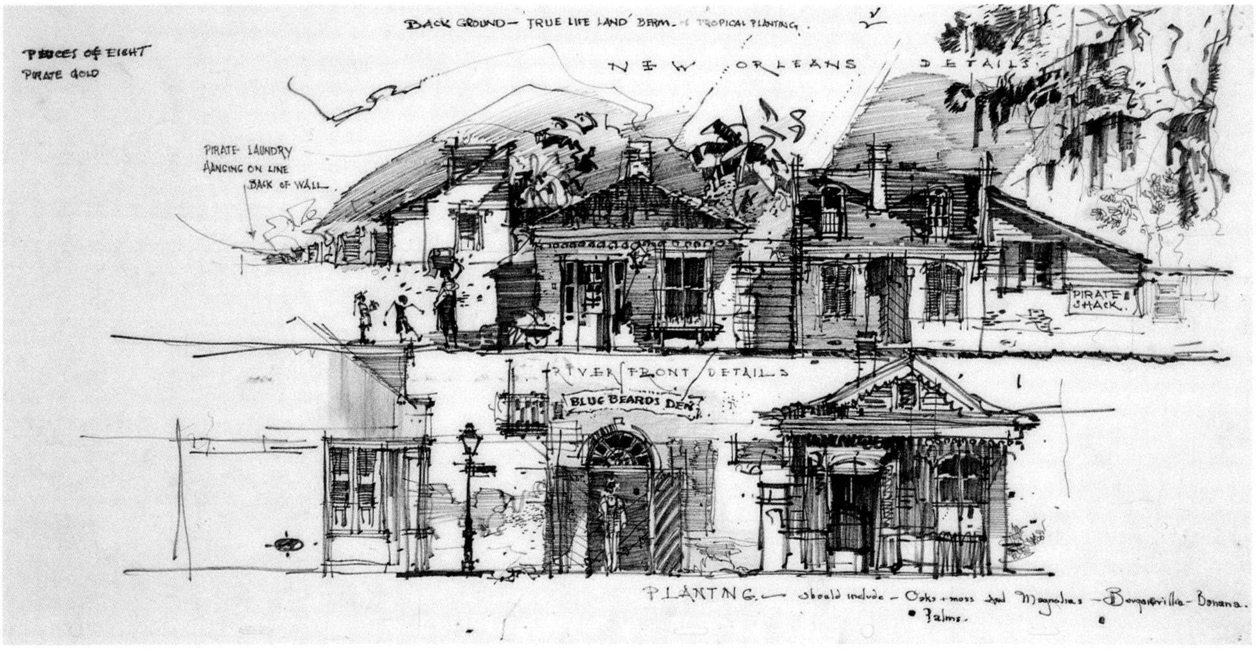

LEFT: Sam McKim created this 1957 general view of the proposed New Orleans Square. The "Haunted House" is visible in the top left corner of the rendering; the Pirate Wax Museum would be located in the basement of the multi-use show building seen in the center of the new area. The Swift Chicken Plantation Restaurant can be seen at the bottom of the rendering, on the banks of the Rivers of America. **BELOW:** Imagineer Marc Davis at his drawing table, working on show concepts for Pirates of the Caribbean.

future plans to the public the very next year in 1958, when New Orleans Square appeared as a district of Frontierland on the first Disneyland souvenir map—which had also been drawn by Sam McKim. The concept had become much better defined since Herb Ryman's 1954 sketch and the early riverfront development abandoned by John Hench and Bill Martin. In addition to the existing Swift Chicken Plantation Restaurant, guests could soon expect to find a Thieves' Market, a Wax Museum, and in the heart of New Orleans Square, a Haunted House. But despite all the recent progress, the plans for New Orleans Square were about to change yet again thanks to Imagineering's newest recruit and a wild jungle.

There's Something Funny Going on at Disneyland

In 1961, master animator Marc Davis was between assignments. Marc had been with Walt since 1935, when he signed on as an apprentice animator on *Snow White*. He was considered one of the studio's top character designers and story men—one of Walt's legendary "Nine Old Men" of animation. In 1961, Marc was enjoying his latest artistic triumph, the ultimate Disney villainess Cruella DeVil in *One Hundred and One Dalmatians*. After creating some concept sketches for *Chanticleer*, a feature that was ultimately abandoned, Marc wasn't sure what the future at Disney held for him. He had no idea that he was about to take his craft into the three-dimensional realm.

With the Studio's next animated feature, *The Sword in the Stone*, already well underway, Walt asked Marc to go down to Disneyland and take a "good, hard, critical look" at the Mine Train Through Nature's Wonderland (a major enhancement of the former Rainbow Caverns Mine Train). "See what you think about this thing," Walt said. Marc dutifully made the trip to Anaheim and, as it turned out, he didn't think much of it at all.

"At this time," Marc told animation historian John Canemaker, "the people down at Disneyland were not very happy about the people that Walt sent from the Studio. They seemed very jealous of us and it was like, 'Oh boy, here we go again.'" But Walt had asked him for an honest assessment, so he "looked around and thought there was an awful lot of things wrong with some of the attractions."

In fact, Marc was so disenchanted with Nature's Wonderland that he took the original designs home and redrew the entire attraction, which did nothing to further endear him to his corporate cousins in Anaheim. Each passenger "had two seats on each side of them, and when you sat down, you were staring at three strangers opposite you. Well, people don't like to ride like that." So he redesigned the cars to make them more guest-friendly and then turned his attention to the show's cast of animated bears, beavers, foxes, and other animal stars inspired by Walt's *True-Life Adventure* series. "They had no gags in it, no story at all," Marc recalled to John Canemaker. "One kit fox's head is going up and down, then about a hundred feet away another kit fox's head is going left to right, so I took the two, put them nose to nose, so one is going up and down, the other moves side to side. So immediately, you have humor!"

Not long after Marc's fateful trip to Disneyland, Walt asked him if he thought there was anything they could do to improve the guest experience. "Oh yeah,

I got a lot of ideas," Marc told the boss, explaining that he had made about forty drawings of "how I thought the whole thing ought to look."

"Where are those drawings?" Walt asked. "I've just spent $50,000 on that ride!" Walt called a meeting of his entire Imagineering team. He ordered Marc to take his sketches to the room WED occupied at the Studio and pitch his ideas.

ABOVE: This Marc Davis rendering (1967) of a swashbuckling shipboard battle was featured on the cover of the original Pirates of the Caribbean souvenir book. **BELOW:** This 1962 Marc Davis rendering depicts pirates poring over a treasure map as all sorts of action unfolds around them. This complex show scene was created for the walk-through attraction, but lacked the instant communication required by a ride-through experience.

"Everyone who was important was there, and here I am, a stranger from animation," Marc told Canemaker. "So I stood up and I started explaining piece by piece." His knowledge of human and animal anatomy quickly became obvious, turning the pitch into an impromptu art class. Walt was every bit as captivated as his fellow Imagineers. "He was buying everything I had done," Marc said, "and was quite intrigued with it." In an article for *Disney News*, Marc added, "Walt liked the idea of the storytelling tableaux. But he said, 'You can't tell a story from beginning to end with a climax, as in a film, if you're moving.'"

Walt was so enamored of Marc's take on three-dimensional storytelling and flair for sight gags that he began giving the rookie Imagineer an ever-increasing number of Disneyland assignments. This alarmed some of the pencil pushers who were still smarting from Davis's costly assessment of Nature's Wonderland. "There were a lot of guys there kind of hoping you would fall on your head." Marc gave an example to John Canemaker about a WED executive who once walked by his desk and sneered, "And what are you doing with your little pencil now?"

One of Marc's first big assignments would prove to have serious consequences for the still-evolving New Orleans Square concept and, as a result, the proposed Haunted House and Pirate Wax Museum. It started when Walt happened to overhear a guest dismiss the Jungle Cruise by saying, "I've already seen it." Walt was not about to allow

Adventureland's signature attraction to take early retirement. To him, Disneyland was a living, breathing thing that Walt could "plus" whenever he wanted, so he quickly decided to add a series of new show elements to the attraction.

Marc designed several new and decidedly humorous scenes for the Jungle Cruise that debuted in 1962, including a trunk-in-cheek detour through the sacred bathing pool of the Indian elephant and a trapped safari that seemed to be getting more than the usual point to traveling. The enhancements took the Jungle Cruise away from its realistic, *True-Life Adventure* roots and moved it in a more whimsical direction. Building upon the work he had begun on Nature's Wonderland, Marc's unique style of Imagineering began to emerge—simple stories that were tableaux-driven by strong, well-defined characters, and broad, visual humor the audience could easily read. "When I went down to Disneyland for the first time, I felt from the very beginning that there was very little that was entertaining or funny to me," Marc explained to *The E-Ticket* in 1999. "My designs were some of the first laughs found in any attraction at the Park. After all, people go down to Disneyland to be amused, not to be educated. That was my feeling. You want to take your family down there and have some fun and be entertained, and humor doesn't hurt anybody." *That's* what he had been doing with his "little pencil."

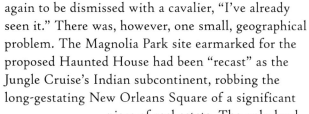

A New Spin

The new additions to the Jungle Cruise were an immediate hit with guests and helped turn the opening day attraction into a perennial favorite, never again to be dismissed with a cavalier, "I've already seen it." There was, however, one small, geographical problem. The Magnolia Park site earmarked for the proposed Haunted House had been "recast" as the Jungle Cruise's Indian subcontinent, robbing the long-gestating New Orleans Square of a significant piece of real estate. The only land left was an unwieldy, horseshoe-shaped section that wasn't big enough to accommodate all of Walt's ideas for the new area.

Walt ultimately decided to "spin off" New Orleans Square into a land all its own, extending its northern border even further to make room for the displaced Haunted House. The loss of Magnolia Park was just as well because, in typical Disney fashion, Walt's plans for New Orleans Square just kept getting more elaborate and he would need the extra room.

The plans for Disneyland's first new themed land since its opening consisted of a series of facades masking an enormous building that housed the Blue Bayou Mart. Inside this enclosed, climate- and light-controlled show building, Imagineers would create a perpetual breezy summer night in the Deep South. The space would be home to the previously announced Thieves' Market shopping district, an elegant restaurant on the veranda of a graceful plantation house overlooking a moonlit bayou, and, far below in the building's dimly lit basement, a walk-through Rogues' Gallery wax museum

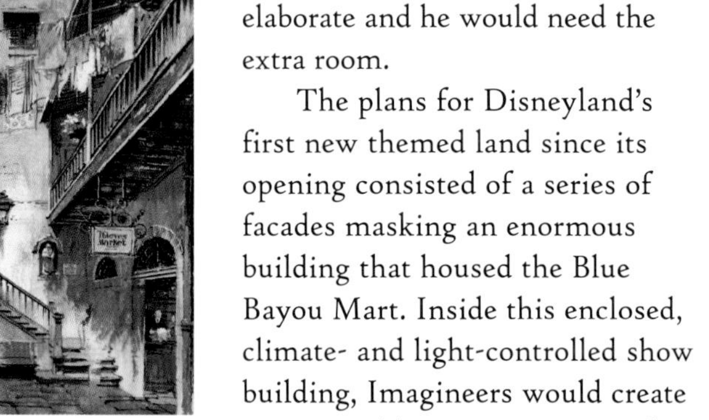

TOP: One of many concepts of the entrance to the walk-through Pirate Wax Museum. **ABOVE:** 1964 Herb Ryman concept painting of the long-proposed Thieves' Market for New Orleans Square. **RIGHT:** Imagineer Sam McKim at work on show concepts for the then-titled Rogues' Gallery.

a

602-21?916

081-POS-?-03-1734557
Time 02:24 PM
Reg?ter POS-081-03

	Description	Amount
	Books	$3.29
93	Books	$2.29
3290	Books	$3.29
002294	Books	$2.29

	$11.16
ment Terminal	$11.16
merican Exp	
*********5008	

Total Money Saved
$0.00

Thank you for shopping at Goodwill and helping us end poverty through the power of work.

Our Return Policy has changed

Goodwill accepts returns within 7 days of purchase. Customers will receive an in-store credit valid for 1 year from original purchase date. Returns must include purchase receipt and original Goodwill tag attached. Customers returning items without purchase receipt or tag attached will receive the last known discount amount of $1. We apologize, no discounts or returns on new or seasonal merchandise.

Complaints or concerns? Please call Goodwill's Customer Care Line: 1-877-200-8500

081-03135324026398

iller & Northern Arizon
Al accept donations!

St
3 Route 152 Phon
AZ

sactio
/2024
ployee 22

Item Code

20146870290
2014687022
2014687000
2014686

Tota
Pa
**

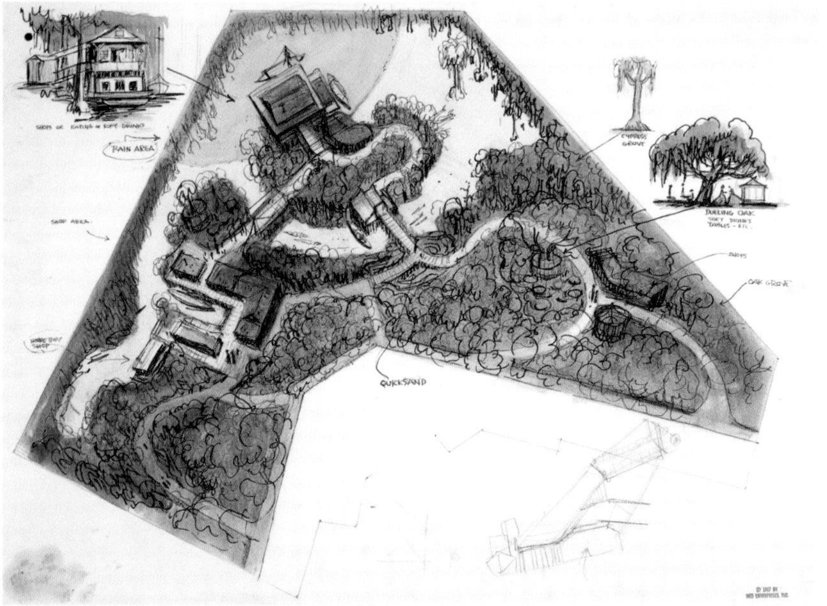

ABOVE: View by Marc Davis (circa 1962-1963) of the proposed Blue Bayou Mart. This space was much larger than the resulting Blue Bayou Restaurant, with areas earmarked for shopping, dining, and snack and soft drink vendors. This elaborate, immersive environment even featured rain and "quicksand" effects. **ABOVE RIGHT:** Herb Ryman on a research trip to the Caribbean. **BELOW:** Herb Ryman concept sketch of a shadowy pirate underworld.

devoted to eighteenth-century pirate history. The Haunted House, meanwhile, was moved northwest near the site of the Swift Chicken Plantation Restaurant.

Although a number of designers, including Sam McKim, Duane Alt, and Dorothea Redmond, contributed to the project throughout the first half of the 1960s, the evocative look of New Orleans Square was largely established by Herb Ryman. Like many of the first Imagineers, Herb was an industry veteran who had worked as an MGM studio artist on such films as *A Tale of Two Cities* and *The Good Earth* and went on to work for the Disney Studio as a sketch and background artist on animated features, including *Pinocchio* and *Dumbo*, as well as to draw the first schematic aerial view of Disneyland in a stunning forty-eight hours.

The Imagineers had been working on New Orleans Square on and off since 1954 when Herb drew a number of sketches depicting life in the old French Quarter and in a sinister pirates' stronghold. His reflections on the origins of New Orleans Square and his own contributions to the project are recounted in a book celebrating his life and work, *A Brush with Disney: An Artist's Journey*: "Walt was making his customary rounds early one morning, having just come from the offices of John Hench and Bill Martin. 'Well, Herbie, I guess you guys have dropped the ball with the New Orleans Square.' I said I had some ideas, I knew how New Orleans ought to look, I knew how it ought to be, but it was

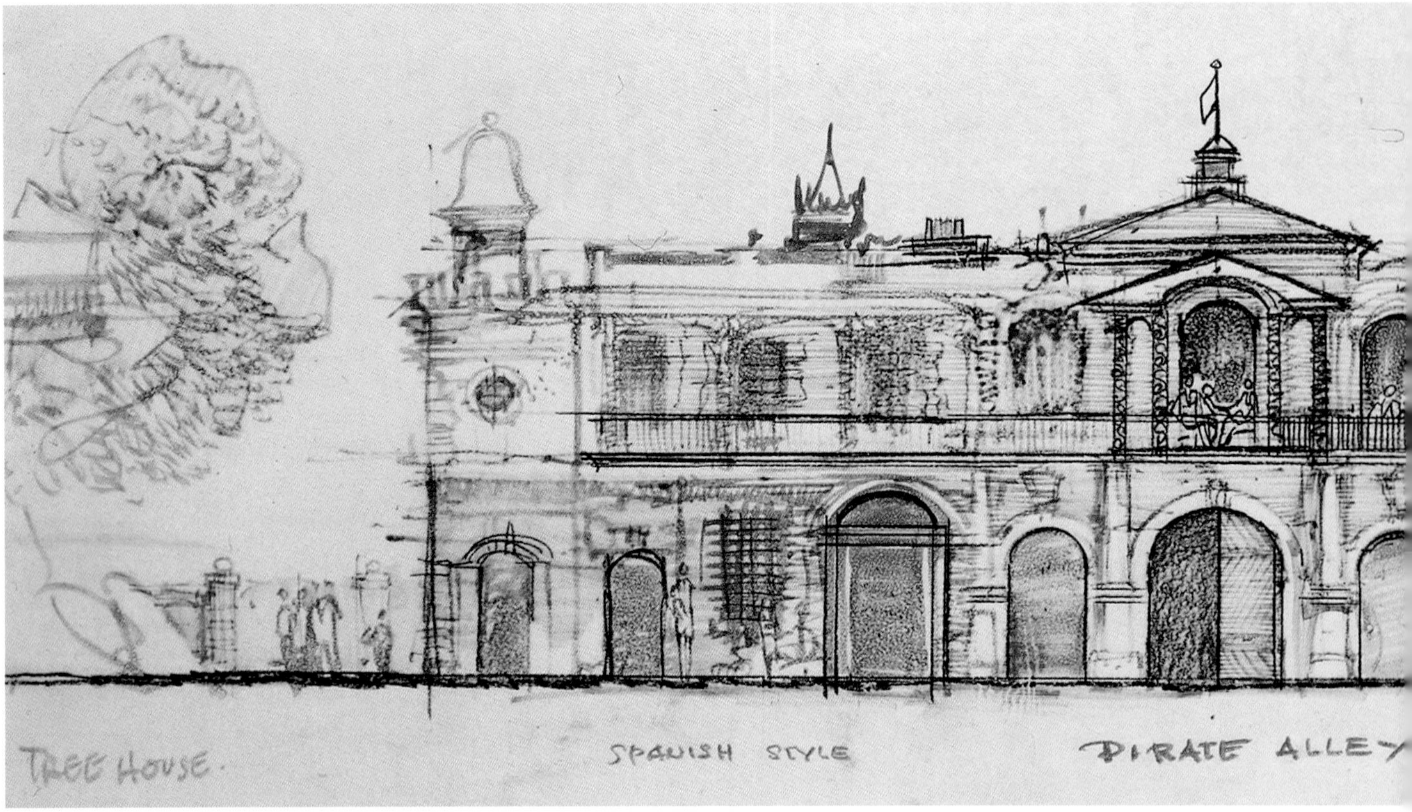

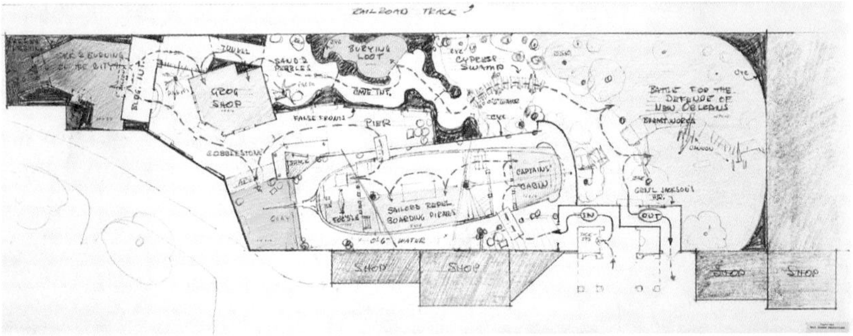

ABOVE: This 1963 Herb Ryman rendering of a "Pirate Alley" illustrates the transition between the Swiss Family Treehouse and the wilds of Adventureland on one side (hence the inclusion of the Delta City's Spanish style) and the graceful, wrought-iron French Quarter on the other. **LEFT:** The first plan view, created circa 1958, of the proposed walk-through Pirate Wax Museum.

not my project. Walt's response was, 'It is now, do anything you wish. I'm coming back at noon tomorrow and I want my Square.'

"Evidently, Walt was pleased with what he saw that next day. I had split the three walls open into three facades. I believed that the winding streets curving out of view would arouse people's curiosity and invite them in to explore."

In his plan, Herb took the largely front-facing facades of the main show building and ancillary structures seen in Sam McKim's 1957 general view, broke them up, and manipulated them into more of a "neighborhood," creating a much more intimate setting and a delightful sense of place for New Orleans Square. Guests could virtually disappear down quaint side streets that would seemingly transport them hundreds of years and thousands of miles away from the hustle and bustle of Disneyland.

Herb's concept sketches and paintings of New Orleans Square are among the most evocative ever created for a Disney park. That had much to do with his painstaking research and meticulous attention to detail. His renderings are filled with story-defining hallmarks of the region and period. "We made many trips to New Orleans in order to get inspiration," Herb recalled on an episode of The Disney Channel's *Disney Family Album* in the mid-1980s. The Sisters of Charity depicted in his sketch "are a ubiquitous part of the scene in New Orleans. I always think that if I can put something in that really belongs there, people will be deceived into thinking I knew what I was doing."

Walt imposed certain limits on reality, however. Just as he had replicated an idealized version of the Main Street of his childhood in Marceline, Missouri, Walt wanted to present a more romantic

and layout of New Orleans Square, other Imagineers focused on the interiors of the various show spaces. Art director and interior designer Dorothea Redmond joined WED in October 1964. Another Hollywood veteran, Dorothea worked with legendary producer David O. Selznick and contributed to the set designs for *Gone with the Wind* and Alfred Hitchcock's *Rebecca*; she later worked on *The Road to Bali* with Bob Hope and Bing Crosby, and on Hitchcock's *Rear Window*.

From fabrics and fixtures to wall coverings and carpeting, Dorothea made sure that the interiors were every bit as rich and detailed as the exteriors Herb was envisioning. She had an intuitive sense of ambience that she was able to capture impeccably in her compositions, especially in the medium of watercolor, which was her preference as well as her specialty. The striking interior design work Dorothea was doing on New Orleans Square's shops and restaurants earned her an even more exclusive assignment: Walt personally commissioned her to decorate a private apartment in which he and his brother, Roy, could entertain business associates and foreign dignitaries. This luxurious suite of rooms, complete with private courtyard, was on the top floor of one of the two main show buildings. The appropriately named Royal Suite's wrought-iron balconies overlooked the streets of New Orleans Square and offered breathtaking views of the Rivers of America. These rooms have since been converted into The Disney Gallery.

In addition to Herb Ryman's new layout of the land, the various show components of New Orleans Square evolved significantly since their first appearance on that souvenir map in 1958. The expansive Blue Bayou Mart became simply the Blue Bayou, a full-service restaurant set on the veranda of an antebellum plantation house that looked out over a moonlit Louisiana bayou. The previously indoor Thieves' Market turned into an outdoor district of shops and boutiques nestled among the winding streets and back alleys, and included everything from a one-of-a-kind antiques shop to a

interpretation of the Big Easy. "Walt would never let us show any sign of aging," Herb Ryman stated. "He said, 'No, I don't want it to look old.' And I said, well, New Orleans is old; it's been there for hundreds of years. And he said, 'I want this to look clean, and the paint is fresh, just like the day it was built.'"

Walt and his Imagineers ultimately split the difference on the aging issue, realizing that a certain amount of "distress" was what gave New Orleans its appeal and sense of romance. So unlike the pristine facades of its Midwestern neighbor, Main Street, U.S.A., the color styling incorporated tonally reserved hues with a wash of "aging" over the fresh paint to obtain the true feel of "Old" New Orleans. This creative compromise wound up contributing greatly to the charm and romance of New Orleans Square.

While Herb Ryman worked on the overall look

LEFT: Dorothea Redmond concept painting of the Disney family's private apartment above Pirates of the Caribbean, a space that has since become The Disney Gallery.

LEFT: Dorothea Redmond's striking watercolor concept painting of The Blue Bayou Restaurant. This romantic and haunting "exterior," housed completely within a show building, is like an elaborate, permanent film set and inspired her fellow Imagineers to faithfully realize the space almost exactly as she had envisioned it. **BELOW:** Marc Davis concept sketch that illustrates how a walk-through attraction might have worked. A "star" figure would tell a pirate story in the foreground as the action is illuminated in the background.

perfumery. The Haunted House was upgraded to a Haunted Mansion, and it sat on a slight rise overlooking the Rivers of America. The Rogues' Gallery was now dubbed the Pirate Wax Museum.

After seven years of on-again, off-again design and development, construction on New Orleans Square finally began in 1961. The newly renamed Haunted Mansion's facade was completed two years later. The rest of New Orleans Square didn't fare quite as well. As of 1963, Walt's version of the Delta City consisted only of an enormous basement—the future home of the Pirate Wax Museum—filled with beams of structural steel and other building materials, and surrounded by a high wooden construction fence. The site was an endless source of fascination and discussion for anxious kids spying from high atop the Swiss Family Treehouse throughout the mid-1960s.

House of Wax

AMONG THE assignments Walt gave Marc Davis when he first came to WED in 1961 was the wax museum in the basement of what was then still the Blue Bayou Mart, an attraction that had been in a more active state of development since 1958, when the first rough site plan was created. Marc designed a second, more detailed view of the Pirate Wax Museum in the early 1960s, shortly after he began working for WED.

The walk-through attraction would showcase the dark side of the Delta City, long known as a land of pirates, vampires, and voodoo, undoubtedly influenced by Madame Tussaud's Wax Museum and its infamous Chamber of Horrors in London. If Fantasyland represented the fairy tale dreams of children everywhere, then New Orleans Square, between The Haunted Mansion and the Pirate Wax Museum, was rapidly shaping up to be a shadowy realm of nightmares, home of Disney's dark side.

In an interview with *Theme Park Adventure*, Marc recalled his first meeting with Walt on the wax museum project: "When I was at WED, Walt came to me and said, 'Marc, you know, there's something I'd like to do. I'd like to do an attraction on pirates.' And he said, 'You know, maybe pirates of the Caribbean.' In that moment, he named it!" Walt may have serendipitously come up with a name for the attraction, but he had only a vague notion of what he

RIGHT: Marc Davis created this plan view of a walk-through experience, circa 1962, shortly after he began working on the attraction. The dotted line represents the route guests would take through the show building. **BELOW:** Concept art by Marc Davis. The caption reads "Enlisting a pirate crew—'FORMAL INVITATION.'"

wanted the experience to be and left much of the show's direction to his newest Imagineer.

"At first, Walt thought it should be a walk-through underneath New Orleans Square," Marc told *The E-Ticket*, "but I think Walt was still trying to find ways to go. They were excavating at that time, and I went to work on designs and ideas for a walk-through attraction." And so Marc went to work on "Monsieur Disney's" Wax Museum.

This would be no ordinary wax museum, however, with figures passively displayed on pedestals. In true Disney fashion, guests would walk through immersive environments and would be transported back to the eighteenth-century Caribbean islands. One of Marc's early general views of the attraction depicts a pathway winding through a series of elaborate tableaux, including a rough-and-tumble tavern, a cobblestoned town square, a burning seaport, shadowy grottoes, a beachfront treasure hunt, and an anchored pirate galleon. The pirates themselves would be displayed in dynamic poses doing what they do best—the raucous pursuit of rum, women, and loot on land and at sea. Since its inception and in all following incarnations, the attraction would be about a crew of pirates ransacking a Caribbean seaport in search of a hidden or cursed treasure.

In one of the earliest walk-through versions of the show, a guide would lead fifty to seventy guests at a time through six or so different vignettes, telling the story depicted in each scene. The Disneyland operations team quickly concluded that it would be difficult to retain the attention of such a large group and decided to let guests gather on their own and then begin the spiel. Such a scenario caused the operators significant concerns about the potential capacity as well as the operational efficiency of the attraction, leading to a walk-through versus ride-through debate with WED that would last for years.

At one point in the attraction's development, Walt realized that his newly dubbed Pirates of the Caribbean should possess at least the same capacity for movement as the animal stars of the Jungle Cruise and the Mine Train Through Nature's Wonderland. That notion would gain even further momentum after the premiere of the first full-fledged Audio-Animatronics show, The Enchanted Tiki Room, in 1963, and the debut of the first Audio-Animatronics *human* figure, Abraham Lincoln, in Great Moments with Mr. Lincoln at the 1964–1965 New York World's Fair.

In this more dynamic incarnation of the show, each scene would feature a "star" animated figure in place of a tour guide, who would tell guests a tale of the golden age of piracy. As the old salt's yarn unfolded, theatrical lighting would come up to reveal additional figures populating an intricate tableau in the background. Those figures would then come to life and act out the scene in a more limited form of animation, similar to that of an elaborate department store window display. It would give the typical wax museum experience a distinct Disney difference.

As intrigued as he was to be working on the project, Marc struggled at first with how to bring history's most notorious bad boys to the Happiest Place on Earth. "I thought, none of this is 'Disney,'"

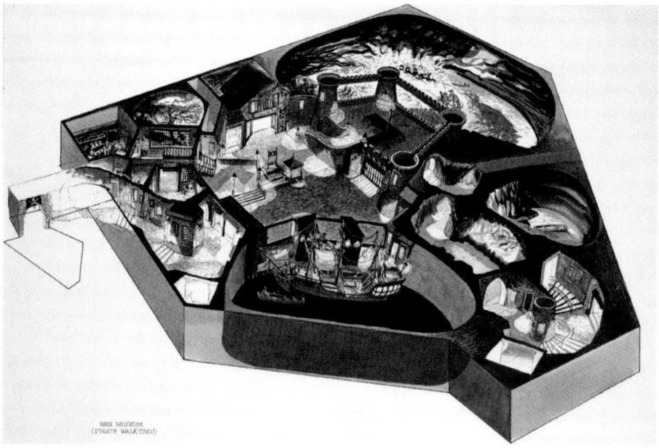

LEFT: Marc Davis's third and final plan of a walk-through pirate attraction, circa 1963. This version featured several show elements that would wind up in the final ride-through attraction, including a dark grotto, a moonlit beach, and a burning seaport.

Marc once told fellow Imagineer Randy Bright. Undaunted, Marc set out to learn everything he could about his cast of characters, personalities that were colorful in every sense of the word. "When Walt was talking about this, the first thing I did was to get a few books on pirates," Marc told *The E-Ticket*. "You know, the artist who really invented pirates as we see them now was an illustrator by the name of H[oward] C. Pyle. He was the guy who really decided how pirates should look. Most of the pirates were descended from the Spanish, but there were a lot of Englishmen, too. I knew a lot about pirates myself, having lived down on the Gulf Coast. I lived in Galveston, Texas, where there was a lot of interest in pirates and locating pirate gold. Somebody was always trying to find Captain Kidd's treasure around there, you know."

With his own boyhood experiences in mind, Marc initially focused on the real pirates of the Caribbean, legendary buccaneers such as captains Morgan and Kidd, and perhaps the most bloodthirsty of cutthroats, Edward Teach, better known as Blackbeard. But as he delved deeper into the truth behind the legends, he discovered that there was a considerable difference between the reality of pirates and the average person's perception of them. Their somewhat false impressions were fueled by scores of artistic, literary, and cinematic interpretations of buccaneers over the years. "These guys would shanghai somebody and force them to become a member of the crew," Marc said to *The E-Ticket*. "They would have to sign the [pirate's contractual] 'articles' with their own blood. It turns out that there were very few battles with pirates at sea. Most pirates died of venereal disease that they got in bawdy houses in various coastal towns. I was sorry to read that because it took a lot of the glamour out of these characters. So at first I wanted to explore the possibility of using real pirates in the show, but later I decided that that wasn't the way to go."

Between the disappointing revelations in the history books and the ironic fact that the pirate "look," as the world knows it, had largely been created by an artist like himself, Marc decided to make a break from reality and have fun with the material. Much as he did with Nature's Wonderland and the Jungle Cruise, Marc looked for ways to inject humor into the show wherever he could, making these barbaric brigands more comical than frightening and the overall experience more family friendly. Pirates of the Caribbean became less of a *True-Life Adventure*

ABOVE: Walt loved this 1965 Marc Davis concept of drunken pirates in a dinghy overloaded with rum bottles, but the gag never made it off the drawing board.
RIGHT: A pirate captain monitors the progress of his crew as Anne Bonny and Mary Read look on in this Marc Davis concept sketch created for the walk-through attraction.

and more like *Treasure Island.*

Although Marc was generating all sorts of characters, gags, and story ideas, he felt as if he wasn't making much progress with Walt. "I filled the walls of my office with all these sketches and concepts, but the funny thing was, Walt never seemed interested in them," Marc told *Disney News* in 1992. "He'd come in and talk with me about pirates, but he wouldn't look at the storyboards. It annoyed me because I knew some of my ideas were pretty good, but I think Walt didn't look at them because he knew the walk-through idea wasn't right." And it wasn't. Thanks largely to Marc Davis and the ingenious work he was doing with that "little pencil" of his, Pirates of the Caribbean was rapidly outgrowing its humble beginnings as a small-scale, walk-through experience.

A New York State of Mind

In 1963, with The Haunted Mansion sitting vacant on its grassy knoll and Pirates of the Caribbean's basement site filled with nothing but a tangle of structural steel, New Orleans Square and its two marquee attractions were officially put on hold yet again as Walt turned his creative resources to one of the grandest experiments and biggest gambles of his career: the 1964–1965 New York World's Fair. No one at WED knew it at the time, but the delay would allow for the creation of the technology that would transform Pirates of the Caribbean into a true marvel of Imagineering and one of the greatest theme park attractions of all time.

Walt's interest in the New York World's Fair can be traced back to as early as 1960, when he announced his plan to key members of his creative team, directing them to meet with the country's top corporations to see who might be interested in partnering with Disney to create attractions for the Fair. "This is a great opportunity for us to grow," he told them. "We can use their financing to develop a lot of technology that will help us in the future. And we'll be getting new attractions for Disneyland, too." He also planned to use Fair visitors as a test audience to see if there was a market for Disneyland-style entertainment east of the Mississippi.

Walt eventually committed to building four attractions, which Imagineers packed up and transported across the country for installation at Disneyland at the Fair's conclusion. Great Moments with Mr. Lincoln took office in the Disneyland Opera House on Main Street in 1965. "it's a small world," an attraction for Pepsi-Cola on behalf of UNICEF, moved into Fantasyland in 1966. The Magic Skyway with Ford Motor Company, a journey through the history of humankind from the primeval world to the space age and beyond aboard "real" Ford automobiles provided the dinosaurs in a diorama on the *Santa Fe & Disneyland* Railroad. And the Carousel of Progress from General Electric's Progressland became the centerpiece of a new Tomorrowland when it premiered in 1967, moving to Walt Disney World in 1973.

Walt's gamble paid off on all counts. The four Disney shows were the hits of the Fair, and Disneyland subsequently received three new attractions and a major addition to a fourth at very little cost. The Disneyland operations team also learned invaluable lessons about capacity and, more to the point, how *fast* they could conceivably move people through their attractions back home.

TOP: This 1962 Marc Davis sketch depicts a life-sized wax figure of Captain Bartholomew Roberts, or "Black Bart," a real-life pirate who was to be featured in the captain's cabin scene of the walk-through attraction. **LEFT:** Walt Disney shows off a model of "it's a small world," one of four attractions created for the 1964–1965 New York World's Fair.

The Pirates Finally Set Sail

The World's Fair brought work on Disneyland to a virtual standstill. "The Pirates were on the drawing boards for years," art director Dick Irvine told Imagineer Randy Bright in 1987. "Back in the late fifties, it was going to be a wax museum. Then we were going to make it a walk-through. We even started construction, but when the New York Fair came along, we just left Disneyland alone for two years." Once the World's Fair shows were up and running, Walt and his Imagineers returned to California re-energized and eager to apply everything they had learned to the projects that had been in the pipeline years earlier, including New Orleans Square, Pirates of the Caribbean, and The Haunted Mansion.

The Imagineers weren't the only ones thinking about Disneyland's future. After nearly ten years of experience, the Park's operators also had strong opinions about any proposed expansion projects. Based on their own experience at the Fair, the Anaheim operations team maintained more than ever that any new attractions had to be "people eaters," capable of accommodating not tens or hundreds, but thousands of guests per hour.

OPPOSITE: Moody Marc Davis concept sketch of Sir Henry Morgan, another real-life pirate to be featured in the walk-through Pirate Wax Museum. **ABOVE:** Imagineers including Herb Ryman (far left), Marc Davis (in sunglasses), Joe Fowler (standing), and Richard Irvine (seated, with hat) join Walt Disney (front row, right) for a ride in a mock-up of the boat-ride system originally created for "it's a small world" by Arrow Development Company.

Just as Walt had prophesied back in 1960, the new technology WED developed for the Fair proved to have a profound effect on the sidelined attractions. Now the Imagineers had the time and resources to focus on that troublesome bend in the river, as well as on new ways to accommodate the high expectations of the ever-increasing guests. One of the most important ones was the innovative boat-ride system the Arrow Development Company had created for "it's a small world," a natural for a show about seafaring swashbucklers, in which guests rode in flat-bottomed boats propelled by silent, unseen jets of water.

An ocean voyage actually wasn't a new idea. Disneyland director of operations Dick Nunis had been lobbying Walt for a ride-through for years. In a memo dated July 19, 1961, Dick maintained that the "Pirates of the Caribbean Wax Museum," as it was referred to, "could possibly be developed into a ride, still using the story ideas of the famous pirates, but having some means of conveyance for the guests." For their part, Imagineers had been looking for a boat system that could ferry guests down into the basement of the Blue Bayou Mart as far back as October 2, 1962, according to one WED memo.

Claude Coats had long envisioned the show as, appropriately enough, a genuine waterborne adventure. "Claude was always saying that it should be real water," Harriet Burns recalls. "But Walt said, 'No, it would be dirty and cause trouble.' Then later he came back to it and said, 'Well, maybe we can use real water.' Claude was always so tactful, and replied, 'Gee, do you think that'll work?' He never said, 'I told you so!'"

Toward the end of 1963, Walt finally agreed to use a variation of the ride system that they were then testing for "it's a small world." In the latest incarnation of Pirates of the Caribbean, guests would ride in "bateaux" similar to the actual flat-bottomed boats used to navigate the shallow waters of Louisiana bayou country.

Walt knew how such a ride-through experience would work story-wise. "I remember Walt talking to Dick Irvine and all of us at lunch one day," Dick Nunis recalls. "And he just laid out his concept of

Herb Ryman created some of the first views of Pirates of the Caribbean as a ride-through attraction, including this 1963 sketch of bateaux traveling up a waterfall at the show's conclusion (left) and this 1965 concept of the Jail scene (below). **BOTTOM:** Walt Disney shares the stage with José, star of the first full Audio-Animatronics show, The Enchanted Tiki Room.

Pirates as a *ride*. He said, 'They'll ride through in boats and drop down a waterfall and go through a tunnel to get under the railroad tracks and we'll put a big show building outside the park.' He had the whole thing figured out."

It was not an inconsequential decision. "Before the Fair, all the steel had actually gone into the New Orleans Square to do a walk-through of the pirates," Walt Disney Imagineering's current Vice Chairman and Principal Creative Executive Marty Sklar, told *Theme Park Adventure*. "After what we learned at the Fair, about moving people and handling people, and being able to direct their attention via moving, Walt said, 'We can't do the pirates as a walk-through. I mean, we can't handle the number of people that are going to want to come, and it's not the kind of show that we really ought to be doing.' . . . Sure it would have 'worked,' but it wouldn't have taken us to another level with Disneyland attractions."

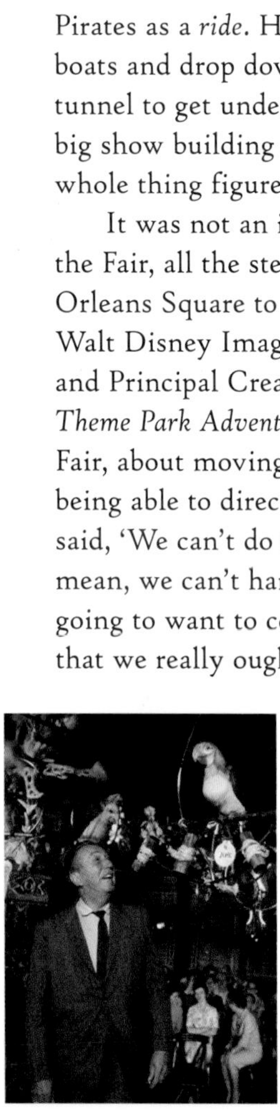

A new ride system was only the beginning of the changes in store for Pirates of the Caribbean. Thanks to the success of Disneyland's first bona fide Audio-Animatronics show, The Enchanted Tiki Room, which premiered in 1963, and the showstopping performance of Mr. Lincoln at the World's Fair, the former wax museum would now feature an all-star cast of fully animated buccaneers who would pillage, plunder, rifle, and loot before the amazed eyes of Disneyland guests. The days of relatively crude animated figures of animals performing simple movements were gone forever. Complex Audio-Animatronics figures were about to invade the Magic Kingdom.

These major upgrades to Pirates necessitated still another redesign of New Orleans Square, one that would create the extra room needed for such an elaborate and high-capacity attraction. Facility architect Bill Martin did some initial calculations, and the news wasn't encouraging, as he related to Imagineers Bruce Gordon and David Mumford. "By the time we sent the boats down into the basement, and then allowed room for a ramp to bring them back up, there'd be no room left for the show!" The Imagineers concluded that a ride-through attraction simply couldn't fit into the basement of the former Blue Bayou Mart.

"The space was very, very small and very tight," Claude Coats told Bruce and David. "So Walt said, 'We're just going to have to go underneath the railroad track and build a big building outside the berm.'"

"Walt just said to Joe Fowler [Disneyland's head of construction], 'We're going to have to tear out that

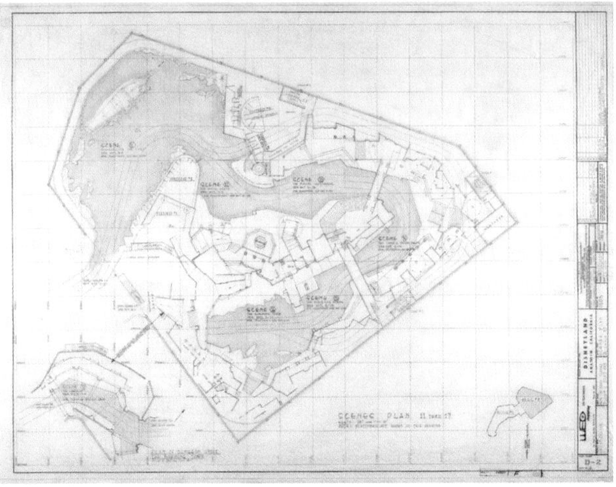

LEFT: This blueprint clearly shows the original basement location of the walk-through attraction, ultimately home to a network of haunted caverns, and the "Ghostly Grotto" transition tunnel that connects it to the mammoth show building erected outside the berm to house the main show. **BELOW:** Early plan view of a scene in the ride-through version of the attraction. **BOTTOM:** Marc Davis working on a concept for the Treasure Room finale of the Walt Disney World version of the attraction.

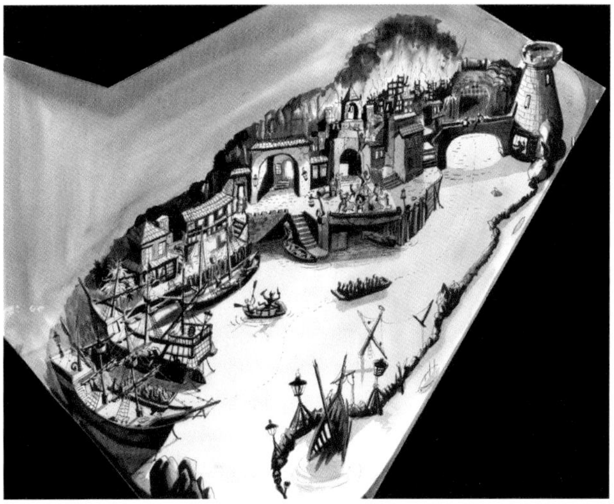

steel; start over again,'" Marty Sklar says. "Boy, that was a pretty hefty decision. That was a lot of money down the drain, but he had a vision, you know."

Walt decreed that guests would board the attraction in New Orleans Square proper, but the bulk of the show would take place in a large, soundstage-like show building outside Disneyland's berm on the former site of Holidayland, a recreation area composed of picnic grounds, a playground, and a baseball diamond, which had been designed to host private functions but never quite took off with the public. Construction on New Orleans Square began—again—in 1965, four years after its initial commencement and two years after the completion of the facade around a tenantless Haunted Mansion in 1963.

A Motley Crew

Marc Davis was still the captain of the Pirates' ship, picking up right where he left off before putting it aside to work on the World's Fair. Walt assigned Marc to come up with a series of lighthearted "pirate gags" that took advantage of the latest Audio-Animatronics technology.

"I did a lot of these drawings and ideas about 1965," Marc told *The E-Ticket*. And this time, finally armed with a solid direction, Walt took such an interest in the sketches and storyboards that began to fill Marc's office that he collaborated on the project, as he had in the early days of Mickey Mouse cartoons. "Walt was his own best story man, and he was very busy at this point in his life," Marc said. "That was one of the most remarkable things about the man . . . that he could go from one project to another and give input to each one of them, and be pleasantly surprised and delighted when he saw things that he liked."

Marc's sketches now possessed a simplicity that his pre-Fair Pirates drawings often did not. Since the pirates would be portrayed by sophisticated Audio-Animatronics performers instead of static waxworks or simplistic figures with limited movements, Marc couldn't afford to employ a large cast, creatively or financially. The characters and gags had to be simply staged in order for the tableaux to read, and that meant cutting down on the clutter to focus the audience's attention on each scene's main story point.

In many ways, Marc felt the scenes had to be simple because they weren't telling a "story" in the traditional sense. Fantasyland's dark rides, such as Peter Pan's Flight and Snow White's Adventures, loosely retold the film stories on which they were based, but Pirates had no such specific frame of reference. Instead, the Imagineers were creating a series of loosely related tableaux that would transport

guests to another time and place and give them an experience they couldn't have anywhere else. "He [Walt] didn't like the idea of telling stories in this medium," Marc told *Disney News*. "It's not a storytelling medium [in the sense of a movie]. But it does give you experiences. You experience the *idea* of pirates. You don't see a story that starts at the beginning and then ends up with, 'By golly, they got the dirty dog.' It wasn't that way. It was scene after scene, and that really works out very well in that attraction. People see it over and over again and they always discover something new every time."

While Marc Davis focused on the pirates themselves, one of his key collaborators turned his attention to the Caribbean. Claude Coats was a veteran background painter who had contributed to such classic animated features as *Snow White and the Seven Dwarfs*, *Fantasia*, *Dumbo*, *Cinderella*, and *Peter Pan* before joining WED in 1955. Claude focused on the layout of the ride system's flume and designing the attraction's interior environments, constructing a set on which Marc's cast of characters could play.

TOP: Claude Coats evocative rendering of the Well scene. **ABOVE:** Claude Coats at work at his drawing table, surrounded by his renderings of show sets for Pirates of the Caribbean. **RIGHT:** Rare Claude Coats gag sketch of a pirate barely avoiding both a sword-wielding soldier and some cannon shot.

Claude began staging the characters in a variety of moody settings, from haunted caverns to a pirate galleon to a ransacked Caribbean seaport. John Hench, who worked with Claude on many of the same animation backgrounds, also contributed design and layout ideas.

Coats was well aware of the role he played in the design of Disneyland attractions and likened set design to his earlier work as a background artist, creating rich environments to support Marc's colorful characters and the business in which they engaged. "I always realized, from working in backgrounds, that the story is the thing," Coats recalled. "The animation, then, is what really tells the story. The background has to support all that, it has to add the proper mood and give the characters the proper space and lighting to work in. But the backgrounds had to be balanced carefully. You can't make them overdone to the point of being distracting."

Walt had a knack for combining his Imagineers' skills to achieve something no individual could do on their own. The wisdom of this collaborative approach is most evident in the work Marc Davis and Claude Coats did together on Pirates of the Caribbean and later The Haunted Mansion.

"The sequence of scenes was just a natural evolution of ideas," Marc told *The E-Ticket*. "Lots of us were working together and we'd say, 'Let's do this

over here.' I'd say that Claude Coats was definitely the layout man for the attraction, but I had a hand in it, too. Everybody was there, and everybody made suggestions, and some of them were used. Claude Coats laid out that section where the chase scenes are . . . that big scene. I did the planning of what the pirates were, and what they were doing, and what they looked like."

"Claude was excellent at laying out rides," Harriet Burns agrees. "He was always the best at getting the most out of a space."

As an increasing number of independent show elements continued to emerge, from characters and gags to sets and tableaux, Marc developed a rough written treatment based on his own sketches and storyboards to tie them all together. Then, when the attraction's overall story line began to solidify, Walt called in still another animator with an apparently hidden talent to write the script.

Creative Writing 101

Francis Xavier "X" Atencio had joined the studio as an assistant animator on *Fantasia* in 1938 and was dabbling in stop-motion animation with future Audio-Animatronics programming wizard Bill Justice when Walt surprised him with the offer—really an order—to join WED in 1965. "I got a call from Walt and he wanted me to do a script for the pirate ride," X told *Disney News* on the occasion of Pirates of the Caribbean's twenty-fifth anniversary in 1992. "I'd never done any scripting before. I'd worked in the Story Department, mostly as a sketch artist. But I said, 'Oh, all right, I'll give it a try.' So I put on my pirate hat, dug out a bunch of pirate books, and watched *Treasure Island*, trying to get the feel of pirate jargon."

"To set the mood for a show like this, you had to sort of become a pirate yourself," X said in *Disneyland: Inside Story*. "I think my Spanish background helped me to write the exchanges between the Pirate Captain and the defenders of the fort."

In addition to Walt's own 1950 live-action classic, a number of other classic pirate films influenced X's script as well as some of the sets and scenes in the attraction, including *Captain Blood* and *The Sea Hawk*, starring Errol Flynn, *Captain Kidd* with Charles Laughton, *Blackbeard the Pirate*, starring Walt's own Long John Silver, Robert Newton, and *The Buccaneer*, starring Yul Brynner and directed by Anthony Quinn.

The cinematic influence was no accident. "We do try to use the material that's in film because people know it and recognize it," John Hench said in a 1984 episode of *Disney Family Album*. "It helps a great deal to have something they already know, something we know they already love." One of the most distinct characteristics about movie pirates is their unique and often heavily accented speech

TOP: Claude Coats rendering of the Auction scene. **LEFT:** Bob Sewell, X Atencio, and Dave Snyder share a laugh with Walt Disney World's "Barker Bird."

LEFT: The Auction scene in model form. The Auctioneer and the plus-sized wench up for bids would ultimately end up on the opposite end of the scene next to the infamous Redhead. **BELOW:** Concept art by Marc Davis.

pattern, along with their use—and misuse—of the language. Such filmic touchstones would guide X as he helped bring Marc Davis's characters to life and enhance his sight gags though the spoken word.

Working from Marc's storyboards and treatments as well as a detailed scale model of the entire attraction, X plunged headlong into this strange new world of beggars and ne'er-do-wells, choosing to script first one of the most dialogue-heavy scenes in the entire show. "The first scene I did was the Auction Scene," X said. "I went through the model and figured out what these guys would be saying. When I was done, I took it over to Walt and he said, 'Fine, go ahead, keep going.' I loosened up after that and went with it."

X couldn't have chosen a better scene for his writing debut, considering its questionable and potentially inflammatory basic conceit: innocent women getting bound up and sold off to the highest bidder. It doesn't take much to figure out what the pirates are actually doing in the scene, but Atencio tried to soften the impact as much as he could through the dialogue and, in this case, a very clear signal—literally a sign. "We made a big banner, 'Auction—Take a Wench for a Bride,' at the Auction Scene to get the point across that these guys weren't 'taking advantage' of the ladies. They were auctioning them off to be brides."

"[Walt] came in one time and even said, 'This will be all right, won't it?,'' Claude Coats told *The E-Ticket*. "He was just a little doubtful of auctioning off the girls. Was that quite 'Disney' or not? We added some other signs around, 'Buy a Bride' or something like that, that augmented the auction scene as though it was a special big event. Marc had done some drawings of the other girls who were tied up and shivering. The way the girls were done, it's not an offensive scene at all, but it probably could have been if it hadn't been handled in an interesting way."

The scene seemed to bear out Marc Davis's initial, overall concern about the project: the distinct possibility that "None of this is 'Disney.'" The Imagineers were concerned that guests might perceive them essentially to be celebrating violent criminals dedicated to the pursuit of wine, women, and song. "The thing we had to do was get across the fact that here are some pretty raunchy old pirates chasing these ladies around, and we couldn't come out and blatantly say that they were doing bad things to these ladies," X related in an episode of *Disney Family Album*. "They were having fun; they were just a bunch of fun-loving pirates." X's light touch with the script was definitely a step in the right direction, but the show element that would do the most to take some of the edge off the debauched pirates was yet to come.

A Song in the Key of X

Like Marc Davis, Walt was concerned about how guests would react to some of the pirates' more lecherous behavior. It was X who convinced him that a rousing sea chantey might be a good way to help soften up these hardened criminals. X also felt that a song would help create a strong sense of continuity for the show. The novice songwriter's approach was simple: "I just came up with some dialogue that the pirates might have said and set it to music," X said. "Yo-ho-ho and a bottle of rum—that was a big part of the inspiration, that classic phrase."

Although X had confidence in his musical brainstorm, he never expected to be the one to actually write the number. "I had an idea for the lyrics and a kind of a little melody for a song for the ride, but I thought Walt would probably get the Sherman brothers ["It's a Small World (After All)," "Chim Chim Cher-ee"] to do it," X declares. "So after one meeting I said, 'I've got a little idea for a song for the pirate ride, Walt.' He said, 'Let's hear it.' I half recited and half sang it and he said, 'Hey, that's great! Get George [Bruns] to do the music.' That was my first attempt at writing lyrics and that's how I became a songwriter." "Yo Ho (A Pirate's Life for Me)" helped the Imagineers turn their band of bloodthirsty brigands into more family-friendly rapscallions just out to have a little innocent fun.

X's lighthearted lyrics were then set to music by veteran studio composer George Bruns, best known for "The Ballad of Davy Crockett." "When I did 'Yo Ho,' we couldn't have a beginning or an end," George said, "because you didn't know where you were going to come into the song in the ride. Each verse had to make some kind of sense, no matter when you heard it." Thus the music cues are in perfect length and synchronization to avoid an aural overload inside the attraction.

The first-time lyric writer would go on to become a first-time director when he oversaw the recording of the attraction's dialogue and music tracks (with a little help from a young WED writer named Marty Sklar). Many of the vocals, including those of the Pirate Captain and the Auctioneer, as well as the show's signature "Dead men tell no tales" warning, were provided by legendary voice actor Paul Frees, who also performed the roles of Disney's own Ludwig Von Drake, Bullwinkle's longtime nemesis Boris Badenov, and the Ghost Host for The Haunted Mansion. Veteran character actor J. Pat O'Malley also voiced a number of memorable characters, including the hook-handed Pirate at the Well and one of the jailed buccaneers. O'Malley is perhaps best known to Disney fans as the voice of Mr. Toad's noble steed, Cyril, in *The Adventures of Ichabod and Mr. Toad*, Tweedledee and Tweedledum in *Alice in Wonderland*, and Colonel Hathi in *The Jungle Book*. And, always one to get into his work, X Atencio himself supplied the voices of the talking skull and crossbones and the drunken pirate on the bridge whose hairy leg dangles above guests as their bateau sails beneath him.

Under the baton of George Bruns, "Yo Ho (A Pirate's Life for Me)" was recorded by the Mellomen, a singing group who had performed in a number of Disney film projects, including *Alice in Wonderland* and *Lady and the Tramp*. At the time of the Pirates recording session, the group was comprised of Bill Cole, Bill Lee, Max Smith, and bass singer Thurl Ravenscroft, who would go on to take the lead on "Grim Grinning Ghosts" as a singing bust for The Haunted Mansion, as well as provide the distinctive voice of Tony the Tiger.

X's songwriting debut turned out to be just as successful as his first script. "It's such a play on words and they come so fast, that even I couldn't sing the song without looking at a lyric sheet. But it's nice to know it's become so well known. I was down in Laguna Beach one time several years ago and there were some kids in a little dinghy out there on the water singing, 'Yo ho, yo ho, a pirate's life for me.' That made me feel good."

ABOVE: Concept art by Marc Davis. **RIGHT:** First-time lyricist X Atencio (right) collaborated with veteran studio composer George Bruns to create "Yo Ho (A Pirate's Life for Me)," one of the most memorable Disney theme park songs of all time.

LEFT: Disney animator-turned-Imagineering sculptor Blaine Gibson puts the finishing touches on the bust of a pirate figure. **BELOW:** All of the pirates began life as scale maquettes that enabled Blaine and his team to establish the pose of a character before creating the full-size figure.

The Pirates Take Shape

One of the key distinctions between the work that former animators such as Marc Davis were doing at WED and their previous line of business was that, at some point, their creations would have to leap off the drawing board and come to life in the three dimensions of the "real" world at Disneyland. It should come as no surprise that the man primarily responsible for that was also handpicked by Walt from his animation studio. Artist and sculptor Blaine Gibson joined the studio in 1939 as an in-betweener on *Pinocchio*, and was later an assistant animator on such films as *Bambi*, *Peter Pan*, and *Lady and the Tramp* before becoming a lead animator on *Sleeping Beauty*. In his spare time, Gibson was an accomplished sculptor.

"I started out using sculpting more as an illustrator would, finding out how you would approach different character types. Back then I would read a novel, and the author would describe a character and so I would sculpt a little head that would fit that. There was an exhibit of my sculpture up in the studio library in the late forties, and Walt had seen it," Blaine told *The E-Ticket*. "Walt had a memory that you can't imagine, and if somebody had done something he'd sort of file it away." Walt recruited him to work on Disneyland in 1954.

Blaine first created a variety of models, miniatures, and sculptures of characters, including the mermaids for Submarine Voyage, dimensional devils for the hellish climax of Mr. Toad's Wild Ride, and elephants for the Jungle Cruise's sacred bathing pool. He worked on Disneyland projects on and off until 1961, when he transferred to WED full-time to run the sculpture shop. One of his primary responsibilities was overseeing the creation of models, full-size mock-ups, and ultimately the heads of the Audio-Animatronics figures.

For Pirates of the Caribbean, it was Blaine Gibson's job to bring Marc Davis's characters to three-dimensional life through his sculpture. "We start off by making little wire armatures," Blaine told *The E-Ticket*. "These little wire skeletons are the start of the animals and figures that we do. Then we build it up with material. We originally used clay. Now we use a material called polyform, which you cook in an ordinary oven and it gets hard. The models we did for Pirates, for instance, were all done in clay. Ken O'Brien and I did all of those. I guess I did some of the painting but mostly we had people like Harriet Burns, who I consider to be one of the top painters."

Blaine and his sculptors added clay to the armature piece by piece, and carved and shaped the material until it gradually became a pirate. The team then took plaster casts from the clay figures and refined the details until they were satisfied that they had captured the character in Marc's original sketch. These casts would serve as the permanent record of the characters, and as the forms from which other molds could be made.

Blaine's task was critical, because his sculpture was literally the only way to shape the personalities of the pirates, townspeople, and animals in three-dimensions and still capture all the attitude and emotion present in Marc Davis's drawings. And because they were dealing with human figures, they had to create heads that were typical of real people as opposed to the more forgiving features of cartoon characters. Since guests pass through the scenes relatively quickly, seeing the characters for such a short time, the characters and the business in which they are engaged had to "read" immediately, with no ambiguity as to who they are and what they want. If a pirate was slated to whistle in the show, for example, he had to be sculpted all puckered up and ready to blow. The Auctioneer, on the other hand, had to be extremely sophisticated in his facial movements in order to convincingly mouth his considerable lines of dialogue.

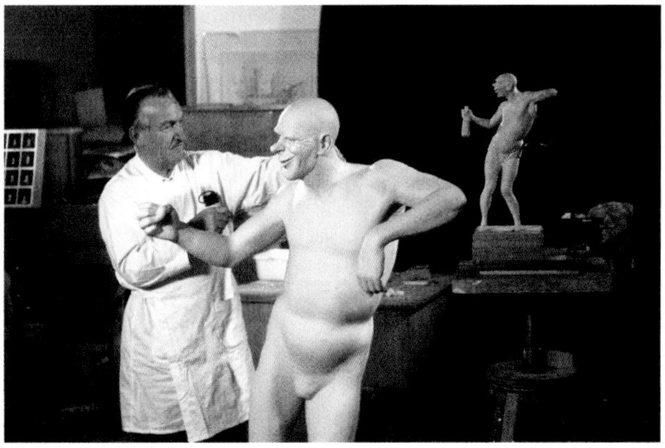

"In a ride system, you only have a few seconds to say something about a figure through your art," Blaine told Randy Bright. "So we exaggerate their features, especially the facial features, so they can be quickly and easily understood from a distance. If you examined them closely, you'd find the nose, the cheekbones, the ears, the eyes all somewhat exaggerated. The frowns and the grins are all exaggerated, too, because we have to instantly communicate 'good guy' or 'bad guy.' We try to provide the illusion of life."

Just as he chose actors for particular parts in his films, Walt personally cast all of the Audio-Animatronics performers. A variety of creative considerations dictated which heads were to be used and where, including whether or not the character had any dialogue, their body size, and their role in the show. Once the roles had been determined and the final characters selected, the small replicas became the guides for the actual sculpting of more than 120 life-size figures. Based on the models, Gibson and company created full-size mock-ups of the bodies and sculptures of the various pirate heads, which were then recast again and again for use throughout the show.

Although it would go unknown by guests, almost all of the pirate heads are composites of real people that Blaine and his fellow sculptors knew, both inside and outside of WED, automatically adding to the realism of the characters. Blaine would borrow an Imagineer's nose here or a particularly striking set of ears there, to create the hyper-realistic appearance of his pirates. In fact, the pirate who is perhaps best known and loved by guests, the Auctioneer, is a rather thinly veiled caricature of a fellow Imagineer, whose identity to this day Blaine prefers to remain anonymous.

There was a method to Blaine's madness. "I think that Walt was extremely interested in getting something that looked alive and believable, whatever it was," he says. "His goal, whether it was with animals or human figures, was to make them as believable as possible." Whether Walt was telling stories in a feature-length animated film or a fifteen-minute ride-through attraction at Disneyland, the illusion of life was a critical component of his audience's willing suspension of disbelief. "I really don't like to leave a sculpture until it has a feeling of life," Blaine Gibson has said of his art, and Pirates of the Caribbean is a living monument to that philosophy.

ABOVE: Working from a scale maquette, WED sculptor George Snowdon shapes the full-size mock-up of a pirate figure. **BELOW:** Blaine Gibson attempts to capture the staging and humor of Marc Davis's sketches in a scale model of a pirate duo in the Burning Town scene.

ABOVE: The Well and Auction scenes in scale-model form.
BELOW: Harriet Burns, "The First Lady of Imagineering" and one of the founding members of the WED Model Shop.

Model Citizens

Blaine Gibson's miniature pirate figures were to be the stars of an elaborate scale model of the entire attraction that the Imagineers began to assemble in 1964. A study model is the only way to see the work in three dimensions before actual construction begins, and it's a lot less time-consuming and expensive to find out something doesn't work when it exists only in model form as opposed to a multimillion-dollar installation at the Park.

One of the cornerstones of the model shop was quite literally "The First Lady of Imagineering," Harriet Burns. WED's first female employee came from the world of television, where she worked in color styling, props, and set design and construction on *The Mickey Mouse Club*. She had been with the show less than a year when Walt drafted her to help open Disneyland in 1955. Harriet is considered one of the co-founders of the model shop, along with Wathel Rogers and Fred Joerger. "We were definitely the oddballs when WED started," Harriet says. "At first there were only a few of us, in a warehouse at the back of the Studio. Later on there were thirty and our department was called Dimensional Design."

Harriet was an artistic Jill-of-all-trades. Her work in the WED model shop would call upon any and every skill she had ever learned, and if she didn't know how to do something she figured it out on the fly rather than say "no" to Walt. "You just didn't know what you were doing because it had never been done!" Harriet says. "I did preliminary sculptures in Styrofoam or other materials, made molds and cast them, used saws, lathes, and sanders, painted and enameled."

Blaine Gibson collaborated with Harriet, Fred Joerger, and their cohorts to create a scale model of Pirates of the Caribbean so Walt and his Imagineers could study every aspect of the attraction in detail and view the entire show as guests would later see it. "We did the model set by set, scene by scene," Harriet says. "We knew the whole story line."

"I was given artists' drawings of an interior set

LEFT: In a testament to WED's attention to detail, even the splashes made by cannonballs were depicted in this model. **BELOW:** An Imagineer applies a coat of paint to one of the diminutive brigands that populate the scale model.

or a building and interpreted them into models," Fred Joerger recalls of his work in the model shop. "It's very easy to make something look good on paper, but if you don't get it into three dimensions first, you may have a disaster. Well, my job was to create the model to avert disaster."

Blaine's nine-inch clay figures were placed on the model sets to stage the pirates as they would appear in the final, full-size version of the show. These detailed figures could be moved from place to place in the model, much as a movie director would stage his actors, so that every aspect of the action could be thoroughly envisioned. In fact, each scene in the model had a strategically placed ring through which Walt and the Imagineers could see the show from the point of view of guests in their bateaux.

"We did the whole darn set-up and it took a long time—it was the longest model we'd ever done," Harriet says. "It was forty feet long. We did it section by section and put it all up on sawhorses. We put Walt in a desk chair with rollers and we pushed him through the whole thing at eye level. In fact, Evie Coats, Claude's wife, said she thought it was more fun than the real pirate ride!"

"We built a model later, set up like a walk-through," Marc Davis also recalled in *The E-Ticket*. "We made the model with openings where you could walk in and get a view of the scenes as if you were in the boats. That way you could get the effect of the stage of the ride scenes, and decide if they were going to work or not. I worked with Blaine Gibson and his people when they were sculpting the little model figures. And the model pretty much portrayed the way the ride would be built. Walt made suggestions all the way along, and he seemed to be satisfied with the way the thing was coming together."

The scale model was a work of art unto itself. It enabled the Imagineers to make changes cheaply and easily by simply moving a character or prop, redesigning a set, or even adding or cutting an entire show scene. This gave the show's design a flexibility the Imagineers would not have otherwise enjoyed. Scenes could be added or deleted with ease, and the order of their appearance could be changed until Walt was happy with the flow of the show, giving new meaning to the phrase "economy of scale."

Alice in Disneyland

DISNEYLAND'S FIRST cast of human Audio-Animatronics figures meant that the Imagineers were going to need a costume designer. Walt decided to keep the position in the family and hired Marc Davis's wife, Alice Estes Davis, an accomplished artist in her own right, who had worked on a WED project before.

Years earlier, Walt Disney had made a surprise appearance at the Davis's table while they were dining at a favorite Southern California restaurant. "We are going to work together one of these days," Walt told a surprised Alice, whom he knew was an experienced costume designer. Alice figured Walt was

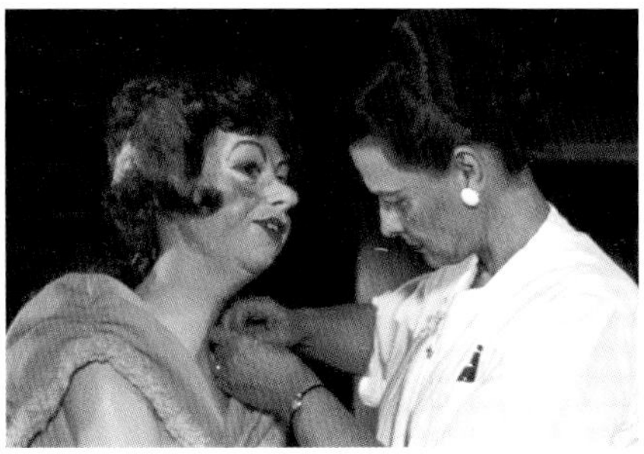

LEFT: Costume designer Alice Davis, wife of artist Marc Davis, works on the costume of one of the village "wenches."

just being polite, but sure enough, two years later she was called to design costumes for the Audio-Animatronics children of "it's a small world." Walt was so pleased with her work on the World's Fair show that he eagerly called upon her again when the time came to dress his pirates. The irony was not lost on Alice Davis. "I graduated from sweet little children to dirty old men overnight," Alice said during her induction as a Disney Legend in October 2004.

If either Davis was concerned about extending their partnership to the workplace, their concerns quickly proved to be unfounded. Alice enjoyed every minute of interpreting her husband's sketches and helping bring his characters to life through her own art. "Working with Marc was an absolute joy," Alice recalls, "and we didn't have a single argument on the whole show."

Audio-Animatronics performers pose a unique set of problems for a costume designer. The costumes have to look like they are covering a normal human body, but the forms beneath the fabric are often anything but natural; the "Redhead" in the Auction Scene, for example, does not even nearly possess the shapely figure one might expect from the waist down. "The redhead was a real problem because from right below her bust to her hips there was nothing but a two-inch tube," Alice recalls. "So I had to sew a complete corset that would fit with grippers on the butyrate underneath the bust and at the top of the hips. She's all hollow inside."

It would be up to Alice and her team of costumers to help Blaine Gibson and Wathel Rogers pull off a convincing anatomical illusion. Since all the figures were bolted to the floor or to a prop, such as a crate, barrel, or cannon, Alice and her team made liberal use of Velcro so costumers could easily dress and undress the characters. And even though Audio-Animatronics figures don't sweat like their human counterparts, they do have a tendency to leak oil and a disquieting red hydraulic fluid, which means the costumes deteriorate from the inside out as opposed to the outside-in effects of normal "human" wear and tear. The figures' constantly moving Audio-Animatronics innards also caused considerable wear, so steps had to be taken to minimize their contact with the material. After her experience with the large international cast of "it's a small world," however, Alice Davis was accustomed to such uniquely Disney challenges, and she and her team of four designed and built costumes for the entire show in less than a year.

Davis's greatest costuming trial came shortly *after* the show opened. "As a costume designer, there are two things you can't do without. You have to have a perfect pattern, and a set of backup costumes." Unfortunately, the WED accountants wouldn't approve funding for a second set of costumes. Artistry takes many forms, however, and Alice solved the problem herself. "I simply told the bookkeeper that the costumes cost twice as much as they actually did and made a second set." Her foresight

LEFT TO RIGHT: The infamous Auctioneer as depicted in one of Marc Davis's original sketches, being outfitted in Alice Davis's costume shop, and as he appears in the final show scene.

LEFT: An Auctioneer's-eye view of the inventory in the Auction scene. **BOTTOM:** Wathel Rogers, the "Father of Audio-Animatronics," with some friends.

amount of time. "Humor is so important in the rides that people remember," Alice told *Theme Park Adventure*. "You ask them about what they like; they always speak of the funny parts. The other is the staging. And if they're staged right, leave them alone. Don't clutter them. Simplicity. You can read things so much better with simplicity."

and creative accounting practices would help Disneyland narrowly avert disaster.

"The show had just opened and sure enough they had a fire—and it started in the Burning Town scene of all places!" Alice explains, of a fire that occurred about two months after the attraction opened. "Three of the costumes were burned and quite a few others were damaged when all the sprinklers came on. Oh, you've never seen anything more ghastly than one of those figures burned!" The Park's operators were panic stricken and immediately called in WED for a damage assessment. "Dick Irvine asked me how long it would take to replace the costumes, and I told him I could have them changed out overnight because I had gone ahead and made a second set. He didn't know whether to kiss me or chew me out me for putting one over on the bean counters. Now they make *three* sets of costumes!"

Alice often went above and beyond her call of duty as a costume designer, especially where the female characters were concerned, and she made her own unique contributions to the Audio-Animatronics figures' illusion of life. "I had the machinists make some wires for bras," Alice remembers, "and fix a contraption on it so in the Chase Scene, when the girls were running, their bosoms would bounce!"

Ultimately, Alice Davis did as much as anyone else to help bring her husband's characters to three-dimensional life. She subscribed wholeheartedly to Marc's vision of the themed show, with his emphasis on humor, and on characters and situations that are clear and easy for an audience to "get" in a short

Keeping to the Code

When the time came to program the Pirates figures, the Imagineers discovered that just because you *could* do something doesn't necessarily mean you *should* do it. In theory, their ever-advancing Audio-Animatronics figures were capable of all kinds of theatrics by that point, but the "forced dignity" of Great Moments with Mr. Lincoln had transformed into a "voluntary simplicity" for the pirates and their assorted enemies and victims. "Most of the figures were very simply animated because we didn't truthfully know how much we should put into these things," Marc Davis told *Disney News*. "The simplicity was fine because you are moving, and you have to have things you could 'read' quickly and enjoy and are not confusing. Then you can move on to another idea. But one figure that has some of the subtleties of the Mr. Lincoln figure is the Auctioneer. He has all

the lip purses and spread of the mouth that Mr. Lincoln has. But then all of a sudden I realized that you're in a boat and you won't see all those things. I mentioned that to Walt and he said, 'You know, each time you go through—and people will go through many times—this is going to be something they haven't seen before.'"

Wathel Rogers led the team that engineered, installed, and programmed the Audio-Animatronics figures. Like Blaine Gibson, Wathel was a former animator whose after-hours interest in sculpting made him a natural choice for the three-dimensional world of WED. He co-founded the model shop in 1954 and went on to help construct the first architectural models of Disneyland. His work on Walt's various early attempts at dimensional animation, such as Project Little Man (a small wooden figure that danced an animated jig) and its descendants, prepared him well for his work as one of the lead programmers of the Pirates figures, leading to his unofficial title at WED, "Mister Audio-Animatronics."

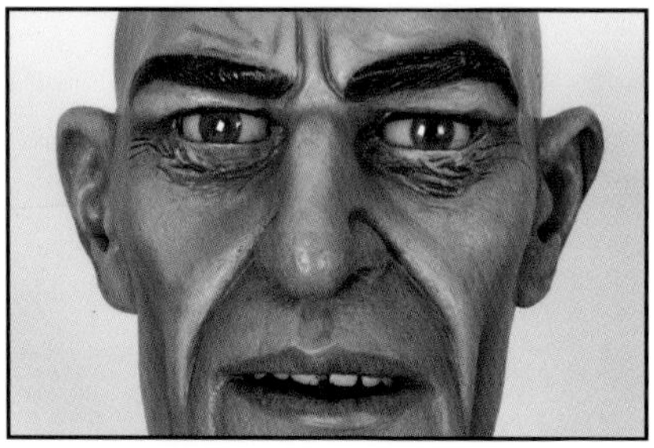

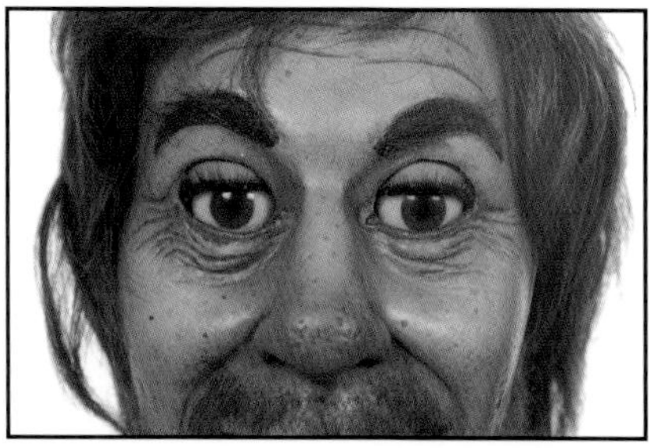

"Wathel was always making everything come to life," John Hench once said of Rogers. "If it was stationary and we wanted it to move, all we had to do was call Wathel and in his quiet, calm way, he'd make it work." Wathel was joined by his model shop co-founder, Fred Joerger, former studio machinist Roger Broggie, and still another former animator, Bill Justice, who had been working with X Atencio on stop-motion animation projects when they both got the call to join WED.

The Audio-Animatronics figures would be produced en masse by a new subsidiary of WED, MAPO, which alternately stood for *MAry POppins*, whose profits paid for its inception in 1965, or Manufacturing and Production Organization, which tied what the organization actually *did* to its patron film's title. In fact, the Pirates of the Caribbean souvenir magazine sold at Disneyland during the attraction's early years officially credits MAPO with "the prototype research, development, testing, and fabrication of the Audio-Animatronics systems and characters."

Wathel Rogers and the MAPO team built and programmed the figures. In developing and programming the various motions, the Imagineers used a coded reference system to plan and track the animation of each character. The Pirate Captain, for example, had eleven functions. These codes represent broad motions such as "left arm swing" and "right arm forward," "torso twist," "body side sway," and "body fore sway." The function codes ranged up to thirty-seven movements for the body (including ten codes for the fingers alone) and another thirteen codes for the head. Examples of the head functions included "eye blink," "mouth pinch right" and "smile left." Another group of thirty-seven codes were used for the various animals and birds throughout the show. Some of the pirates had as few as three or four motions, while most had about seven or eight. When Pirates of the Caribbean's opened, there were twelve pirates and villagers with ten or more of these animation functions.

The Captain at the Well's animation involved fourteen movements, including "torso twist," "right arm out," "head nod," "eye blink," and one, his left elbow, which is known as "free animation." This is an extra motion, usually in an anchored part of a figure (such as the captain's left arm on the well), which moves on its own as a result of other animation. The Auctioneer opened with twenty-five functions, and his performance has only improved with each subsequent generation of Audio-Animatronics figures over the years.

ABOVE: The "illusion of life," as reflected in the special attention paid to the facial features of the attraction's Audio-Animatronics figures.

LEFT: An Imagineer at work on one of the show's many animal figures. RIGHT: An Audio-Animatronics figure awaits its protective "skin" and costume pieces. BELOW: Imagineer Ken O'Brien literally gets into his work capturing the expressions of an Audio-Animatronics figure.

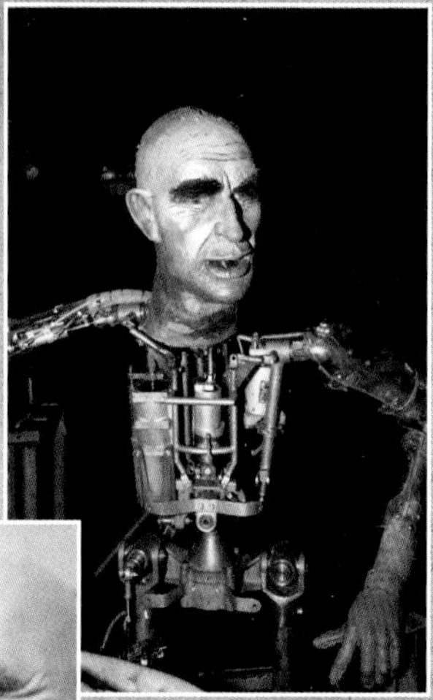

ABOVE: The Redhead gets a touch-up from Imagineer Leota Toombs, whose face would be used to portray Madame Leota in The Haunted Mansion. RIGHT: Bill Justice, former Disney animator and master Audio-Animatronics programmer, practices his craft for the Walt Disney World Pirates installation.

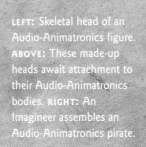

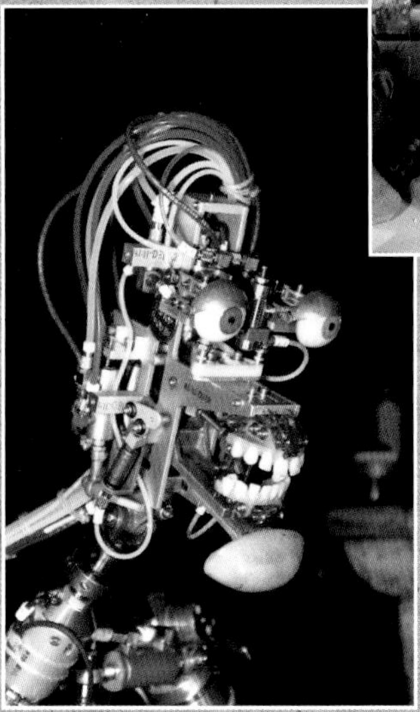

LEFT: Skeletal head of an Audio-Animatronics figure. ABOVE: These made-up heads await attachment to their Audio-Animatronics bodies. RIGHT: An Imagineer assembles an Audio-Animatronics pirate.

Burn, Baby, Burn!

As Blaine Gibson, Wathel Rogers, and the MAPO team were bringing Marc Davis's characters to three-dimensional life, and Claude Coats was supervising the construction of an elaborate stage on which they could play, fellow Imagineer Yale Gracey was experimenting with a variety of special effects that would ultimately complete the delicate illusion of life they were creating. Yale had signed on with the Disney Studio in 1939 as a layout artist on *Pinocchio* and *Fantasia* and joined WED full-time in 1961. He had a reputation as a mechanical genius and master model builder, creating models of experimental airplanes, trains, and other self-proclaimed "funny little things," exactly the kind of out-of-the-box thinking Walt was looking for in his Imagineers.

"That's how Walt worked," Harriet Burns says of Gracey's recruitment. "He just said, 'I'll bring Yale in—he's a putterer.' So Yale did the fire for Pirates of the Caribbean, with a hubcap he found on the freeway and double-crinkly Mylar." Yale's inveterate "puttering" would ultimately give the characters, the environment, and the story they told the final touch of magic they needed.

For an attraction that would be contained entirely within a show building but takes place largely "outdoors" and at night, it was crucial that guests see a realistic sky above them rather than a ceiling and believe it. The solution was yet another legacy of the New York World's Fair. Yale had developed a moving cloud effect for the General Electric Skydome Spectacular. For Pirates of the Caribbean, the master "illusioneer" used the same projection effect to simulate the clouds of an ominous night sky in constant motion. The effect was uncanny, and to this day many guests are convinced that they enter the show building only to find themselves outside again when they step onto Laffite's Landing at the edge of the Blue Bayou.

A burning seaport had been part of the attraction since Marc Davis's early general views of a walk-through wax museum, but no one was ever really sure how elaborate such a scene could be. Taking his

cue from some of Marc's sketches as well as Walt's oft-spoken desire for a truly ransacked town, Claude Coats began developing his own renderings of a quaint Caribbean village slowly burning to the ground. Once Yale saw Claude's concepts for a flaming cityscape, he became more determined to realize the vision with a safe and convincing fire effect. When Claude, in turn, saw the progress Yale was making, he pulled out all the stops to create the ultimate fiery finale for the show. "I remember Yale Gracey fooling around with some Mylar, and a light and a fan," Wathel Rogers recalled. "So he made it a little larger and a little better and Claude Coats came along and designed an entire burning city scene around that one effect."

The result was one of the most realistic special effects ever created for a Disneyland attraction. In fact, the illusion would prove to be *so* convincing that Anaheim fire chief Edward Stringer asked that the effect be programmed to shut off in the event of a real fire alarm.

"I think the fire scene has always been a wonder to me, because I remember when we had to first get the permits from the Anaheim Fire Department," Marty Sklar recalls. "They went in there, and they said, 'Well, how are we ever going to know whether it's a real fire or not?' What a great compliment to Yale Gracey."

"After the chase scenes, you go into the big room with the fire scene," Marc Davis told *The E-Ticket*. "That was Yale Gracey . . . thank God for him . . . coming up with the way to create fake fire. I tried to put some humor all the way through there, even in the burning town scene, because you could scare the hell out of people with all that fire. I think it works, and nobody is terrified that they are going into a burning room."

OPPOSITE: Herb Ryman rendering of the newly deemed ride-through attraction's Burning Town scene. **TOP:** Claude Coats concept painting of the Burning Town scene's background. **RIGHT:** Master "Illusioneer" Yale Gracey and Imagineer Chuck Fuson get a feel for the burning embers in the attraction's fiery finale.

CLOCKWISE FROM TOP LEFT: The show building under construction with the majestic Matterhorn rising in the distance (the "Ghostly Grotto" transition tunnel beneath the train tracks and leading into the Bombarding the Fort scene is visible in the foreground); The infamous "hole in the ground" that would become the home of the haunted grotto; The Blue Bayou is filled with water for the first time; The Disneyland monorail glides by the massive show building under construction outside the Park's berm; Construction ramps up on the Bombarding the Fort scene.

LEFT: Jack Taylor, Bill Justice, Marc Davis, and Wathel Rogers work on the "cam cabinets" first used to create the character action in the show. The cam system has long since been replaced by DACS, which sends motion commands electronically. **BELOW:** Walt Disney and Imagineer Claude Coats review a scale model of the Burning Town.

Pirates Run a Mock

By 1966, construction of Claude Coats's sets was well underway inside the gargantuan show building in Anaheim, and the pirates themselves were beginning to overrun both Blaine Gibson's sculpture studio and the MAPO workshops as they made their journey from Marc Davis's drawing board to the "real" world of Disneyland. X Atencio's script was locked, loaded, and recorded; all that remained was to match his words to the characters' lips through the magic of Audio-Animatronics. The Imagineers felt the show was far enough along to give the boss a sneak preview.

Scale models weren't the only way for Walt and his Imagineers to pre-visualize an attraction in three dimensions. A full-size mock up was the only way to most closely approximate the guest experience before installing the show at the Park. In the early days of Disneyland, the Fantasyland dark rides were mocked up on Studio soundstages, but by early 1966 WED was located on a sprawling industrial campus in nearby Glendale, and that is where a cast of rascals, scoundrels, villains, and knaves made its performing debut.

The show was far too large and complex to mock-up in its entirety, and no one was eager to flood WED's workshops with water and sail them in bateaux, so the Imagineers settled on a land-locked version of the Auction scene. And so, for one performance only, Pirates of the Caribbean was indeed created as a walk-through experience—at least for the Imagineers. Walt, on the other hand, would get at least an approximation of a boat ride—albeit jury-rigged.

"We mocked up the Auction Scene in a warehouse at WED with all the figures working and the dialogue," X Atencio recalls. "We rigged up a dolly and pushed Walt through at the estimated time that the boats would be going through. You could hear all this noise from this side and that side and I said, 'Sorry, Walt, I guess it's pretty hard to understand them.' And he said, 'Don't worry about it. It's like a cocktail party. People come to cocktail parties, and they tune in a conversation over here, then a conversation over there. Each time the guests come through here, they'll hear something completely different. That'll bring them back time and again!' And I thought, Now why didn't I think of that?"

The show was coming together at Disneyland as well, although not quite as fast as New Orleans Square proper. As was his custom, Walt made frequent site inspections to see the work in progress. "Walt was around up to the point where we programmed the animation for the Auction scene," Marc Davis told *The E-Ticket*. "Not completely, but most of it was there. One of the last things that happened, just before Walt passed away, was his tour of our work at Disneyland. The Pirates building was up, and the water channel was walkable, all the way through. Walt, myself, and a half dozen other guys did a walk-through of the ride. There wasn't much scenery up in there, just some frameworks here and

there. You could tell where you were, and Walt's reaction was very favorable. We had made the Auctioneer pirate so sophisticated that you could watch him move, and it was as good as watching [Mr.] Lincoln. He had all the little mouth movements and all that, and I mentioned to Walt that I thought it was a 'hell of a waste.' Walt said, 'No, Marc, it's not a waste . . . we do so much return business down here, and the next time people come in they'll see something they hadn't noticed before.' That was a good example of the kind of input Walt had to these attractions."

Indecipherable dialogue and dollies as a ride system aside, the mock-up was an overwhelming success, and the Imagineers plunged into their work in Anaheim with renewed vigor. Walt had seen the future at the 1964 New York World's Fair, and it was coming to pass in the workshop and studios of WED and in the new attractions that were premiering at Disneyland. But it would turn out that the Auction would be the only scene of Pirates of the Caribbean actually viewed and personally approved by Walt. For the man who had so many long-term visions, time was running all too short.

TOP: Herb Ryman concept sketch of New Orleans Square, with Royal Street visible near the center of the rendering. **RIGHT:** New Orleans Square's Royal Street under construction, circa 1965.

Welcome to New Orleans, CA

"She was the nation's most colorful and exciting city, America's capital of aristocracy, a bristling port exporting more commodities than New York. Cotton was king and the good life was its decree. Its unique atmosphere will live again in New Orleans Square, Disneyland." That's how a 1966 WED press release billed New Orleans Square, which officially opened on July 24, 1966, after spending at least nine years in active development.

New Orleans Square was the first new land built at Disneyland since its opening eleven years earlier, and the only one ever named after a real city. Walt's

LEFT: Intricate design details such as these elegant wrought-iron balconies give New Orleans Square an evocative sense of place. BELOW: Walt Disney and New Orleans Mayor Victor Schiro preside over the opening of New Orleans Square on July 24, 1966. BOTTOM: Elevation of the entrance to Pirates of the Caribbean.

long-gestating riverfront development ultimately cost about $15 million, around $8 million of which was spent on Pirates of the Caribbean, the most money spent on a single attraction to date. The price tag is comparable to what it cost to build all of Disneyland in 1955 ($17 million), and equal to the amount the United States paid for the real New Orleans in the Louisiana Purchase. Standing alongside Walt as he dedicated his Queen of the Delta were New Orleans Mayor Victor H. Schiro and Chief Administrative Officer Thomas Heier.

One expected guest that ultimately didn't show up for the grand opening was the Blue Bayou restaurant. In many ways, the Blue Bayou was the world's first truly themed restaurant. In fact, one of Dick Irvine's earliest memos on the New Orleans Square project outlined a program called "Thematic Feeding," a conscious attempt to tie both the method of service and the food itself into the theme of its area. With mint juleps, crab cakes, and jambalaya served by appropriately dressed servants on the veranda of a grand plantation house, the Blue Bayou was designed to be a prime example of Thematic Feeding as well as Disneyland's premiere full-service restaurant.

In most respects, the Blue Bayou was ready to open in the summer of 1966 with the rest of New Orleans Square, but Walt ultimately felt that since Pirates of the Caribbean was not up and running, the dining experience would be incomplete. He told his team that "if the boats wouldn't be cycling through, the guests shouldn't be in the restaurant eating."

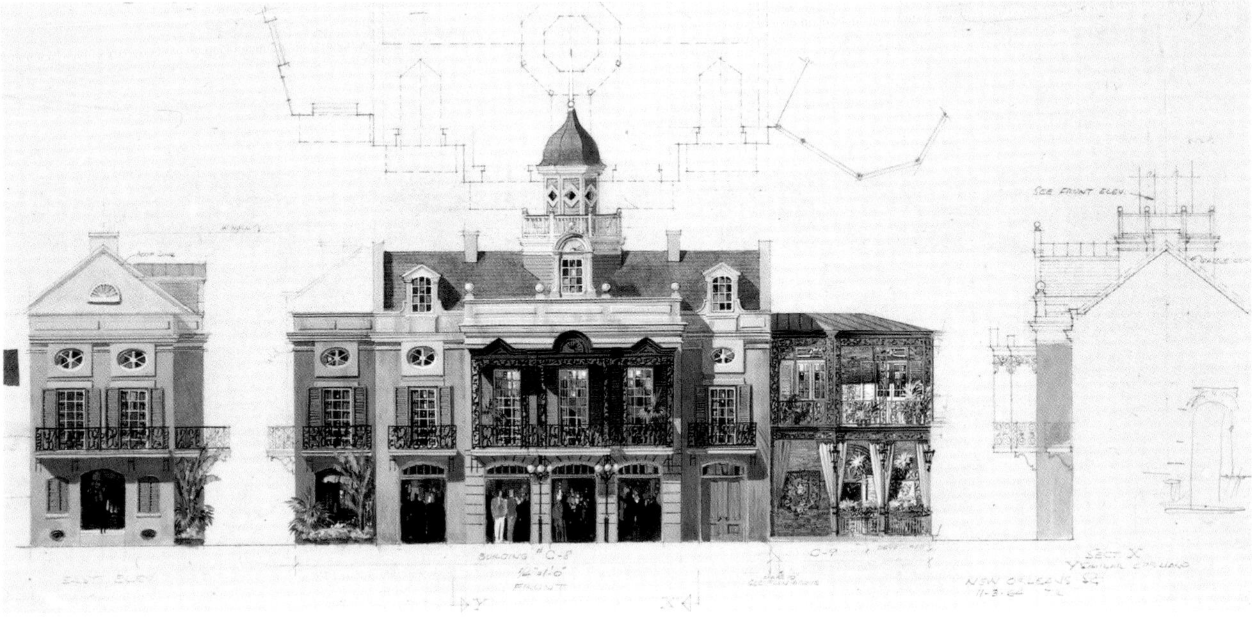

He also wanted every thematic detail to be exactly right, and the old plantation house didn't meet the master's exacting standards. He had lingering concerns about the lighting design and the fact that much of the space had been decorated with faux bougainvillea as opposed to what he considered to be the more regionally appropriate wisteria. Although many of his creative issues were quick fixes, the Blue Bayou's opening was officially postponed to coincide with that of the Pirates attraction.

And there was still plenty of work to do, as film production designer and WED consultant Emile Kuri said in an August 1966 interview to promote *The Happiest Millionaire*. "Well, we opened it last Sunday, not complete. It will take two or three years to finish New Orleans Square. We have the pirate ride in the basement to be done yet. We have the upstairs private clubs. We have a royal apartment to do. We have many things to do in New Orleans Square."

The pirates were definitely getting closer to their maiden voyage, literally and figuratively, than ever before. Although there was nary an Audio-Animatronics buccaneer in sight, at one-thirty in the afternoon on Halloween of 1966, the Pirates channel was filled with water and a bateau set sail for the first time, plunging into the darkness of that infamous basement and the unknown beyond. The Imagineers would soon be doing the same.

The Crew Loses its Captain

Everyone knew Walt Disney was sick; they just had no idea how sick. Walt attributed his increasingly frequent doctor visits and hospital stays to the correction of an old polo injury, but his staff suspected and feared there was much more to the story. By late autumn of 1966, his appearance had grown so

haggard and his once indefatigable spirit so dim that his family and employees alike knew something was very, very wrong.

On November 2, X-rays revealed a tumor on Walt's left lung. The cancerous lung was removed but the prognosis was grim—Walt's doctors gave him six months to two years to live. Only the immediate family, including his wife and children and Walt's brother, Roy, knew of the seriousness of his condition when Walt returned to the Studio after a two-week stay in the hospital.

On his first day back at work, Walt made the short drive over to WED for an update on all the projects in development. During what would be his last meeting with the Imagineers, Walt asked Roger Broggie about the status of Pirates of the Caribbean. Roger replied that the attraction had been completed and shipped to the Park for installation. Disneyland's operators and the company's financial officers were pressing hard for a Christmas opening even though WED was still scrambling to work out the attraction's last few bugs. Just as he had done with the Blue Bayou several months earlier, Walt decreed that Pirates of the Caribbean would not open until it was ready. "Broggie, don't tell them you can do it; the show isn't ready," Walt instructed Roger and the rest of his Imagineers. Walt Disney's final executive decision regarding Disneyland would deprive him of seeing Pirates of the Caribbean open to the public.

Walt then sat down with Marc Davis and went over designs for what would become the Country Bear Jamboree. "He had been in the hospital, and he

TOP: Walt Disney and friend at WED. **LEFT:** Walt lends a head to a Rogues' Gallery of pirate busts. **OPPOSITE:** Walt gets acquainted with Blaine Gibson's three-dimensional realization of one of Marc Davis's town officials, who are doomed to be dunked in the Well scene.

looked terrible," Marc Davis told *Disney News* in 1992. "He had lost a lung and he had lost a lot of weight. One thing about Walt—he was interested as long as you could keep showing him something. So I kept showing him drawings of a project I was working on. He laughed and enjoyed them."

Dick Irvine and John Hench then joined Walt and Marc to see the mock-up for the Flight to the Moon attraction. As usual, Walt had no shortage of ideas for ways to improve the experience. At the mock-up's conclusion, the Imagineers noticed that Walt was visibly worn by his first day back at work. "I'm getting kinda tired," Walt said to Dick Irvine. "Do you want to take me back to the Studio?" Then he did something he had never done before.

"I stopped back in my office," Marc continued. "Walt went down the hall about fifty feet. Then he stopped and turned and looked at me, and said, 'Good-bye, Marc.' That was a killer. I'd never heard him say 'Good-bye'—it was always something like 'See you later.' I was afraid."

His health failing faster than anyone could have anticipated, Walt checked back into St. Joseph's Hospital the following week. Two weeks later, at nine thirty-five on the morning of December 15, 1966, Walt Disney died of an acute circulatory collapse.

Walt's death sent shock waves around the world, but none more pronounced than those on the Studio lot and in the halls of WED. No one was quite sure if they, or the company, could go on. Walt Disney Productions had lost its founder and guiding creative force, the visionary who had the final say on everything that bore his name.

"When Walt died, we felt that we'd lost the drive that was always there before," Blaine Gibson told *The E-Ticket*. "We didn't have anybody around with the vision that Walt had. I felt so strongly about it that I even explored the possibility of working in some other area."

X Atencio spent part of the day reminiscing about Walt with John Hench, but the gravity of what had happened didn't hit him until he had returned home. "It was the day I got our Christmas tree. I came home with it and then it just hit me. I sat down on the couch and just started bawling; uncontrollable sobbing. It was really a touching and amazing part of my life that I was associated with such a great man."

Walt Disney Imagineering's Senior Vice President of Creative Development Tony Baxter has his own vivid memories of the day Walt died. Tony was working as an ice-cream scooper at Disneyland at the time, and preparing a portfolio for a job interview with WED. "I was on my way to the Park to pick up my paycheck. When I pulled into the employee parking lot, I saw the flag in Town Square lowering to half-staff and I knew something was wrong. All of the Cast Members were standing around crying, and I knew."

Tony got his paycheck and walked over to check on the progress of Pirates of the Caribbean, as he had for most of the past year. He noticed that they were cycling bateaux and asked the engineer in charge if they could use a "human sandbag." The Imagineer agreed and sent Tony off alone in a bateau. "There were no Audio-Animatronics figures, no waterfalls, no effects, and no sound except for one solitary 'Yo Ho' guitar track. I remember gliding through this big empty, eerie city and thinking to myself, I'm riding Pirates of the Caribbean, but Walt Disney's dead and now there will be no WED and no job for me to get. I had no idea what the future held, for me or for Disneyland."

The truth was that no one knew what the future held for Walt Disney Productions, inside or outside the company. But Disneyland remained open that day—at Lillian Disney's insistence—and work continued on Pirates of the Caribbean. The Imagineers and the audience for whom they were making one of Walt's last dreams a reality would have to find a way to work through the pain and uncertainty and face the future, if for no other reason than it's what Walt would have wanted.

ABOVE: Walt Disney strolls through the arch of Disneyland's castle.

Carrying the Torch

In the months after Walt Disney's death, the Pirates of the Caribbean finally drew within sight of their home port after spending so many years in a stormy sea of development. As guests enjoyed the quaint shops and sidewalk cafés of the newly opened New Orleans Square, the Imagineers worked their unique brand of Disney magic, out of sight and out of mind inside a grand French manor house and a mammoth show building carefully hidden on the other side of the berm, readying the wildest crew that ever sacked the Spanish Main. Marc Davis and Claude Coats brought their characters and sets together into finished show scenes. X Atencio's script deftly united a tranquil Louisiana bayou; a network of haunted caverns; an epic battle between a pirate galleon and a Spanish fortress; a cutthroat pumping and dunking the town's mayor for information about a buried and cursed treasure; a buccaneer auctioneer "marrying off" town maidens to the highest bidder; rakish brigands in hot pursuit of wine, women, and song; and a seaport in flames.

Blaine Gibson, Bill Justice, and Wathel Rogers brought the entire motley crew to life onstage through their symbiotic arts of sculpture and Audio-Animatronics. Alice Davis made last-minute alterations for her men in uniform, ensuring that her husband's creations would look their finest on opening day. Yale Gracey put his finishing touches on the special effects that would turn every day into an endless summer night and burn a Caribbean village to the ground on cue. Fred Joerger supervised the final phase of construction, and then the show's installation at the Park.

Walt Disney had personally delayed Pirates of the Caribbean's opening because he refused to open an attraction before he felt it was ready, and his Imagineers were intent on keeping that unspoken promise to their audience. They obsessed over the tiniest details, partly because they knew that's what Walt would have done, and partly because his loss was a blow to their confidence and they were leery of forging ahead on their own. "I remember Marc and Claude agonizing over where to put that bird," Dick Nunis recalls, referring to the parrot perched next to the pirate with a dangling hairy leg. "One would come down and move it one way, and then the other would come down and move it the other way. I finally told both of them, 'Hey, guys, that damn bird is going to get worn out because you guys keep moving it! I know why you guys don't want to open the show. You're scared because Walt's not there to say it's okay. . . .What did Walt always say? 'We can always come back and plus the show, but we gotta get it open.' So, that's what happened."

The Maiden Voyage

Pirates of the Caribbean finally debuted with a soft opening on March 18, 1967, its official premiere and press event following on April 19. The waterborne journey was a far cry from Walt's original walk-through Rogues' Gallery wax museum. Those six rather presentational waxen vignettes had become a sprawling adventure starring sixty-four pirates with their assorted enemies and victims, and fifty-five animals, including cats and dogs, pigs and parrots, and chickens and donkeys. The show had outgrown that infamous basement of the Blue Bayou Mart to encompass a 1,838-foot flume weaving through two enormous show buildings totaling 112,826 square feet

ABOVE: Pirates of the Caribbean around the time of its opening in 1967. **RIGHT:** The attraction set an attendance record in the wake of Walt Disney's death, helping ensure Disneyland's future in the process.

and a channel containing 750,000 gallons of water. Disneyland guests had never before experienced anything of its scope, and it would set the standard for everything that would come thereafter.

The show premiered with the expected Disney pomp and circumstance, a spectacle befitting the last hurrah of the world's greatest showman. A pirate crew led by veteran Disneyland performer Wally Boag, star of the Golden Horseshoe Revue, shanghaied the press corps aboard the sailing ship *Columbia* and set a course for New Orleans Square. When the ship pulled in to port, screen siren Dorothy Lamour broke a bottle of Mississippi River water over an anchor reputed to be once owned by Jean Lafitte to open the attraction. Then Boag and his buccaneers smashed through the faux front door of the stately manor house that contained the attraction.

Like Disneyland itself, Pirates of the Caribbean was an instant hit with the public—minus the disastrous opening day, thankfully—and erased any doubts about the future of Walt Disney Productions without its founder at the helm. And, like all entertainment phenomena, it had legs, growing in popularity as time went on. The attraction enjoyed its highest attendance on August 24, 1968, setting a new Park record in the process. "Pirates of the Caribbean literally saved Disneyland," Alice Davis recalls with no trace of hyperbole.

"You always hope that anything you build will be a big hit," Marc Davis told *Disney News* on the adventure's twenty-fifth anniversary in 1992. "And I think we had a feeling that this one would be a success. But to be as popular now as when it opened? That was too much to hope for back then."

ABOVE: Sam McKim created this 1968 "fun map" of the attraction, which featured prominently in the original Pirates of the Caribbean souvenir book. **BELOW:** Imagineers and Disney Legends John Hench and Marty Sklar help the pirates chart a course for the future at Walt Disney World in Florida.

There is no one explanation for the immediate success and enduring appeal of Pirates of the Caribbean. It is a magical alchemy of creative factors and design decisions, each a testament to the considerable talents of the individual Imagineers and the overwhelming cumulative effect of their collaboration. If you were to ask the guests on the queue why they love Pirates of the Caribbean, each one of them would have a different answer. For some it is Marc Davis's cast of memorable characters and the miracle of their realization by Blaine Gibson and Wathel Rogers. For others it is the sheer virtual reality of Claude Coats's irresistibly immersive environments. Still others like to quote X Atencio's dire pronouncements about a cursed treasure and the consequences in store for those who don't heed the cryptic warning or sing along with their favorite sea chantey.

If you were to try and point to one common denominator, it would probably be the meticulous attention to detail exhibited by each Imagineer in every discipline. It is that quality that enables guests to discover something different every time they board a bateau and sail into the darkness. "Even though they know it well, there's so many things that people haven't seen," John Hench recalled in *Disney Family Album.* "It's abundant in its details. I think that's another thing. We put more and more into it. But I suppose it's an old favorite. It's like a good musical, like *Pirates of Penzance*, maybe. It has everything in it: music, a little thrill."

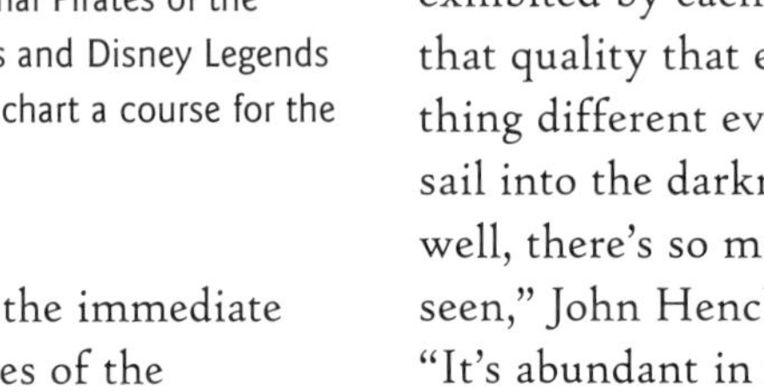

"Pirates is Disney's quintessential, signature attraction," Marty Sklar says. "We measure everything we do against Pirates of the Caribbean."

Perhaps Blaine Gibson sums up the enduring appeal of Pirates of the Caribbean better than anybody: "It boils down to just one man—Walt. It just verifies how right he was. We were all just going along for the ride."

It was an important benchmark that would set a new standard as the Imagineers embarked on their own grand adventure: the pursuit of Walt Disney's last and greatest dream on a distant peninsula due nor'-nor'west of the Spanish Main.

Setting Sail for Florida and the Far East

Caribbean Plaza

Pirates of the Caribbean quickly took its place as Disneyland's signature attraction, the crown jewel that saved the Park in the tumultuous times immediately following Walt's death. It represented the pinnacle of the art of Imagineering, the ultimate synthesis of creativity and technological know-how, a testament to Walt's singular vision of three-dimensional storytelling. So Pirates would obviously be one of Walt Disney World's anchor attractions when the planet's second Magic Kingdom opened its gates in 1971, right? To the contrary, in the late 1960s Pirates of the Caribbean was nowhere to be found on the developing Magic Kingdom's menu of attractions.

The decision to omit Disneyland's runaway hit from its younger sibling was a combination of realization and rationalization. The Imagineers and their operational partners both realized that the inclusion of Disneyland's most expensive attraction might deal a fatal blow to a budget that was already stretched to its limits. In addition to a Magic Kingdom that was much larger than the Disneyland original, the Walt Disney World team had two resort hotels, a complex and costly transportation system, and hundreds of acres of resort amenities to build. The hefty price tag also created an intractable capacity issue. "To add that one attraction we would have had to eliminate five others," says Dick Nunis, Disneyland—and soon to be Walt Disney World—operations chief. The Park couldn't risk losing the critical people-eating capabilities of that many attractions in order to make the numbers work on just one—even one as popular as Pirates of the Caribbean.

The Imagineers dealt with this dawning realization by employing a creative rationalization: Florida was so steeped in its own true-life pirate history, and

BELOW: Marc Davis concept sketch of the Hurricane Lagoon scene in the Walt Disney World version of the attraction.

LEFT: The Walt Disney World attraction is housed in El Castillo (The Castle), an ancient citadel that stands in the shadow of Torre del Sol (Tower of the Sun). **BELOW:** Marc Davis concept sketch of Pirate's Bay, a rocky Caribbean beachfront where guests board their bateaux. Since Caribbean Plaza already establishes the story's setting, the Florida attraction's load area stands in for both Laffite's Landing and The Blue Bayou at Disneyland.

so close to the real Caribbean, that residents and tourists alike would have little interest in a simulated pirate experience. At the same time, however, they didn't want to deprive their East Coast audience of such an elaborate and immersive story. So the Imagineers tried to view the omission of Pirates as an opportunity to take the state-of-their-art to the next level and dethrone their reigning champion in the process. It was Marc Davis himself who spear-headed an ambitious E-Ticket adventure slated for the Magic Kingdom's first expansion phase: Western River Expedition, a rip-roaring waterborne journey through the American West, starring cowboys and Indians in place of buccaneers and brigands. But Marc and the rest of the WED team didn't count on one thing: cross-country word-of-mouth and the undiminished power of Disney's Sunday night television show.

In just four years of operation, Pirates of the Caribbean had become a fundamental part of the Disneyland experience and like Main Street, U.S.A., rockets to the moon, and a fairy tale castle in the sky, it was expected to make the transcontinental move to Florida. The Imagineers quickly discovered that most Walt Disney World guests had either experi-enced the attraction for themselves in Anaheim, heard rave reviews from people who had, or seen it featured on *Walt Disney's Wonderful World of Color*, in a TV hour written by Marty Sklar, and *none* of them could understand why it wasn't part of Florida's Magic Kingdom. They expected to see Pirates of the Caribbean at Walt Disney World, and they weren't at all happy when they discovered that they wouldn't.

Walt Disney Productions CEO Card Walker per-sonally decreed that Pirates of the Caribbean would be added to the Magic Kingdom, and fast. The Imagineers tried to explain that they were working on a new adventure even bigger and better than Pirates, but Card wouldn't hear of it. The guests had asked and they would receive. An Adventureland site for Pirates of the Caribbean was chosen in the spring

of 1972, less than six months after Walt Disney World's grand opening, and construction was underway by that fall. Cast Members in City Hall, who were on the front lines fielding guest complaints about the AWOL buccaneers, began wearing buttons proclaiming, "The Pirates Are Coming! Christmas 1973!" Better late than never, they thought, and hoped guests would agree.

One person who most certainly didn't agree was Marc Davis. He wasn't at all happy about scuttling WED's would-be masterpiece, Western River Expedition, to cover what he felt was the same ground, his own creative triumphs and popular demand notwithstanding. But he knew Card Walker wouldn't budge, so he began campaigning for substantial changes and improvements to the latest version of Pirates. Marc had never been happy with his hastily created solution for that ultimately obsolete basement in New Orleans Square: the haunted caverns "prologue," and he knew that the Imagineers had made significant advancements in Audio-Animatronics technology and programming in the five years since the attraction's premiere. "Let's at least top Pirates with Pirates," Marc reasoned. But it was not to be.

The attraction's move to Adventureland dictated a number of other design alterations as well. The pirates' new home port would be Caribbean Plaza, a sun-bleached district of Adventureland styled after the English and Spanish colonies of the eighteenth-century West Indies. The attraction itself would be housed in El Castillo (The Castle), an ancient Spanish citadel. Guests would pass through its labyrinthine dungeons and arsenals on their way to the bateaux docked at Pirate's Bay, a rocky Caribbean beachfront that stood in for the Blue Bayou. The bateaux would then proceed directly into the shortened haunted-grotto scenes, but from the Bombarding the Fort scene on, the experience would be almost identical to the Disneyland original.

One scene new to the Florida show was a more suitable grand finale, which Marc Davis moved from a subterranean arsenal at Disneyland to the sacked town's Treasure Room. Drunken pirates still shoot at one another—and guests in their passing bateaux—but their incursion into the Treasure Room, complete with bound and gagged colonial guards, did bring some closure to the story as the pirates finally obtain their golden and bejeweled objects of desire when the curtain comes down.

Despite the lack of time and enhancement opportunities, Marc did enjoy one major creative victory in the Florida show: the elimination of the "upramp" that brings the bateaux back to the load area. It was a design element that had always bothered him about the Disneyland version, still another direct result of the quick-fix haunted caverns and the two drops that carry guests deep underground—after all, what goes down must come up. With its perilously high water table, Florida could hold only one waterfall drop, and even that was included solely for the thrill element; it was not an operational necessity like Disneyland's trip under the berm.

"I don't like the fact that when the ride is over, you have to sit at the bottom of that ramp and then go chug, chug, chugging up this hill and then out, wondering what the hell you're going to do next," Marc Davis told *The E-Ticket*. "In Florida we got the people out of the boats, and then they go up a speed

ABOVE: A "Barker Bird" welcomes guests to the attraction, offering hints of the adventure to come. **RIGHT:** Concept sketch by Marc Davis of a scene unique to Florida: The Treasure Room, where the pirates finally find the plunder for which they've been searching throughout the attraction.

LEFT AND BELOW: The Treasure Room guards, bound and gagged as the pirates clean them out in the final show scene. BOTTOM: Guests encounter a pirate that transforms into a skeleton and back again in a scene, possibly proposed for the boarding area, which was ultimately cut from the final attraction.

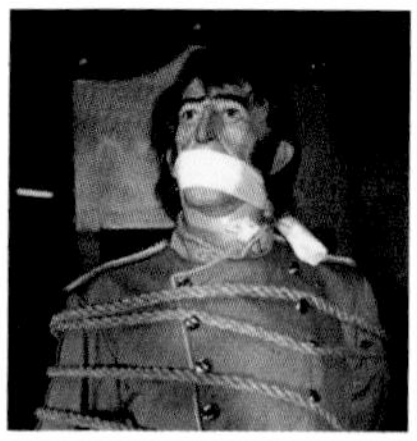

ramp and out. But then, we didn't really think about it [the ending] at Disneyland. We were just trying to get the ride system to work."

Although Marc Davis couldn't make as many enhancements as he would have liked, sketches hint at the Pirates of the Caribbean that could have been. One proposed scene would have bridged the narrative gap between the pirates in their "yo-ho" heyday and the grisly fate awaiting them in the haunted grottoes but alas, Marc's Island of Lost Souls never made it off his drawing board. "Something I tried to do for Florida was a pirate that would turn into a skeleton," Marc said in *The E-Ticket*. "It's a sort of Pepper's Ghost effect. Florida was going to have a kind of island, but this stuff was never done." The effort was far from wasted, however, and the notion of pirates that transform into skeletons and back again would go on to play a major role when the attraction set sail on the big screen thirty years later.

Pirates of the Caribbean opened at Walt Disney World's Magic Kingdom on December 15, 1973, and ranked as one of the Park's most popular attractions. The Imagineers had now designed and built Pirates of the Caribbean twice. For their third performance, they would attempt a seamless thematic blending of the first two incarnations.

LEFT: Attraction art that presents the name and location of the show with Japanese "subtitles." **BELOW:** At Tokyo Disneyland, the attraction is located in a New Orleans–themed subset of Adventureland.

"No Mouth on a Dead Person"

The 1970s were tumultuous years for Walt Disney Productions, a longer than expected transitional period that began with Walt's death in 1966 and ultimately ended with the arrival of a new management team in the form of Paramount's Michael Eisner and Frank Wells, formerly of Warner Bros. But it was also a time of ambitious and unprecedented expansion for the Disney theme parks, seeing the openings at Walt Disney World of Magic Kingdom Park, on October 1, 1971, and Epcot Center, on October 1, 1982, and the company's first international destination, Tokyo Disneyland, which welcomed its first guests on April 15, 1983.

The Tokyo project in particular would prove to be a major milestone for the company, laying the foundation for an international expansion that would continue well into the twenty-first century. It proved to the Disney management team, then led by CEO Ron Miller, Walt's son-in-law, that there was a considerable audience with an insatiable appetite for Disney theme park entertainment outside the United States. Japan's deep interest in a Disneyland of its own, formally ratified in an agreement with the Oriental Land Company, also demonstrated that the magic of Disney translated well into any language, and the Studio's characters and stories knew no boundaries—international, cultural, or otherwise.

That translation would fall as it always had to the Imagineers, now led by Marty Sklar, who Walt had brought to WED from Disneyland to work on the World's Fair, and comprised of old hands such as John Hench, Ken Anderson, Herb Ryman, Marc Davis, Claude Coats, Blaine Gibson, Sam McKim, and X Atencio, and newer recruits such as Randy Bright, Eric Jacobson, Michael Sprout, John Horny, Bob Weis, and Chris Tietz. The apprentices were learning at the feet of the old masters, and they were doing so on the first international iteration of Walt Disney's original Magic Kingdom concept. And as it turned out, exporting the Disneyland experience to Japan would prove to be more difficult than it first appeared.

The Imagineers went to great lengths to accommodate Japan's climate and culture, covering Main

LEFT: Pirates of the Caribbean as background photo op for these visitors to Tokyo Disneyland. **BOTTOM LEFT:** Concept sketch of the costumes proposed for Tokyo Disneyland. **BOTTOM RIGHT:** The Auctioneer points the way in the Tokyo version of the show.

Street, U.S.A., with a glass canopy to create the more weather-friendly World Bazaar, and presenting the history of Japan in an ambitious Audio-Animatronics theatrical presentation, Meet the World. They reasoned that the Japanese audience would want a theme park experience tailored to their culture and tastes, reflecting their own unique view of the world. To the designers' surprise, however, the Japanese preferred their Disneyland unadulterated and decidedly American, which meant hamburgers and hot dogs on the menu and direct lifts of classic attractions such as Jungle Cruise, The Haunted Mansion, and Pirates of the Caribbean.

The Japanese, like most everyone else who experienced it, were particularly enamored of Disneyland's Pirates of the Caribbean. A carbon copy was going to be a challenge without New Orleans Square, which wouldn't be making the trip to Tokyo, once again leaving Adventureland as the only logical choice. But in the same way the Imagineers had created a Caribbean district exclusively for Pirates at the Florida park, they decided to carve a literal French Quarter out of Tokyo's Adventureland, preserving the New Orleans location and the popular Blue Bayou restaurant of the Disneyland flagship. It made perfect story sense; for the Tokyo audience, nineteenth-century New Orleans, with its mélange of French, Spanish, Creole, Cajun, and, yes, American influences, was an exotic port of call, and that made it a perfect fit for Adventureland.

Tokyo's water table isn't much lower than Florida's, however, and that necessitated the only two cuts made to an otherwise direct lift of the full Disneyland show. As in the Florida version, there is only one drop over a waterfall; and the Captain's Quarters, a vignette featuring a skeletal Pirate Captain reading in bed inside an ornate, subterranean

chamber, was the only scene absent from the haunted caverns.

The show may have looked almost exactly the same as its Anaheim predecessor, but the way it sounded was a completely different story, as X Atencio quickly found out. Cinderella Castle may not be subject to any cultural barriers and Mickey Mouse stands for the same things in any language, but X discovered that at least one classic Pirates show element was literally getting lost in the translation, as he recalled on an episode of *Disney Family Album* in 1984. "For the Tokyo version of the attraction, we found out that instead of saying, 'Dead men tell no tales,' the ghost voice was saying, 'There is no mouth on a dead person.' Well, that doesn't make sense, that wasn't what we were trying to do. There's no Japanese equivalent of 'Dead men tell no tales,' so we had to come up with something along the lines of, 'If you're not careful, you will not pass this way again.'"

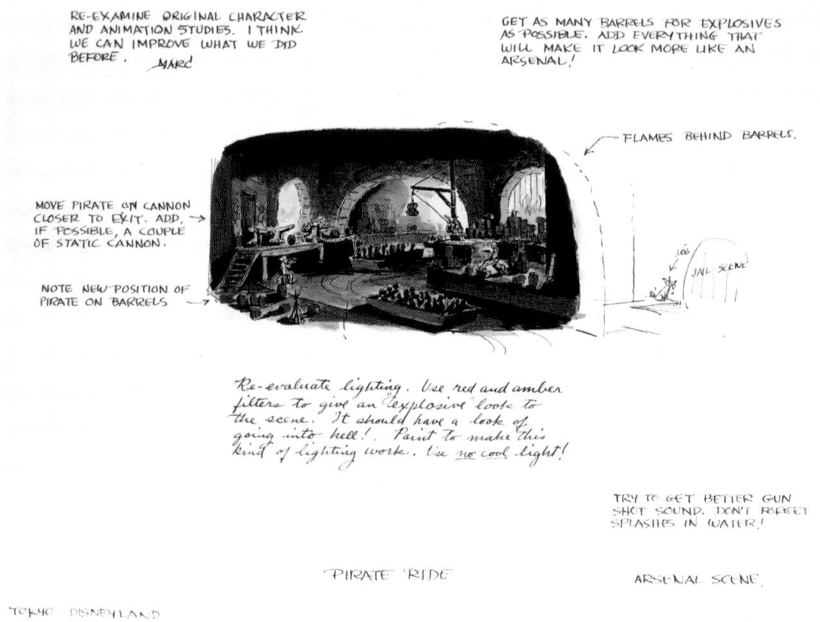

Although the show featured largely the same audio tracks as the Anaheim original, the talking skull was a notable exception. And just as X Atencio had literally gotten into the act in the American versions of the show, the voice of the skull—along with The Haunted Mansion's Ghost Host—was supplied by Teichiro Hori, a former movie producer at the home of *Godzilla*, Toho Studios, who had been brought in to serve as a Japanese counterpart to the Imagineers.

As it turned out, Disney magic didn't require a translator. Pirates of the Caribbean was a crowd-pleaser on Tokyo Disneyland's opening day and ever after, and quickly found a special place in guests' hearts, just as it had done almost exactly sixteen years earlier in Anaheim. The Tokyo project proved to be an invaluable learning experience, because Walt Disney's original team of handpicked Imagineers was slowly retiring, one by one, and a new generation of dreamers and doers was about to embark on one of the biggest and most challenging international endeavors in Disney history.

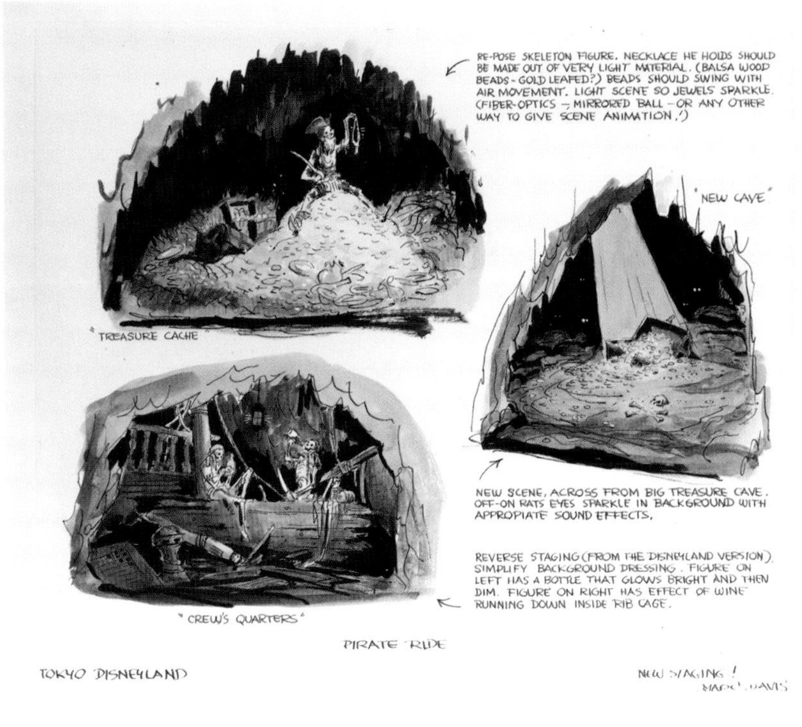

ABOVE AND LEFT: Marc Davis concept sketches of now-familiar scenes newly adapted for the Tokyo Park, including the Grotto sequence and The Arsenal.

The European Invasion

How Do You Say "Aargh!" in French?

Far from closing its doors or selling out to a larger corporation, Walt Disney Productions survived the deaths of its co-founders, and the Parks and Resorts division actually flourished under the alternately cautious and ambitious stewardship of Card Walker, Ron Miller, and the rest of their management team. The precedent they set with Tokyo Disneyland in particular left an invaluable legacy for incoming CEO Michael Eisner and President Frank Wells when they arrived at the company in 1984. They didn't shy away from the challenge, and one of their first orders of business was the launch of a European park.

Dick Nunis and his parks team had already done extensive research and exhaustive site surveys, narrowing the company's options to sites outside Barcelona, Spain, and Paris, France. In 1984, Michael Eisner personally selected a Paris location and plans were set in motion to build Euro Disney—later renamed Disneyland Resort Paris—a Walt Disney World–style theme park and resort destination located in Marne-la-Vallée, a verdant agricultural region twenty miles east of the City of Lights.

The centerpiece of the resort would be a new interpretation of Disney's flagship park in Anaheim. Second-generation Imagineer and Disneyland veteran Tony Baxter was assigned to lead the creative team that would once again reinvent the Magic Kingdom experience, this time for a European audience. Unlike their Japanese counterparts, French officials weren't interested in a wholesale reproduction of Disney's American parks, which meant that Imagineers would have to take special care in the translation of their stories to appeal to this very different culture. This reinvention enabled Imagineers to revisit some of their own signature attractions and draw from more than thirty years of experience to create the ultimate expressions of those stories. In the case of Pirates of the Caribbean that meant turning the experience completely on its head, and in the

ABOVE RIGHT: Imagineer Tony Baxter, lead creative designer for Pirates at Disneyland Paris.
BELOW AND RIGHT: Concept sketch of the Pirates exterior facade, and a view of the fortress under construction.

process, finally addressing any lingering creative issues over those hastily contrived haunted caverns.

As with the last two Magic Kingdoms, an Adventureland location was the natural choice for a pirates hideout, but Tony Baxter and Chris Tietz, the attraction's lead creative designer and show producer, were intent on taking their story's setting to the next level. The attraction would be housed in a Spanish fortress, much like the Walt Disney World show. But unlike Florida's El Castillo, which is somewhat quaint and charming, even pretty, this buccaneers' redoubt would be an intimidating and physically imposing edifice that would have the Jolly Roger flying high and proud above it.

The show building was only the beginning. The ancient fortification sat across an exotic lagoon from Adventure Isle, a tropical playground that was home to Ben Gunn's Cave of *Treasure Island* fame, as well as Skull Rock and Captain Hook's pirate galleon from *Peter Pan*. The sprawling Pirates location was also situated directly between Adventureland and Fantasyland, corresponding with the similarly themed Peter Pan's Flight just across the border. And so this hearty trio of Adventure Isle, Peter Pan's Flight, and Pirates of the Caribbean formed a distinct thematic triangle that immediately spoke to guests—most of whom spoke different languages to begin with. "The area speaks to you no matter what language you speak. It's the visual language of pirates," Tony Baxter says. With thousands of English, Dutch, French, German, Italian, and Spanish-speaking guests in the Park at any given time, such potent visual literacy was a necessity in the stories the Imagineers were telling at Disneyland Paris.

In addition to the striking visual statement made by a bastion looming so ominously over guests, the attraction's exterior design had a practical consideration as well: the show building *had* to be tall in order to accommodate the experience the Imagineers were creating inside. "We wanted to take the best elements of the Disneyland original as well as duplicate the thrill of that design," Chris Tietz recalls, referring to that attraction's breathtaking plunges down two waterfalls. "We couldn't do the drops at Walt Disney World and Tokyo Disneyland because of the high water table. Well, Paris has a high water table, too. We couldn't go down, so we knew we had to get the audience up."

"You go two feet down and you've got a lake,"

TOP: Map-like view of the attraction, similar to the piece Sam McKim created for the Disneyland original in 1968. **RIGHT:** Chris Tietz, Imagineer and show producer of Pirates of the Caribbean for Disneyland Paris.

Tony Baxter agrees. "We built it up so we wouldn't have to dig a hole down." Armed with the height needed to restore two drops to Pirates of the Caribbean for the first time since the Anaheim flagship, Tony and Chris were determined to spend their thrills wisely. "We wanted to save some of the fun and excitement for the end of the show and not have it all at the beginning," Tony says. The Imagineers would accomplish that by completely reversing the Pirates story as various audiences had known it until that time.

The changes begin almost immediately upon entering the old pirate stronghold. After winding their way through the flickering gloom of the fort's dungeons and arsenals, as in the Walt Disney World version, guests find themselves on the shores of a tropical lagoon at twilight. "We wanted the same feeling as the Blue Bayou," Chris explains, "but we had a Caribbean story line, so we adopted something of a castaway theme." The resulting Blue Lagoon proved to be the perfect stand-in for its Cajun cousin thousands of miles away at Disneyland.

Once guests are safely aboard, the bateaux glide through this serene lagoon, passing lush tropical foliage, soothing waterfalls, and a foreboding shipwreck on their way to another great stone fortress on the opposite shore. Unlike a conventional roller-coaster or water-flume ride, the lift mechanism itself is completely story driven, with the bateaux proceeding up an incline that colonial soldiers would use to transport supplies to the installation's upper levels. This clever and convenient story point also helped explain the system of chains, pulleys, and winches that haul the bateaux up and inside the old fort.

On the fort's upper level, Chris and his creative team staged a scene in which a familiar band of jailed pirates are trying to coax a key from a "guard dog" and escape from their cells. From their bateaux, guests can see silhouettes of pirates climbing over a wall to attack the fort and Spanish soldiers trying to fend them off. The prisoners, meanwhile, are making every effort to free themselves so they can rejoin their pirate crew and plunder the town.

"That's where we reversed the entire story," Tony says. "The pirates are coming to *free* their comrades in jail. So we start with what our American audience has come to know as the ending and that sets everything else into motion."

In this case, the Jail scene literally sets the story—and the guests—into motion, and, for the first time, even the attraction's first big drop serves the narrative. A cannonball has shattered an aqueduct and flooded the fort, which helps explain why the bateaux are able to "cruise" through the jail in the first place. The bateaux pass through a gaping hole in the wall created by cannonball fire and plummet over a parapet into the harbor, where guests find themselves in the middle of an epic battle between the fort and a pirate ship anchored offshore. Unlike the three previous incarnations of the attraction, this time the guests are not invisible to the story's characters; the buccaneers actually see them and target their bateaux with cannon fire, making the scene more immersive than its predecessors. "It's the only time when the cannon fire is synchronized to the bateau's arrival in the harbor," Tony Baxter states.

Once the bateaux sail into the town, the attraction follows much the same course as the Disneyland original, until the fiery climax. The most notable addition is a pair of sword-fighting pirates dueling to

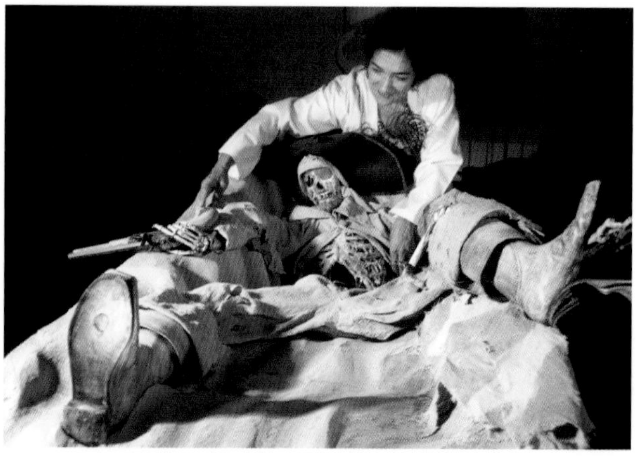

ABOVE AND RIGHT: An Imagineer ages the model of the attraction's facade with a touch of character paint while one of her colleagues helps a pirate settle into his final resting place. **OPPOSITE:** The attraction poster, with the show's name and location in English and the tagline in French.

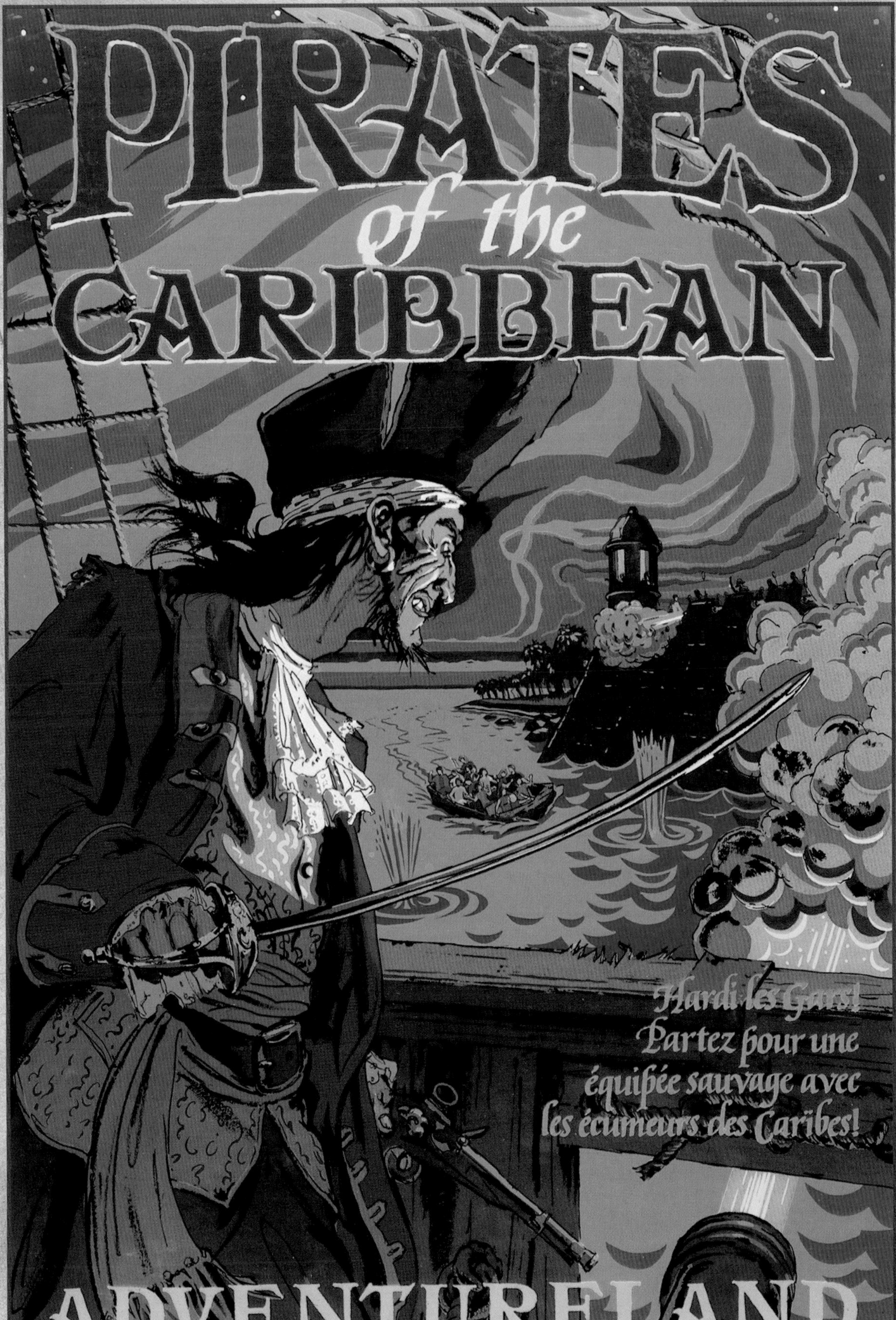
PIRATES
of the
CARIBBEAN
Hardi les Gars!
Partez pour une
équipée sauvage avec
les écumeurs des Caribes!
ADVENTURELAND

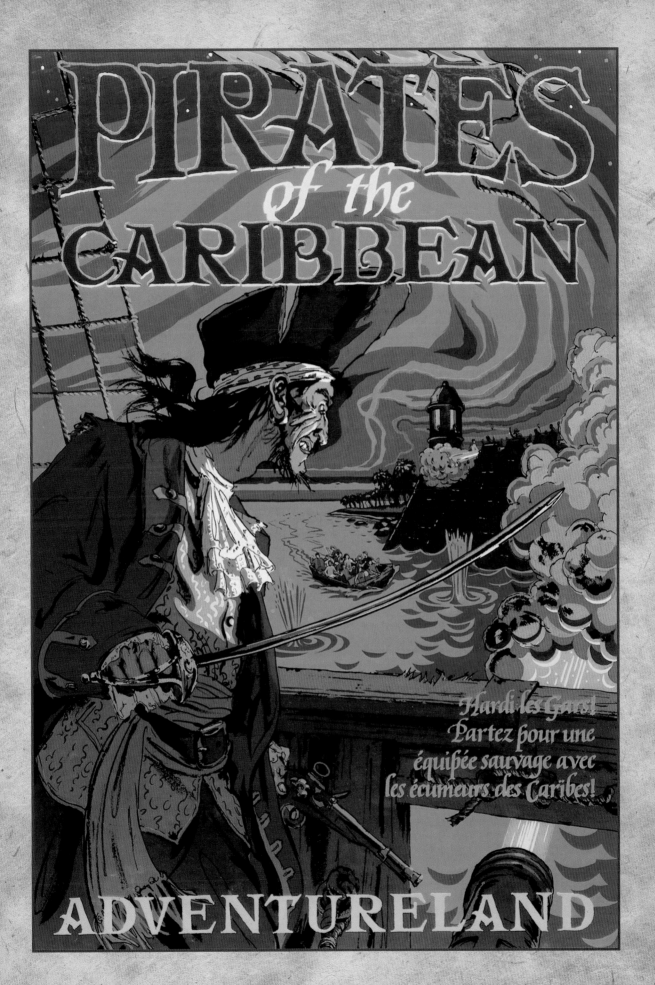

the death in the Chase scene. "I asked the team if we could have the pirates do something that I as a human being would be afraid to do, and that's how we came up with the sword fight," Tony says. "We saw an opportunity to advance the state of the art of Audio-Animatronics; that's a big part of what we try to do at Walt Disney Imagineering. We always try to give the guests a little more." The duelists, whose swords actually cling and clang as they make contact—an Audio-Animatronics first—quickly became the talk of the attraction.

The Imagineers saved their second drop for the traditional climax of the show, the Burning Town scene. Once the bateaux pass under the drunken pirate with the dangling hairy leg and enter the burning arsenal, there is a tremendous explosion, and guests sink into oblivion as the town's gunpowder supply goes up in smoke. The placement of the second drop wasn't exactly a new idea; it was inspired by some creative editing in a preview of the original Pirates of the Caribbean on *Walt Disney's Wonderful World of Color*.

"When Disney previewed the attraction on the Sunday night TV show, they placed the second waterfall right after the pirate with the dangling leg," Tony says. "I guess they thought it was a great way to end the ride, even though it wasn't that way in reality." Tony and his team jumped at the chance to finally deliver on that false promise in their version of the show. "By putting a waterfall there, it also gave us a chance to synchronize some of the effects to the bateaux."

"As you enter the burning arsenal, we drop you down into an inferno as though the whole arsenal is going up," Chris Tietz says. "We've been waiting thirty years for those barrels to blow, and it finally happens at Disneyland Paris. The force of the blast sends you into a dark cave. The explosion washes over you and echoes back to you as thunder. That's where you enter the haunted caverns, and that's when you first hear, 'Dead men tell no tales.'"

Guests then experience all the familiar vignettes of the Disneyland original, from the skeleton sailing his ghostly galleon through a hurricane to the eerily ornate Captain's Quarters to the Treasure Cache overflowing with pirate loot that can never be spent. But this time, the prologue has become an epilogue, a fitting conclusion to this tale of pillaging and plundering.

"That explosion in the arsenal is what happens to pirates who get carried away," Tony says of their big finish, "and the haunted caverns is where they end up." The concussive sounds turn into the wailing

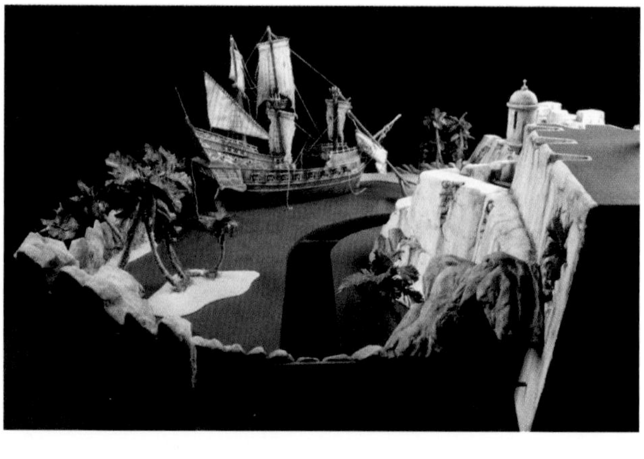

TOP: General view of Pirates of the Caribbean's exterior facade and queue area. **LEFT AND ABOVE:** Like the Disneyland original, each scene of the Paris show was laid out in an elaborate scale model.

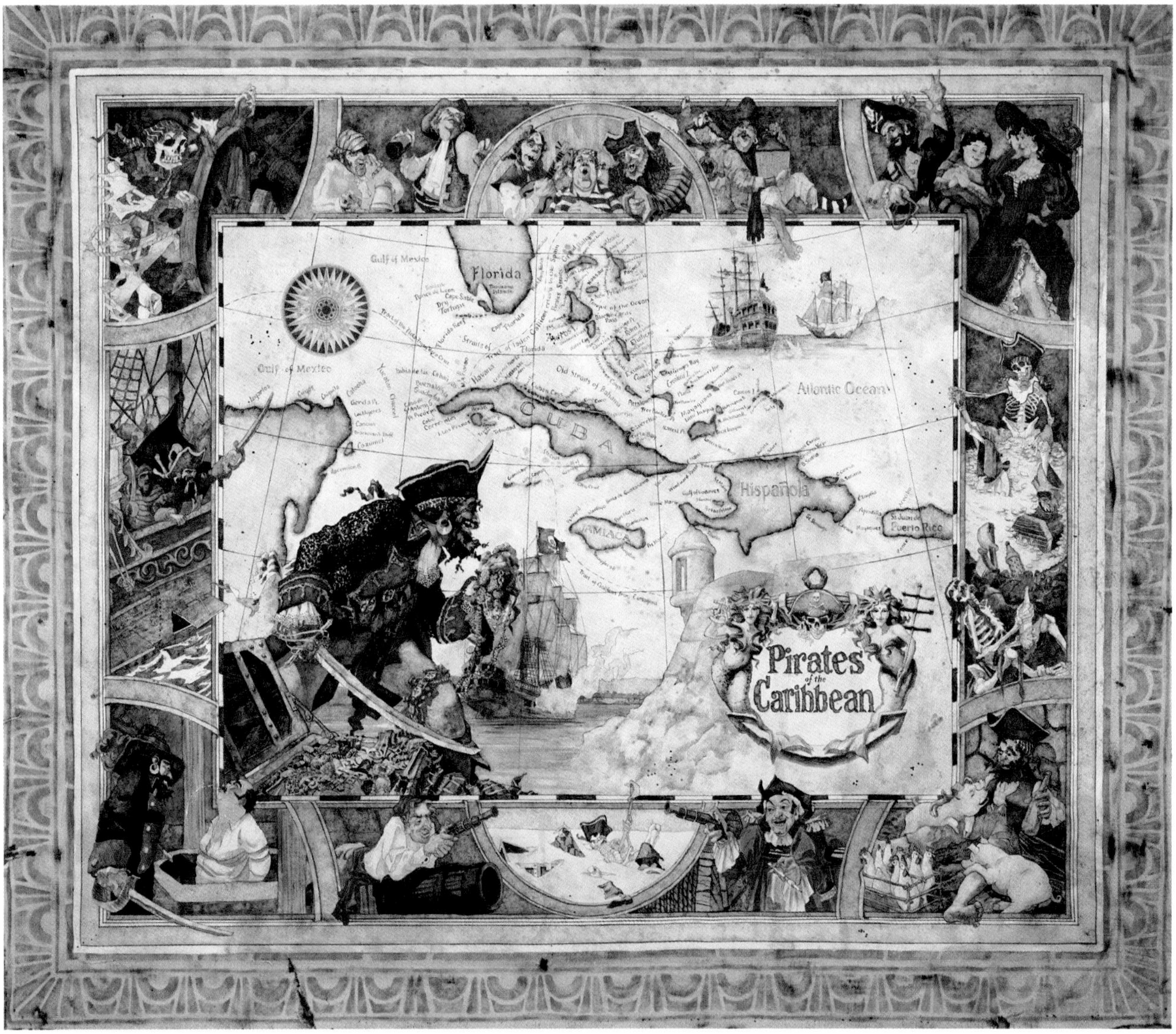

of the wind and a ghostly voice admonishing, "Dead men tell no tales." When the smoke clears, guests are in the haunted caverns, filled with the treasure that has thus far proved so elusive. The climax then turns into a "metaphorical 'meeting your maker' epilogue," as Tony explains. "That's the moral of the story. What good is all the treasure if you're so frivolous and careless? You can't spend it if you're dead. The end result, the whole 'Crime Doesn't Pay' moment, takes place at the end."

"The haunted caverns have always represented the pirates' 'comeuppance' in one form or another, the consequences of a life of greed and pursuing a cursed treasure," Chris adds. "We just put it at the end of our story."

In a fitting coda to the revised story, the last thing guests see before disembarking is the attraction's signature talking skull embedded in the rocks overhead, and it delivers the now-extinct pirates' ominous parting message: "Dead men tell no tales."

ABOVE: A striking piece of art created by Imagineer John Horny. The pirate just beneath the name of the attraction is a caricature of Marc Davis, a subtle tribute to an old master.

Since guests are back at "ground level" after two drops from the lofty heights to which Imagineers have taken them, there is no need for them to navigate an up-ramp of any kind, in a bateau or on foot. Marc Davis would have been proud.

Pirates of the Caribbean opened with the rest of the Paris Magic Kingdom on April 12, 1992, a full quarter-century after the debut of the Disneyland original. The Imagineers had indeed taken the very best of that classic show and reinvented it for a new generation and an international audience. It is unsure where and when the Pirates of the Caribbean will drop anchor again, but one thing is certain: the spirit of Walt Disney's final masterpiece will continue to guide his Imagineers on their ongoing voyage of adventure and discovery.

Course Heading

The Spanish Main

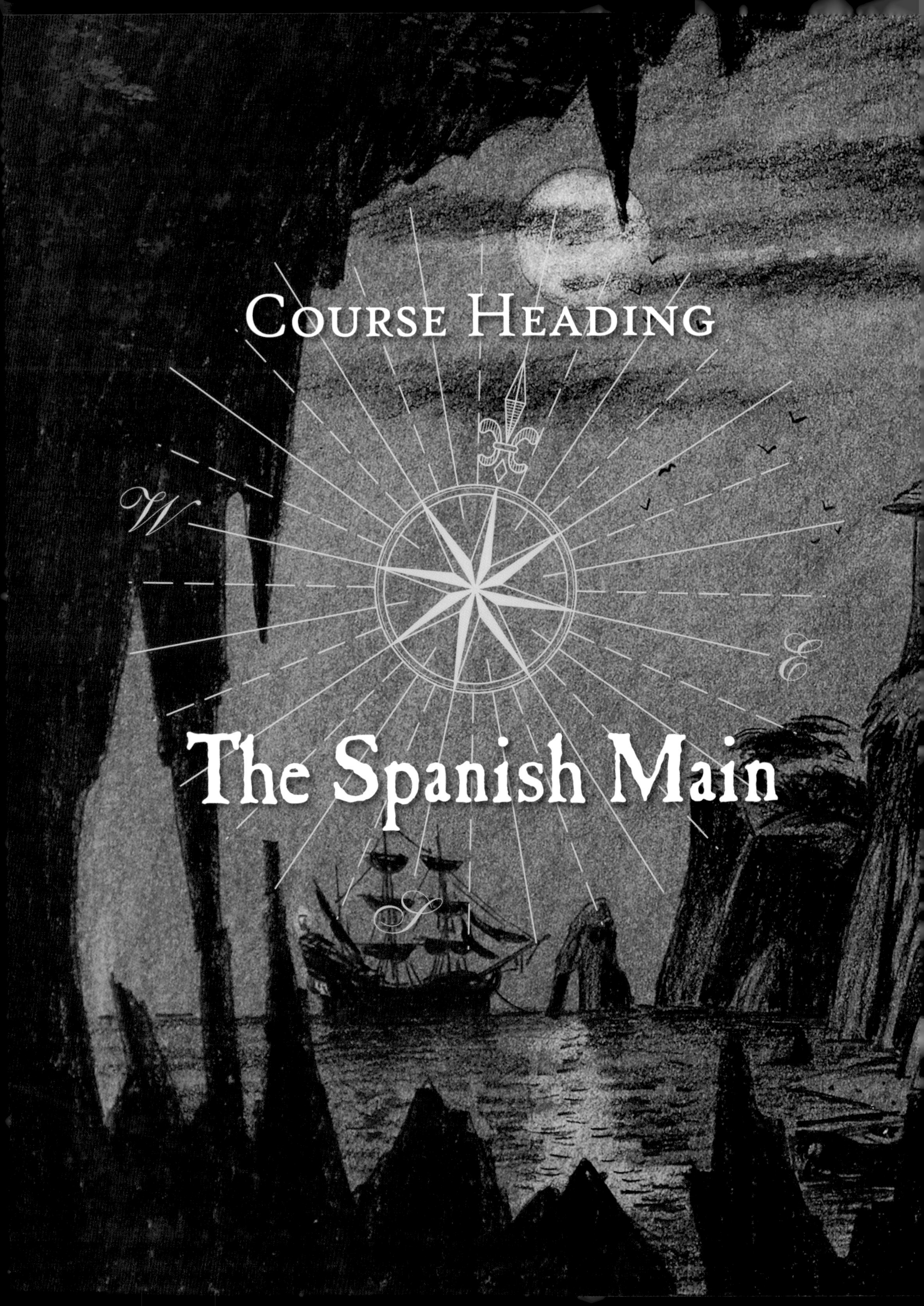

The Port of NEW ORLEANS

OUR ADVENTURE begins in the French Quarter of old New Orleans, which stands proudly at a wide bend in the Rivers of America. With its lacy wrought-iron balconies, shuttered windows, French doors, and pastel-colored stucco, the architecture of New Orleans Square reflects the Queen of the Delta in the 1860s, when the bustling port city was a cultural mélange of French, Spanish, Cajun, Creole, and Early American influences. This tranquil journey back in time continues as guests approach a stately manor house at the head of Royal Street, its genteel appearance standing in stark contrast to the hidden dangers that lurk inside.

Guests entering the manor house are greeted with an improbable sight, a brick canal in which bateaux sail around a tropical sandbar, strewn with treasure chests, a weathered Jolly Roger, and an unfurled treasure map. A green parrot wearing a pirate hat and an eye patch perches atop an old chest, quizzically watching the bateaux as they sail past him. As guests make their way past this scene-setting tableau, the attraction's title materializes across the treasure map in an eerily glowing script, as if glittering gold dust has been scattered over the ancient parchment by an invisible hand. They proceed onto a wooden walkway that leads to a nearby boat landing.

ABOVE: A view of the Pirates of the Caribbean facade, taken from the bridge that was added to allow guest traffic to flow above the attraction's frequently crowded exterior queue. **PAGES 66-67:** 1963 Collin Campbell concept sketch of a pirate galleon anchored off the coast of a Caribbean seaport.

HIDDEN TREASURE

In-Spire-ations

The spire atop the Pirates of the Caribbean facade is, well, "inspired" by the famed Cabildo in New Orleans's Jackson Square (left, circa 1912, courtesy of the Louisiana State Museum). The Cabildo was built in 1799 to house the Spanish colonial government, and is perhaps best known as the site in which the Louisiana Purchase was signed in 1803.

RIGHT: Marc Davis concept sketch of a sandbar the bateaux sail around as they make their way back to the load area. In later years, the scene was enhanced with a parrot similar to Walt Disney World's Barker Bird, and a treasure map "marquee" upon which fiber-optic effects spell out the attraction's name.

HIDDEN TREASURE

Walking the Plaque

Gracing the front exterior wall of the manor house is a plaque (above) honoring Pirates of the Caribbean's thirtieth anniversary in 1997, which was unveiled as part of a major enhancement. Although Disney attractions typically do not feature such opening credits, the plaque bears the names of the key Imagineers who brought the attraction to life, forever commemorating their significant contribution to the Disneyland experience.

HIDDEN TREASURE

Real Characters

The caricatures on the manor house's interior walls are based on some of Marc Davis's earliest renderings of nautical personages Sir Francis Verney, Sir Henry Mainwaring, Anne Bonny and Mary Read, and Captain Charles Gibbs. Marc drew the sketches while researching pirate lore, but abandoned these and other real-life personalities to take the show in a fictional and humorous direction.

Tokyo Disneyland
The Grand Foyer

Although Tokyo Disneyland's manor house is similar in almost every respect to the Disneyland original, it does possess one unique feature: an ornate grand foyer on the first floor. Disneyland's exterior queue winds beneath an expansive bridge in front of the show building, constructed in 1987 so guest traffic could flow smoothly above Pirates' often-congested exterior queue. Its Japanese counterpart invites guests to come in from the often-inclement weather and explore the home's finely appointed lobby while they wait. Paintings of pirate ships and epic sea battles and a map of the Western Hemisphere adorn the walls, along with portraits of an aristocratic gentleman and his lady, presumably the master and mistress of the house. A decorative birdcage (perhaps inspired by a mechanical bird in a cage Walt picked up on a trip to the Delta City in the mid 1940s), an old sea chest, and a scale model of a galleon complete this picture of Southern gentility, while offering hints of the nautical adventure to come.

Walt Disney World
Caribbean Plaza and El Castillo

Pirates of the Caribbean's move to Adventureland at Walt Disney World necessitated a new show building and environs. The pirates make their East Coast home in Caribbean Plaza, an island seaport reminiscent of the British and Spanish colonies of the seventeenth- and eighteenth-century West Indies. The attraction itself is housed in El Castillo (The Castle), an ancient Spanish citadel based on the Castillo de San Felipe del Morro in San Juan, Puerto Rico, which stands in the shadow of Torre del Sol (Tower of the Sun), a Caribbean-style watchtower that guards the entrance.

HIDDEN TREASURE

The Barker Bird

A green parrot in a pirate hat, sporting a peg leg and a tattoo of an anchor on his feathered chest, greets guests as they approach El Castillo. This "barker bird," much like a similar avian spokesman at The Enchanted Tiki Room at Disneyland in its early years, "sells" the show to passing guests, setting the stage for the adventure to come. In this case, it was by necessity. The Florida version of Pirates of the Caribbean, unlike its Disneyland predecessor, was not pre-sold to the public on television, which meant that most guests had no idea of what to expect inside El Castillo, the attraction's marquee notwithstanding. The barker bird tells guests point blank that the old fortress is home to a swashbuckling pirate adventure.

TOP: The Grand Foyer, part of the interior queue in the Tokyo version of the show. **RIGHT:** El Castillo and Torre del Sol in Caribbean Plaza, home of the Walt Disney World attraction.

HIDDEN TREASURE

Check, Matey!

Once inside El Castillo, guests pass through a dimly lit labyrinth of arsenals and dungeons that serves as the attraction's interior queue, home to one of the most brilliantly conceived and least appreciated of Marc Davis's sight gags. Guests who peek through the iron bars of one of the cells find two skeletal inmates hunched over a chessboard, concentrating on their game even in death. The contest is in a state of perpetual check, in which the only available move leads to a sort of loop that can never be broken. Apparently both buccaneers would rather die than declare a tie, and fate has obliged them.

When the tableau was refurbished in the 1990s along with the rest of the attraction, the chessboard was inadvertently swept clean and the Imagineers realized they had no idea how to re-create the game. Fortunately the project team discovered that Marc Davis had drawn a diagram of what the board should look like on the back of his original sketch of the scene.

ABOVE: Marc Davis concept sketch of a chess game that will never end. **BELOW:** A view of the Fortress at Disneyland Paris.

Surrounding El Castillo is a collection of dockside shops, merchant stalls, and converted storehouses filled to overflowing with imports—obtained legally and otherwise—from around the world, including Plaza del Sol Caribe Bazaar, the appropriately named House of Treasure, and The Crow's Nest. Directly opposite the attraction is El Pirata Y el Perico (The Pirate and the Parrot), a restaurant in the guise of a rough-and-tumble tavern typical of a Caribbean seaport during the golden age of piracy. Just across the plaza from Torre del Sol is La Fuente de la Fortuna (The Fountain of Fortune), into which guests can cast "pieces of eight" in the hope of good luck. Not only does Caribbean Plaza serve as a geographically appropriate pirate hideout, its red clay–tiled roofs and Spanish-influenced architecture provide a seamless visual transition between this Caribbean district of Adventureland and the old American Southwest region of Frontierland that borders it.

Disneyland Paris
The Fortress

Taking its cue from El Castillo, the Disneyland Resort Paris show can also be found inside a Spanish fortress straight out of the eighteenth-century West Indies. But where Walt Disney World features a scaled-down castle citadel in relatively pristine condition, with a tattered Jolly Roger the only indication something may be amiss inside, the massive stone fortress in Paris is portrayed in the battle-scarred state in which it might appear *after* the pirates have taken over. This dramatic increase in both scale and atmosphere not only helps present Pirates of the Caribbean as Adventureland's anchor attraction, but instantly communicates the pirate story line to the Park's multilingual population in a clear and direct visual language.

Guests enter a rocky grotto at the base of the installation and proceed into the secret underground entrance to the fort's armory. They make their way through the shadowy bowels of the fortress past dungeons, arsenals, and hidden treasure caches before getting a glimpse of the Crew's Quarters and its skeletal occupants, a disquieting hint at the pirates' ultimate fate in the adventure to come. The Paris attraction is the only one in which a major show scene is visible from the interior queue.

Laffite's LANDING

A BOARDWALK leads guests to a rickety, wooden boat landing on the edge of a quiet Louisiana bayou in the early 1800s, continuing their journey back in time. It is a balmy and breezy summer evening, with bright shining stars dotting the dark rich blue of the night sky, and a full moon reflecting off the cool waters of the bayou. Flickering lantern light illuminates a crude, handpainted sign that announces the dock as Laffite's Landing. Guests step into the waiting bateaux and set out onto this serene Blue Bayou.

Laffite's Landing at Disneyland is named after the infamous French pirate Jean Lafitte (though not spelled the same way), who made his secret headquarters in Louisiana bayou country. Lafitte was the scourge of the Gulf of Mexico in the 1800s, and although he was a known smuggler in New Orleans, he consistently hired the city's best lawyers to acquit him of piracy charges. Lafitte later fought against the British with Andrew Jackson in the Battle of New Orleans, further cementing his place in the city's history. In an ironic twist of fate and allegiance, Lafitte became a spy for the Spanish, who were desperate to crush the Caribbean piracy that was wreaking havoc on their trade with America. The story of Jean Lafitte is one of the "true-life

HIDDEN TREASURE

The Road to Adventure

Sitting near the water's edge is an anchor that supposedly came from one of Jean Lafitte's ships. Screen legend Dorothy Lamour broke a bottle of Mississippi River water over the anchor to officially open the attraction to the public, the perfect way to send guests off.

TOP: An early photograph of guests boarding their bateau at Laffite's Landing.

adventures" that inspired Marc Davis when he began researching pirates in 1961.

Disneyland operations chief Dick Nunis won a key battle with WED head Dick Irvine by insisting that the landing be long enough for two bateaux to line up at a time, effectively doubling the number of guests that could board the attraction per load cycle. Dick Irvine contended that too much conveyor belt would be visible to guests in such a long load area but Walt easily reassured his lead designer. "What's the difference, Dick? That belt's gonna be covered with boats. No one's gonna see it anyway!"

Walt Disney World
Pirate's Bay Boarding Dock

In the Walt Disney World show, guests emerge from the subterranean passageways of El Castillo on the shores of Pirate's Bay and make their way along a rocky beachfront that stands in for Laffite's Landing. A pirate ship is anchored far out in the bay, and moonlight reflects off the surf as it rolls gently toward the shore. Pirates can be heard digging for buried treasure in a nearby cave and the plaintive cries of distant seagulls echo through these beachfront caverns, playing off the pulse-quickening sound of rushing water in the grotto ahead. Safely seated inside their bateaux, guests then set sail into the cavernous abyss before them.

Disneyland Paris
The Landing

At Disneyland Paris, a passageway leads guests out of the pirate stronghold onto the white-sand beach of a lush tropical island in the West Indies. The air is cool and the night sky is clear, save for a few clouds that pass across the face of a full moon. Crickets can be heard chirping in the distance, along with the soothing sound of breaking waves. Guests board their bateaux beneath palm trees that sway gently in the summer breeze and set sail across a tranquil Blue Lagoon.

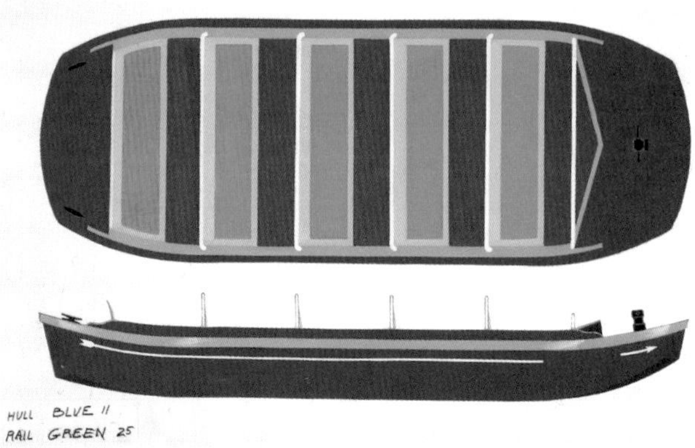

HIDDEN TREASURE

Les Bateaux

Guests make their waterborne journey in small, 22-passenger boats reminiscent of the flat-bottomed "bateaux" that were used to ply the shallow waters of the Louisiana bayous. The original fiberglass boats, which could seat only nineteen guests, were reconfigured in the late 1980s to accommodate an additional row of passengers. Today there are fifty-two bateaux in all, up from the opening-day fleet of forty, each of which is christened with either a woman's name that reflects the French and Spanish influences on the region, or the name of a famous pirate. The names had been vanishing one by one as the original boats were replaced, only to return during a routine refurbishment of the attraction in 2003, when the bateaux were repainted to look as though they were built of wood salvaged from a shipwreck.

TOP: Ride vehicle color elevation. **BELOW:** The Landing load area at Disneyland Paris.

HIDDEN TREASURE

How High the Moon
Although the night sky above the Blue Bayou appears to soar into space, the ceiling is actually only forty feet high. The "bayou" itself is two feet deep.

The Blue BAYOU

THE BATEAUX pull away from Laffite's Landing and glide through a picturesque Louisiana bayou on the perfect soft, Southern summer night. Mangroves rise from the water and stretch into the cloudy sky, casting eerie shadows that dance in the light of a full moon. Fireflies bob and weave in and out of the high swamp grass. A small wooden houseboat lists ever so slightly to and fro in the wake of the passing bateaux. And other than the water softly lapping against the hull of the bateaux, chirping crickets and the occasional, almost otherworldly croaking of a bullfrog are the only sounds that break the silence of this natural wonderland.

The bateaux continue deeper into the bayou, and guests looking off to the right can see diners enjoying a romantic meal by candlelight on the wide veranda of an elegant Southern plantation. To the left is the seemingly infinite wilderness of Louisiana bayou country, a verdant landscape dotted by shrimp boats and swamp shacks. A banjo can be heard strumming somewhere in the distance, offering a counterpoint to the crickets' song. As the bateaux leave this picturesque scene, they pass a lone homesteader sitting in a rocking chair on the porch of his ramshackle cottage, a good pipe his only company.

The Blue Bayou creates a strong sense of place that firmly connects the show to its New Orleans Square location. The scene also provides a vital spiritual and geographical link between the fabled backwoods hideout of Jean Lafitte and the distant Spanish Main with its promise of infinite, if illicit, wealth for anyone who dares to pick up a cutlass. It lulls guests into a false sense of security while quietly setting the stage for the swashbuckling adventure to come as guests leave the relative safety of the Blue Bayou for the lawless waters of the Gulf of Mexico and beyond.

The romance and charm of the Blue Bayou evolved from the sumptuous concept paintings of

LEFT: Herb Ryman concept painting of The Blue Bayou Restaurant. The bateaux can be seen on the left, sailing past an elegant plantation house where guests are dining on the veranda.

Dorothea Redmond and Herb Ryman. With its chirping crickets, twinkling stars, and dancing fireflies, this sleepy little swamp is one of the most realistic environments ever created by Walt Disney Imagineering. More than a few Disneyland guests have been thoroughly convinced that they've entered a grand French manor house only to exit it again immediately upon their arrival at Laffite's Landing. The illusion is especially persuasive after dark, when guests go from a real nighttime environment into the faux-summer evening of the Blue Bayou without missing a beat.

The Blue Bayou is also the attraction's first showcase for Yale Gracey's special effects magic. In a projection effect first pioneered at the 1964–1965 New York World's Fair, even the most skeptical guests become convinced that they are in fact gazing up at the real night sky rather than at a man-made blanket of clouds over rural Louisiana. The dancing fireflies have also long been a guest favorite; they are, in reality a tiny fiber-optic lighting fixture at the end of a wire moving to and fro on a light current of air.

Songs of the South
Two banjo solos were recorded for the Blue Bayou scene: "Oh, Susanna" and "Camptown Races," but only the former is currently used in the show.

TOP: Marc Davis concept sketch of Cajun Joe's, an old grog shack in the Blue Bayou that didn't make it into the final show. **ABOVE:** Concept sketch of a shipwreck in the Blue Lagoon, an old fort looming in the distance. **RIGHT:** A view of the old fort and a pirate galleon in the harbor beyond.

Disneyland Paris
The Blue Lagoon

THE BATEAUX depart from the boarding dock and glide through a serene Blue Lagoon off the coast of a West Indies island, passing lush tropical foliage and soothing waterfalls on their way to another great stone fortress on the opposite shore. The hulking remnants of a shipwrecked pirate galleon rest amid the palm trees on a white sandy beach, where "islanders" are taking advantage of the mild weather and enjoying a meal by moonlight. The bateaux then sail right through the partially submerged shipwreck, where an octopus is laying claim to the remains of the ship's cargo as a bold crab challenges him for a piece of the action.

"The octopus-versus-the-crab gag always gets a big laugh," show producer Chris Tietz says with a smile. "The guests eating at the Blue Lagoon restaurant can't see inside the shipwreck, so they have no idea what everyone's laughing at and it makes them want to go on the attraction to see for themselves."

Emerging from the wreckage, the bateaux carry their human cargo toward the distant fort and the unknown dangers lurking inside.

LEFT: 1963 Collin Campbell concept sketch of guests sailing through a watery grotto, among the first to depict the attraction as a boat ride. A pirate crew in a dinghy searching for treasure is seen in the distance. In the final show, the only pirates depicted are long dead. **BELOW:** The talking skull voiced by Imagineer X Atencio.

Approaching THE WATERFALL

"... Ye comes seeking adventure and salty old pirates, aye? Sure ye've come to the proper place. But keep a weather eye open, mates, and hold on tight ... with both hands if you please. There be squalls ahead ... and Davy Jones waiting for them what don't obey. ..."

THE BATEAUX leave the serenity of the Blue Bayou and enter a brick-lined passageway illuminated by flickering gas lamps. A talking skull affixed to the wall overhead issues a series of ominous admonitions that culminates with the chilling prophecy, "Dead men tell no tales." With those words still ringing in guests' ears, the bateaux spill over a waterfall and splash down into a long, dimly lit passage. The bateaux slip over a second waterfall and coast into a subterranean grotto carved by the underground stream. A ghostly voice repeats the warning, "Dead men tell no tales," which echoes throughout the caverns as the bateaux sail even further into the past.

HIDDEN TREASURE

What's Your Angle?
The two drops in the Disneyland show are both 21-degree angles; the first is fifty-two feet and the second is thirty-seven feet.

HIDDEN TREASURE

Don't Look in the Basement!
When guests enter the Grotto, they are seventy feet below ground level in the original "basement" of the old Blue Bayou Mart, the space initially earmarked for the walk-through Pirate Wax Museum.

Entering THE GROTTO

"Yo ho, yo ho, a pirate's life for me. We pillage, plunder, we rifle, and loot. Drink up, me hearties, yo ho. We kidnap and ravage and don't give a hoot. Drink up, me hearties, yo ho!"

THE BATEAUX drift into a cavernous grotto dimly illuminated by moonlight spilling into the catacombs from the surface high above. Waterfalls cascade into underground pools through jagged fissures in the rocks. And through the gaping mouth of a cave, guests can see storm clouds forming the ghostly image of a skull and crossbones in the night sky beyond. From out of the gloom comes the sound of pirates singing a rousing sea chantey, "Yo Ho (A Pirate's Life for Me)."

The grotto was something of a hasty addition to Pirates of the Caribbean. When Walt made the decision to turn Pirates into a ride-through attraction, the original basement was no longer large enough to accommodate the experience he now envisioned, and his Imagineers weren't sure how to deal with their big hole in the ground. "What do we do with that basement?" John Hench asked.

As usual, Walt had an answer, albeit a vague one, at the ready: "Oh, just put in some caves or something." It wasn't an inexpensive decision. Construction crews had to rip out all of the structural steel that had been sitting there since 1961 in order to fill Walt's cave order. Undaunted by such an abrupt change in their course, Marc Davis designed a number of scenes for the grotto, and Claude Coats helped fill up the space artificially by putting a number of switchbacks in the flume.

Regardless of the circumstances of its birth, the Grotto, with its eerie warnings, skeletal pirate inhabitants, and the first performance of the show's rousing theme song, is one of the guests favorite environments in a Disney park, and the sequence of scenes has been included in one form or another in every subsequent adaptation of Pirates of the Caribbean. The Grotto went from a prologue in the Disneyland original to an epilogue with a fitting "Crime doesn't pay" message at Disneyland Paris.

LEFT: Another 1963 Collin Campbell rendering of a waterborne voyage through eerie caverns. In this scene, pirates attempt to haul up their prize from its subterranean resting place. Although the grotto would go on to play a crucial role in the show, "live" pirates were ultimately replaced with skeletal remains.

Disneyland Paris
The Cargo Dock

The bateaux disappear through the ocean-side entrance to the embattled old fortress, passing an abandoned loading dock where supplies were once received for transport to the various stations throughout the stronghold. Guests see that an old winch once used to hoist cargo to the fort's upper levels is still in operation, and their bateaux get ensnared in a chain-lift mechanism and hauled up a dark "cargo ramp." The faint sounds of a distant battle grow louder as the bateaux reach the top of the ramp and slip into the fort's upper level, which has been flooded by an aqueduct damaged by an errant cannonball.

The Flooded Fort

On the fort's upper level, the bateaux pass a familiar band of jailed pirates who are trying to coax a key from a "guard dog" and escape from their cells. From their bateaux, guests can see silhouettes of pirates climbing over a wall to attack the fort and Spanish soldiers trying to fend them off. The prisoners, meanwhile, are making every effort to free themselves so they can rejoin their pirate crew and plunder the town. The thunderous sound of falling water fills the air as the bateaux drift perilously close to a gaping hole in the wall created by cannonball fire.

Escaping the Fort

The bateaux slip through the breach and splash down into the sea below, thrusting guests into the middle of a ship-to-shore battle between the fort and a pirate galleon sitting in the harbor. The captain immediately targets the new "combatants" and guests find the ship's guns trained on them as their bateaux make for the relative safety of the port.

These concept sketches and show scene depict the reversal of show flow that Imagineers employed as they adapted the story in the Paris attraction. The journey begins in a flooded fort (above), where pirates are held prisoner in a repositioned Jail scene (right), followed by a thrilling splash down into the Bombarding the Fort scene (top).

Dead Man's COVE

"Dead men tell no tales!"

THE BATEAUX glide by a lonely beach littered with the skeletal remains of pirates who fell short in their search for buried treasure. One lies sprawled facedown in the sand, a cutlass protruding from his back. Another, a captain, by the look of his decaying uniform, stands impaled on a rocky outcropping, a sword having been run through his chest. A seagull squawks at guests from its nest in the dead Pirate Captain's tricornered hat as the bateaux pass by this lonely graveyard of lost souls.

What's My Line?

GHOSTLY VOICE #1: *"Hear ye a dead man's tale o' a dastardly deed. Brave seamen, these . . . Helped bury the gold they did, then silenced forever. Har! So thought that black 'earted divil! . . . But stay, I told their tale 'afore . . . now I be tellin' it again. Here be where the gold . . . Dead men tell no tales !"*

GHOSTLY VOICE #2: *"Dead men tell no tales, Harrr, heh-heh-heh! Look there upon these pirates bold, take heed whilst I tell ye the gruesome details o' their slight misfortune . . . and the treacherous act what did them in. Unsuspectin' rogues, unmindful . . . Dead men tell no tales!"*

If that dialogue doesn't sound familiar, it shouldn't—it was ultimately cut from the show. Each scene in the Grotto sequence originally featured ghostly narration and even witty dialogue for its skeletal performers, performed by Paul Frees (Voice #1) and J. Pat O'Malley (Voice #2) in what was to be a ghostly counterpoint to Frees's recurring warning, "Dead men tell no tales." Walt and his Imagineers ultimately concluded that the moody visuals spoke for themselves and packed more punch without dialogue. We finally let these involuntarily mute pirates have their say now, proving once and for all that perhaps dead men *do* tell tales!

TOP, ABOVE LEFT, AND BELOW: Marc Davis renderings of Dead Man's Cove, including a 1962 concept for the walk-through attraction in which Anne Bonny and Mary Read can be seen admiring their treasure. The women were ultimately cut, but the rest of the scene remains largely intact in the final ride-through version.

"What poor hulk lies smashed on the cruel rocks, pounded by the angry sea? Who knows the gallant efforts o' the wretched crew to save the ship? I knows, 'cause I were there! 'Twas the royal fortune, bound for the Spanish Main, with enough treasure aboard to . . . Dead men tell no tales!"

(from deleted narration)

Hurricane LAGOON

GALE-FORCE winds and sheets of blinding rain lash the catacombs (though not the guests) as the bateaux come upon a ghost ship sailing a storm-tossed lagoon. Brilliant flashes of lightning illuminate a ghastly skeleton clutching the ship's wheel, dead set on steering his vessel into any port in this particular storm. The tattered remains of his uniform flail in the howling wind as the skeletal steersman weathers the worst of the storm on his eternal voyage.

HIDDEN TREASURE

Skeletons in the Closet—and the Basement
Because the original Imagineering team felt that the faux skeletons of the period were just too unconvincing, the Grotto sequence originally featured real human remains obtained from the UCLA Medical Center. The skeletons were later returned to their countries of origin and given a proper burial when a new generation of Imagineers replaced them with equally convincing facsimiles.

LOST TREASURE

Distant Sea Battle
In an early draft of the script, the scene also featured a distant sea battle raging on the lagoon in the background behind the wrecked ship. Flashes of flame and puffs of smoke could be seen in the turbulent skies of the squall as the telltale sounds of cannon fire joined the howling wind and raging surf.

TOP: 1965 Marc Davis concept sketch of Hurricane Lagoon. **ABOVE RIGHT AND RIGHT:** Views of the final show scene, including an "alternate angle" of the ghost ship's skeletal captain.

Crew's QUARTERS

FAIRING FAR better than their cursed comrades are the two skeletal crewmen having the time of their afterlives in the ruins of a dockside tavern filled with every whiskey, rum, and grog known to piratedom. Even though they obviously drank themselves to death a long time ago, the party goes on for these debauched buccaneers. Guests can even see the firewater flowing down one pirate's gullet as he takes an endless pull from a bottle of rum. Crudely handcrafted signs warn patrons to "Stow Yer Weapons" and proclaim that "Thar Be No Place Like Home." More attentive guests can hear girlish giggles and the lecherous laughter of pirates emanating down a stairway decorated with discarded petticoats.

ABOVE AND INSET: 1965 Marc Davis concept sketch of the Crew's Quarters and a view of the final show scene that illustrates how closely the attraction approximates Marc's renderings.

"Shipshape this anchorage for pleasure-seekin' rogues . . . Aye! After months at sea, facin' the perils o' their adventurous trade . . . they was inclined to traffic their ill-gotten wealth for the pleasure of a lovely lassie's voice and . . . Dead men tell no tales!"

(from deleted narration)

Hanging above the bar is a painting of a lady buccaneer enjoying her own interpretation of the high life. The color of the wench's hair is no coincidence. In the concept sketch on which the painting is based, Marc Davis portrayed the ever-popular "Redhead" from the upcoming Auction scene as she might appear after many years of presumably happy marriage to the pirates. A pirate's life for her, indeed.

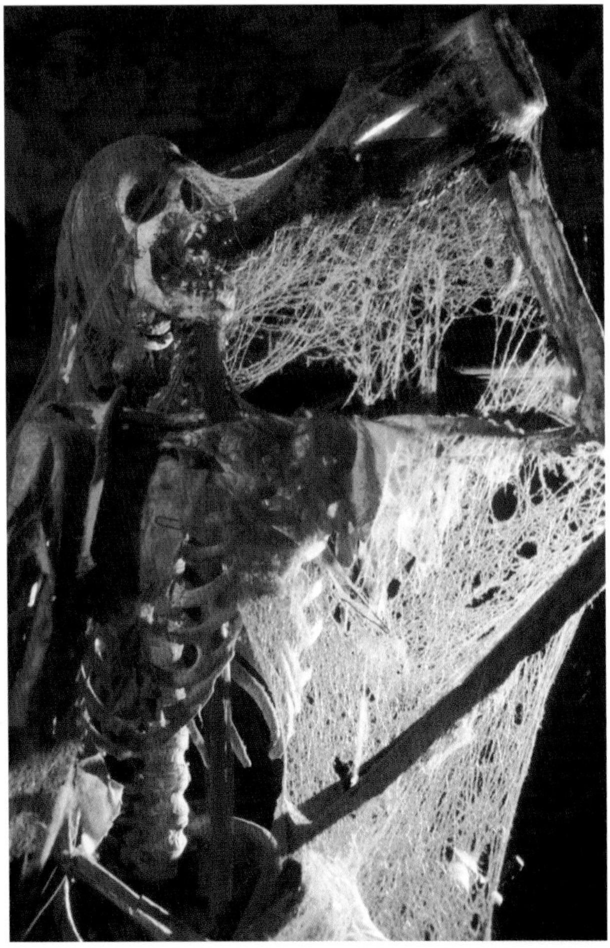

ABOVE: Marc Davis concept offering a "portrait of things to come" for the infamous "Redhead." **LEFT AND BELOW:** This popular gag depicting rum pouring down a skeletal gullet would go on to become an equally magical moment in the 2003 feature film.

Makeshift Crew's Quarters in a Pirate's Camp

Before the action was moved to a subterranean tavern, an early draft of the script cast a makeshift pirate's camp as the Crew's Quarters. The scene was more of a companion piece to Hurricane Lagoon, with water from the storm leaking into the camp through the grotto's ceiling and collecting in an assortment of strategically placed buckets, pots, and pans. At this point, the music was to segue into a "raindrop tune" as the numerous leaks came together to form a melody. According to X's script, this scene would be where "We hear voices for the first time—a variety of different voices as if from a distance. The squawks of a parrot are intermixed with the pirate talk."

Captain's QUARTERS

Our bateaux carry us into the finely appointed private quarters of this ghost crew's captain. Guests find what remains of the Pirate Captain reading in bed, surrounded by the spoils of a lifetime of treachery and ill-gotten gains. The bony buccaneer holds a magnifying glass over his reading material—a treasure map, naturally—the lens magnifying his empty eye socket to grotesque proportions. A nearby harpsichord plays the now-familiar pirate anthem as the bateaux glide on into the grotto.

ABOVE AND BELOW: 1965 Marc Davis concept sketch of the Captain's Quarters and detailed views of the final show scene, including the version at Disneyland Paris (bottom left).

LOST TREASURE

The Meeting Room and a Parrot's Life for Me

"Morgan says the streets are paved with gold! Storm the fort and steal a fortune. Squawk! Drink up, me cutthroats, time to sail! Avast there, mates—wait for dark! Squawk! Our fortune's made, lads. Quick now—we're keepin' the ladies waiting! Aye, Captain, your heart's as black as your beard. We'll have a hot time in the old town tonight."

In that same early draft of the script, the Pirate Captain was not made to spend eternity entirely alone. A parrot perched atop a high-backed chair pulled up to the table in an adjacent meeting room, where the captain and his crew would plan their next attack. This first mate most fowl would repeat conversations of his human compatriots, some famous, such as Captain Morgan, to passing guests. The parrot's mimicked lines dropped ominous hints of the pillaging and plundering to come.

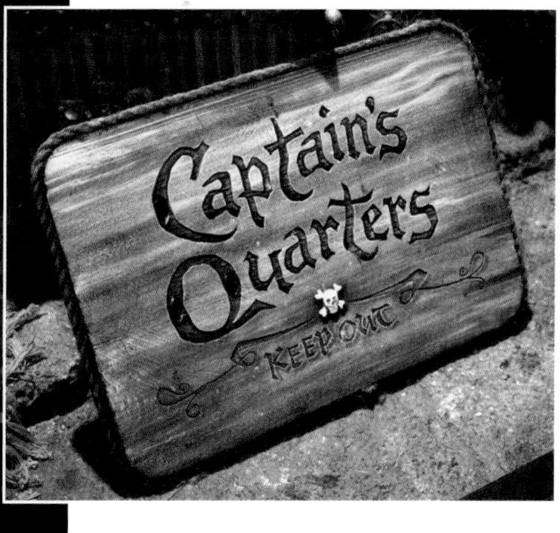

Treasure ROOM

"Pretty baubles, think ye, and a king's ransom in gold. Aye, blood money, and cursed it be . . . cursed by the black-hearted rogues what left it. Who knows what evil spell lurks 'neath each cursed chest?"

1965 Marc Davis concept sketch of the Treasure Room and scenes from the final show, including the skeletal pirate from Tokyo Disneyland (above). The Treasure Room would have a major influence on the filmmakers when they designed the secret treasure cache on Isla de Muerta in the feature film.

As THE bateaux continue on their perilous voyage, guests stumble across the object of many a pirate's desire, the legendary Treasure Room of this secret grotto. Sitting atop a mountain of gold doubloons, jewels, and pieces of eight is the last member of this doomed crew. The brigand clutches a stack of doubloons in his gnarled hand, basking in his fleeting glory for all time. In leaving this elusive cache, guests succeed where so many pirates have failed: casting their eyes upon this cursed treasure and living to tell about it . . . at least for now.

LOST TREASURE

The Talking Salesman

"Avast there, mates! Look here—I can get it for you wholesale! The Captain's away, mates—special discounts today. . . . Guaranteed only from the finest homes . . . And you never pay retail at Peg-Leg Pete's!

"Perhaps something from the bargain basement? Low overhead, mates . . . Every one's a steal. . . . Keeps the prices down and the values up . . . Who'll give me twenty doubloons for these earrings? Ten doubloons for a golden necklace? Five doubloons for the whole store!"

In an early draft of X Atencio's script, three hungry alligators guarded the Treasure Room against any would-be pillagers. The reptiles strained against their chains and snapped at passing bateaux, literally looking for a handout. The scene was also to feature a pirate "salesman" standing at another entrance to the cache. The huckster would open his long coat, first his right side, then his left, to reveal his wares—rings, necklaces, gold pins, and earrings—as he hawked the cursed booty to guests sailing by in their bateaux.

Ghostly GROTTO

"No fear have ye of evil curses
sez you . . . HARRrrr–HU–HUMmm.
Properly be warned, sez I.
Who knows when that evil curse will
strike the greedy beholders
o' this bewitched treasure . . .
Dead men tell no tales."

WITH VISIONS of forbidden riches still dancing in guests' heads, the bateaux leave the haunted caverns behind and drift down a long, dark tunnel as the sounds of distant cannon fire and shouting fill the air. Two ghostly voices warn guests of the ancient curse placed on the treasure, and the grim fate awaiting anyone who dares disturb it or take it from its subterranean resting place. Guests sail even further back in time to the golden age of piracy, when these very same cursed pirates first invaded this unsuspecting island colony in search of the legendary treasure.

Although the disembodied narration and dialogue were cut from most of the scenes in the Grotto, the warnings in this transition tunnel tell guests everything they need to know about the cursed treasure and set the stage for the action to come. This provides a narrative connection between the ultimate fate of the buccaneers that guests have just seen, and the initial ransacking and search for treasure that led to this fate so long ago, which guests are about to witness. The structure of the story grew out of the decision to make Pirates of the Caribbean a ride-through experience, and Walt's subsequent direction to fill its original basement location with "caves or something." X Atencio's script was a practical way to make up for any narrative complications brought on by the sudden inclusion of the haunted caverns. At Disneyland Paris, the order of the show scenes was reversed to tell a more cause-and-effect story.

This transition tunnel is one of the most significant pieces of real estate in Pirates of the Caribbean, for it is the conduit through which guests travel from that original basement under the tracks of the Disneyland Railroad to a massive show building outside the Park's berm, where most of the show takes place. The Imagineers also used the tunnel as an opportunity to narrow guests' focus and create a claustrophobic feeling that would contrast sharply with their sudden expulsion into the wide-open space of the upcoming Bombardment scene.

"We had just finished doing the World's Fair

RIGHT: 1963 Collin Campbell concept sketch depicting another proposed grotto scene, this one featuring rival brigands fighting over treasure as a trio of musicians look on.

HIDDEN TREASURE

So What's the Story?

In its various incarnations as a walk-through and ride-through attraction, Pirates of the Caribbean was always designed to be a collection of loosely related vignettes that would transport guests back to the golden age of piracy. As the concept developed in Marc Davis's sketches and storyboards, then later in the scale model and X Atencio's scripts, the experience ultimately evolved into the story of a pirate crew that lays waste to a Caribbean seaport in search of hidden treasure. Little do they know that the treasure carries a terrible curse and that the pirates must pay for their prize with their very souls, spending eternity in a graveyard of haunted caverns.

Imagineers and guests alike have speculated as to exactly when the story takes place. The entire experience is officially considered one long journey from 1860s New Orleans back in time to piracy's golden age in the late 1700s. But some prefer to think of the Grotto and the Caribbean seaport as existing in the same time period, with the attacking pirates simply being the latest crew to come searching for the cursed treasure, ultimately destined to suffer the same grim fate as the poor souls who have come before them in the haunted caverns.

things after interrupting the pirate walk-through," Claude Coats said in an interview with *The E-Ticket*. "By then Walt had decided that it would be a ride. I'd gotten information from MAPO about what the boats would do, and what curves and radiuses it would take, and I tried to put it in the space that already had columns in it. It was very, very small and very tight. . . . Once again we rerouted the track through that area which is now Grotto. It gave us a chance, as we went under the railroad track, to do some good story development. X Atencio got into it about that time with the words, 'Dead men tell no tales,' and the hollow voice in a rather confined passageway opened up into a very large scene with the boats. It seemed to [have] an interesting impact to go right through a battle, with cannonballs supposedly going over heads and hitting the water and splashing. Our first introduction to the 'real' pirates was at that point, really about six or seven minutes down into the show."

Bombarding THE FORT

"Strike yer colors, ye bloomin' cockroachers!"

GUESTS EMERGE from the Grotto to find themselves in the middle of a fog-enshrouded harbor under cloudy night skies, their bateau caught in the middle of a fierce battle between a pirate galleon, *The Wicked Wench*, and a Spanish fort on the shore of an island colony. They have arrived in the late 1700s, the golden age of piracy. The Pirate Captain barks orders to his crew as they fire the ship's guns and cannons into the water around the passing bateaux. Colonial defenders can be seen manning the fort's cannons, barking orders to each other in Spanish and shouting threats at the invading pirates. As the bateaux slip through an inlet and enter the seaport itself, the silhouettes of two duelists are seen sword fighting atop a rampart in the distance.

The Bombarding the Fort scene is a prime example of the cinematic influence on the art of Imagineering. All recruits from the Walt Disney Studio, the early Imagineers thought in those terms and spoke in that language, a practice that continues today. Guests first see the scene in a "long shot," a wide angle that encompasses the pirate ship and the fort firing upon each other against a sprawling background of Caribbean sea and sky. "Claude [Coats] wanted to 'iris in' and the Grotto get smaller and tighter so the reveal of the open sea would be bigger and more shocking," Blaine Gibson recalls. Then the bateaux, acting as the camera, slowly "push in" for a medium shot that puts guests in the middle of the action. Finally, a series of close-ups reveal intricate details such as sudden splashes of actual water and handpainted, faux stone walls that look like the genuine article even from a few feet away.

HIDDEN TREASURE

Blackbeard's Ghost

Although none of the characters in the show is a depiction of an actual historical figure, the Captain, voiced by Paul Frees, is inspired by Edward Teach, better known as the infamous Blackbeard. The only things missing are the lit fuses that Teach would braid into his beard to give himself a demonic appearance that helped to cower his foes. If you look closely, however, you'll see that this captain does have bows tied into his whiskers, which is something Blackbeard did, too, presumably when he wasn't trying to scare his enemies to death. Coincidentally (or was it?), one of Walt Disney's last productions was *Blackbeard's Ghost*, starring Peter Ustinov and Dean Jones, which, like Pirates of the Caribbean, premiered shortly after Walt died in 1967. That film would go on to play a small role in a major refurbishment of the attraction in 1997.

LEFT: Marc Davis rendering of Captain Edward Teach, the infamous Blackbeard.

ABOVE: Concept sketch by Kirk Hanson of the Spanish soldiers who were added to the scene in the 1999/2000 rehab. **LEFT AND BELOW:** Marc Davis sketches for the Bombarding the Fort scene.

HIDDEN TREASURE

A Mouse in the House

Cannonballs have left craters in the wall of the fort, creating a Hidden Mickey.

Disneyland Paris
Splash Landing

In the Paris show, the bateaux enter the scene from inside the fort itself. Floodwater from the blasted aqueduct pours from a gaping hole created by cannon fire, taking the drifting bateaux with it. Guests splash down into the harbor to find themselves in the middle of an artillery battle between the fortress and a pirate galleon anchored just offshore. Continuing this utter immersion into the scene, the pirates take notice of the bateaux and train their ship's guns on *guests* in addition to their colonial adversaries.

Wicked Wench

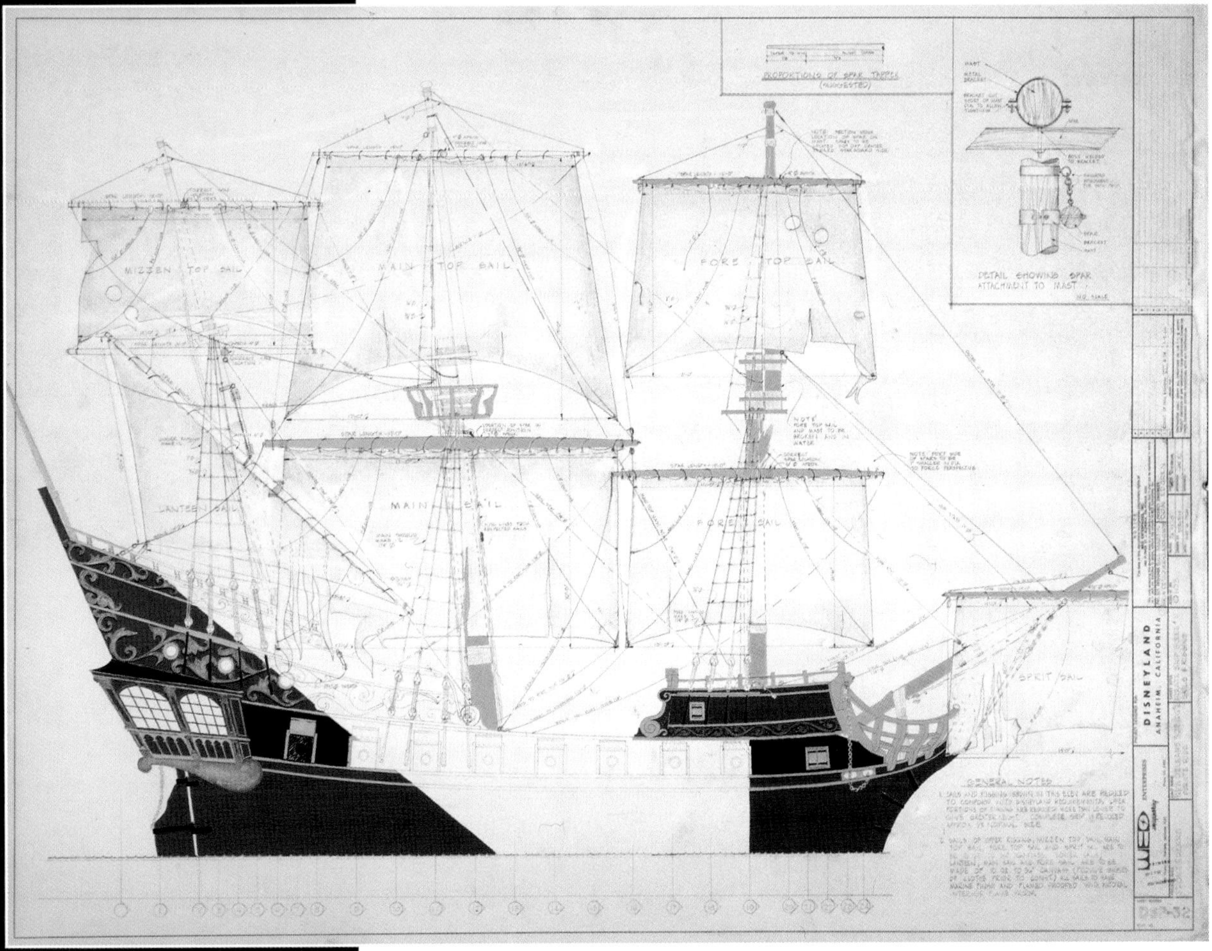

LEFT: The *Wicked Wench*. **OPPOSITE INSET:** Marc Davis rendering of a pirate ship firing on its opponent and taking some hits in return. **TOP:** 1966 Claude Coats exterior color elevation, side view of pirate ship in battle scene. **ABOVE:** 1965 Marc Davis concept sketch of the captain of the *Wicked Wench*, inspired by Edward "Blackbeard" Teach. Note the ribbons tied into the captain's bushy beard, an eccentricity made infamous by Blackbeard.

The WELL

"Pipe the lubber, aloft, matey. Speak up, ya bilge rat! Where be the treasure?"

"Don't tell him, Carlos, don't be chicken!"

AS THE bateaux sail into the seaport, the search for the treasure begins as a surly Pirate Captain (J. Pat O'Malley) tries to extract information from Carlos (Paul Frees), the town magistrate, and other local officials by dunking them in a well. The poor magistrate spits and sputters water as one of the mates pulls him out of the well, a third pirate underscoring the action with a flute. The magistrate's wife appears in an upstairs window of an adjacent building, begging her husband not to talk. Another of the crewmen fires his musket at her and she vanishes back into the house, pulling the shutters closed behind her. The Pirate Captain orders the magistrate dunked again as his crew explodes into laughter and the other townsmen quake in their nightshirts.

As hard as it may be to believe, this scene of Caribbean water torture was almost a musical. In one of the first drafts of the script X wrote pre–"Yo Ho" in 1965, the Captain sang a duet with a parrot on his shoulder as the "gov'ner" (demoted to a magistrate in the final draft) took his dunking. The Captain would sing each verse as the governor went down ("The gov'ner won't tell us where he's hid the golden treasure, so we'll dunk 'im in the well again, besides, it gives us pleasure!") and the parrot would join his master for the chorus as the stubborn politico came back up ("'Ees up again, now watch 'im fall, down, down, down in the well. Stand in line, there's room for all, down, down, down in the well!"). The duo was to be accompanied by three instrument-playing pirates, a trio that was reduced to a solitary flutist as X continued to refine his script.

ABOVE: The Magistrate's wife. **BELOW:** Marc Davis concept depicting the Well scene in a "master shot."

HIDDEN TREASURE

It Figures

The figures currently in the Well scene were originally built for Disneyland Paris, but were instead routed to the Anaheim park for a 1990 refurbishment of Pirates of the Caribbean. A new set of figures was then constructed well in time for the Paris Resort's opening in 1992.

ABOVE: The final show scene is a near-perfect realization of Marc Davis's original rendering. **RIGHT:** Blaine Gibson captured the strain of pulling the portly magistrate out of the well in the hoisting pirate's face, a necessity in order for the gag to be read quickly and easily by guests in passing bateaux. **MIDDLE RIGHT:** Marc Davis concept sketch illustrating the "before" and "after" effects of his Dunking the Magistrate gag.

One anonymous Disneyland guest must have experienced a strange sense of déjà vu when he saw the Well scene during the attraction's early days. In fact, it may very well have seemed like he was looking in a mirror, and if he felt a certain kinship with the magistrate it's because he *was* the magistrate! For that he could thank a chance encounter with Blaine Gibson. "I studied people who had interesting heads," Blaine says, "because Walt's direction was always to make believability part of the entertainment factor. Well, my wife and I were having dinner in a restaurant and I saw a fat guy that looked like he'd be great for the dunking scene. I couldn't take my eye off the man, and my wife would kick me under the table for staring at him. But I think the human face is the most interesting thing in the world."

HIDDEN TREASURE

Slippery When Wet

The Imagineers knew their magistrate would be spending all day every day popping in and out of a well. A *dry* nightshirt would have been a slap in the face of reality, but they couldn't very well dunk a sophisticated Audio-Animatronics figure in real water. They had to make sure the nightshirt itself didn't get too waterlogged, either—anyone who has left clothes in the washing machine for too long knows what happens. Alice Davis and her costume team could smell a potential mildew problem and solved it by putting a coat of mineral oil on the magistrate's nightshirt to make him appear perpetually wet. "It would never go bad because it's natural," Alice explains, effectively guaranteeing that the magistrate's nightshirt will be able to hold out a lot longer than he ever will.

The AUCTION

"Shift yer cargo, dearie . . .
Show 'em yer larboard side."

THE BATEAUX drift into the town's bustling marketplace, where an impromptu auction is taking place. AUCTION—TAKE A WENCH FOR A BRIDE, a banner reads. A pirate Auctioneer (Paul Frees) is in the process of selling off women of all ages, shapes, and sizes to an audience of rowdy buccaneers sitting across the waterway. The Auctioneer extols the virtues of a "pleasantly plump" and positively beaming maiden who is clearly pleased to be landing a husband, even by such unorthodox means. The drunken bidders across the way loudly and clearly make known their clear preference for the next lot on the bloc—a sultry redhead of questionable repute. A stern-looking henchman fires a rifle to silence the hecklers, but it does little good as the Auctioneer continues his sales pitch in an effort to unload his excess inventory. The redhead's time will come, though, and if that painting in the Crew's Quarters is any indication, she'll wind up taking to a pirate's life just fine.

In a number of 1965 drafts of the script, X had packed the scene with even more gags. The Auctioneer's original dialogue was more reminiscent of the rapid-fire delivery of a real one, and chickens on display in the marketplace were "continuously clucking in a rapid-fire imitation of an auctioneer's

TOP: This 1965 Marc Davis print establishes the Auction scene in a "long shot," a term derived from Imagineering's motion picture origins. **ABOVE AND RIGHT:** Marc Davis concept sketch of the "wenches" up for bids, and a view of the final show scene as realized at Tokyo Disneyland.

MERCADO
AUCTION
Take a Wench for a Bride

RIGHT: This rare view of the "Red'ead" suggests why she is so popular with her pirate audience. **BELOW:** The portly princess in all her glory. **BOTTOM:** Marc Davis concept sketch of the Auctioneer and the "winsome wench" he is trying to marry off.

HIDDEN TREASURE

Looks Can Be Deceiving

The Redhead may be the most popular girl in town, but looks can be deceiving. Alice Davis reveals that the fiery femme fatale is little more than a pole from the waist down. It is a careful construction of one-of-a-kind undergarments that helps create the illusion of an hourglass figure. Sorry, guys!

chant," according to the script. When the Auctioneer asked his audience who wanted to bid on the plump damsel, he was answered by enthusiastic bleating of the goats tethered near the water's edge. The pirates across the waterway, meanwhile, were too busy "wolf whistling" at the Redhead to place a bid—even the snores of the drunken pirates came out as wolf whistles; they would get more vocal in subsequent drafts. The draft also called for two "Heckler Pirates" who knew they had no chance at the Redhead; they instead tried to put her down with such zingers as "Her father's the tax collector," "Her mother sings opera," "She smokes cigars," and "But she don't drink." Love can be cruel, even for bloodthirsty pirates.

In subsequent drafts, both the action and dialogue were simplified significantly to focus the audience's attention on the main gag: the pirates' obvious preference for the fiery femme fatale over the "stout-hearted and corn-fed" specimen currently up for bids. To that end, the Auctioneer's lengthy sales pitch was cut back and his delivery slowed down, the livestock kept their comments to themselves, and the hecklers focused their ire on the "winsome wench" on the auction block while the rest of the crew put on very public displays of affection for the more "brazen" woman in red. Guests would be spending less than a minute in the scene; the story had to be kept simple so the audience could get it in the short time they had. In the vernacular of Disney animation, it had to read.

HIDDEN TREASURE

Pleasure by the Pound

The pirate rogues may "want the redhead," but the best value for their money would have to be the full-figured damsel currently on the auction block. As designed, with her proportions she would weigh in at three hundred pounds in the real world.

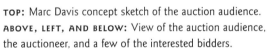

TOP: Marc Davis concept sketch of the auction audience.
ABOVE, LEFT, AND BELOW: View of the auction audience, the auctioneer, and a few of the interested bidders.

The CHASE

"We're beggars and blighters, and ne-er-do-well cads. Drink up, me hearties, yo ho! Aye, but we're loved by our mommies and dads. Drink up, me hearties, yo ho!"

THE BATEAUX drift into the heart of town, where pirates are now invading homes in search of food. A dim-looking buccaneer with a plate piled high with food is caught between a hungry goat and horse, both of which are trying to out-pirate him. The horse has already snatched an apple and is coming back for more. The goat is equally aggressive, sending the bandit back and forth between them like a human Ping-Pong ball. Meanwhile, a deliriously Pooped Pirate, already stuffed from acts of rampant gluttony, sits next to a barrel asking after an errant piece of fish. The lid of the barrel intermittently pops up, revealing a cat holding the bones of the fish in question. In the background, a woman brandishing a rolling pin chases two pirates through her house in an effort to reclaim the food they've stolen.

And across the waterway, an inebriated brigand, "Old Bill," as he introduces himself, does his best to get some stray cats to join him for a spot of rum.

The Chase scene offers one of the best examples of the Imagineers' use of forced perspective, another cinematic technique that allowed them to play with the scale of their show sets to establish an even more convincing sense of place. It also enabled them to add the illusion of depth to what is in fact a rather shallow space. Throughout both the Chase and Burning Town scenes, the pirates appear to be varying distances from the guests in their bateaux, and Blaine Gibson helped create this illusion by downsizing certain figures. "You know, certain elements like the pirate ship would be scaled down to add to the feeling of distance within the ride," Blaine Gibson told *The E-Ticket*. "With the pirate figures themselves, the way we underscaled them was by making some reducing-glue molds of other pirates. This kind of mold is made with a water-based material and every time you make a casting from it, it shrinks because of evaporation. We would make a successive series of castings of three or four of the pirate heads, and finally we got the reduced figures we needed. There was distortion, of course, but that didn't matter because they were pirates! When they were done, they ended up not looking like any of the other pirates, and they were smaller."

TOP: The Chase scene is now populated by ravenous renegades on the prowl for food and drink . . . but not wenches! **LEFT:** Marc Davis devotee and Disney Feature Animation veteran Kirk Hanson designed this vignette depicting a hungry pirate caught between a horse and a goat. The gag is very much in keeping with the Marc Davis style of simple staging and character-driven humor.

LEFT: The Pooped Pirate brandishes a chicken leg instead of a lady's undergarment in the revised incarnation of the scene. **BELOW:** The village maidens don't take kindly to the pirates' kitchen raid. **BOTTOM:** Original Marc Davis concept sketch of the libidinous Pooped Pirate, destined to become a glutton in the controversial 1997 rehab.

Boy Scouts of the Caribbean

THE CHASE scene did not always look this way. Originally, the pirates weren't chasing after food; they were looking for love in all the wrong places. The Pooped Pirate dangled a frilly petticoat as he asked passing guests if they had seen its young owner, none too delicately suggesting that he was willing to share if they helped him find the object of his desire. In the background, the pirates were chasing the mistresses of the house, not the other way around. The sole exception was a spinster-type who chased a pirate obviously not quite that desperate—a conscious attempt to defuse the obvious suggestiveness of the rest of the scene. "We had the girl chasing the guy to try to get the point across that this was harmless fun," X Atencio says of the original scene. "We hoped that would get us off the hook."

And it did for thirty years, but a new generation of Imagineers felt they needed to make some changes to keep pace with the evolving sensibilities of their audience. A creative team led by Tony Baxter and show producer Bob Baranick went to work. They had no problem "tampering" with a classic because both of them felt that the Chase scene was weak to begin with, sexually suggestive or not. Tony and Bob were far more concerned about presenting guests with decidedly underwhelming and largely static figures going round and round on turntables after the show-stopping animation of the two scenes that precede it. They did want to keep the popular Pooped Pirate, so they built a new story line around him, replacing one of the seven deadly sins—vice—with another—gluttony—hence the hungry brigand and his frisky feline companion. Inside the cantina, the pirates are making off with nothing more than an innocent snack, and it is the vengeful female cooks who are doing the chasing.

The controversy surrounding the redesign eventually died down, except among the Imagineers who created the scene. Their reviews are mixed, although softened somewhat by an inherent understanding of a changing world and their successors' motives in responding to those changes. "The show's called *Pirates* of the Caribbean, not *Boy Scouts* of the Caribbean," X Atencio says, with a twinkle in his eye. "They're my babies, you know? I hate to see them fool around with 'em."

"Whether I like it or not doesn't matter," Alice Davis concludes. "Each new generation has the right to come in and do what they feel is best for the show—and that's what they did."

LEFT: In the original Chase scene from Disneyland, the Pooped Pirate brandishes the slip of a maiden he's been chasing. **ABOVE:** Close-up of the hidden maiden at Disneyland Paris. **BELOW:** The highlight of the Chase scene in the Paris show is the first full-contact sword fight between two Audio-Animatronics figures, a scenario dreamed up by Imagineer Tony Baxter and his creative team.

Disneyland Paris
Pirates and Maidens

THE PIRATES and Maidens scene in the Paris show preserves the spirit of Disneyland's original Chase scene, with one pirate chasing a fair young maiden around a balcony while an angry matron wielding a broom turns the tables on a less fortunate older buccaneer. The Pooped Pirate is back in action here, with his quarry furtively peeking out of a barrel, but his dialogue is far more innocent, at least as innocent as a hopelessly debauched pirate can get. This being France, after all, the European audience had no problem with their pirates, regardless of their intentions.

The real stars of the scene are a pair of sword-fighting swashbucklers straight out of an Errol Flynn movie, as a noble townsman sword fights with one of the more agile, younger pirates. While the duelists initially elicited all the expected gasps and "How'd they do that?" queries from their audience, they also worked a little too well, slashing each other's arms and heads and cutting their clothing to ribbons in true pirate form. The aggressive cast-mates were ultimately pulled from the show (for a year and a half at one point), until the European Imagineering team could figure out how to choreograph them so they would perform their stunts without killing each other for real. Now they're back and dueling to the death once again, but with all the split-second timing, agility, and restraint of their human counterparts on the silver screen.

The Burning TOWN

"We kindle and char and inflame and ignite. Drink up, me hearties, yo ho! We burn up the city, we're really a fright. Drink up, me hearties, yo ho! Yo ho, yo ho, a pirate's life for me!"

ABOVE: Marc Davis rendering of the Burning Town, the fiery finale of Pirates of the Caribbean. **RIGHT:** A trio of merry musicians reprise "Yo Ho (A Pirate's Life for Me)" as the show's grand finale begins.

THE BATEAUX pass beneath a bridge and pull alongside a stable, where three pirate musicians are singing "Yo Ho (A Pirate's Life for Me)" as a dog and a donkey bark and bray backup respectively. One member of the trio plays a guitar and another a concertina to accompany their shipmates, who sing their anthem and cackle in a drunken stupor as the town burns to the ground around them. Two particularly inebriated brigands cling to each other for support, one barely holding onto what could very well be the offending torch, as they stagger to the music. Nearby, another blotto buccaneer clutches a lamppost, the only thing keeping him from tumbling to

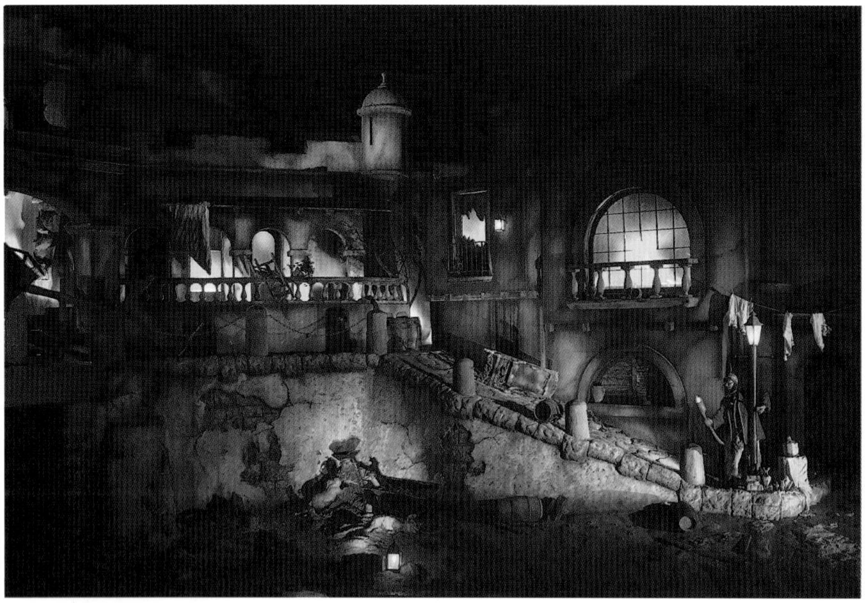

his doom. Behind them the horizon glows an ominous reddish-orange as flames engulf the town and climb ever higher into the night sky.

At the water's edge, one enterprising pirate attempts to make his escape in a wooden rowboat of questionable seaworthiness. He's absconding with everything he can carry and then some, his arms filled with an unwieldy treasure chest and other valuables—even his head is piled high with pilfered hats. The greedy bandit has one foot in the boat and one on the dock, and the uneven weight of the strongbox causes him to teeter perilously between the two. Just across the waterway, a rum-swilling souse lies in the mud with the only creatures in town that will consort with him: a trio of squealing pigs, their legs twitching in soporific contentment. The bateaux pass beneath a bridge, which looks to be the reinforced sewer entrance to the underground parts of the city. A buccaneer clutching a jug of rum sits atop the bridge, one hairy leg dangling above guests' heads. A parrot perches next to him, mimicking his incoherent companion as he giggles and sings, "Yo ho, yo ho, a pirate's life for me." The bateaux disappear into the darkness of the underground tunnel.

The Burning Town is a fitting climax to the grandest theme park spectacle Walt Disney and his Imagineers had ever created. In some respects, it was the only way they could end the show. After all the wonders that guests had just experienced, there was nothing they could possibly do to top themselves other than burn their set to the ground, just as Atlanta had burned in *Gone with the Wind.* The illusion is deceptively simple, yet fools the human eye just as convincingly and effectively as it would the lens of a movie camera. And like so many of Disneyland's ingenious special effects, it came from the fertile mind of master illusioneer Yale Gracey.

Yale took sheets of Mylar, a strong polyester film commonly used in packing, insulation, and recording tape, and cut them into flame-shaped pieces, lighting them from below with red and orange gelled lights. When he aimed a strategically placed fan at them, the Mylar would dance in the breeze like the flickering fingers of hungry flames. Under the controlled lighting conditions of the show building, the resulting effect was almost indistinguishable from real fire.

As it turned out, the burning town really *did* get burned. "Two or three months after the attraction had opened," Marc Davis told *The E-Ticket*, "there was a fire in the fire scene. It burned up several of these figures. It was the most gruesome thing you've ever seen in your life! The heat

TOP: View of the Burning Town scene from Disneyland Paris. **LEFT:** Original Marc Davis sketch of a pair of drunken fire-starters and a close-up of their Audio-Animatronics counterparts. **OPPOSITE:** The stars of the Burning Town scene, from sketch to reality.

HIDDEN TREASURE

X Marks the Spot

X Atencio got into his work as no other Imagineer on the show had, by voicing another character—this one with a bit more skin on his bones, dirty as it may be. X provided the off-key warbling and drunken giggling of the pirate whose hairy leg dangles over the side of the bridge.

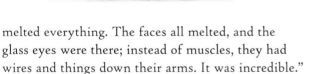

melted everything. The faces all melted, and the glass eyes were there; instead of muscles, they had wires and things down their arms. It was incredible."

Imagineers eventually replaced the Mylar with pieces of shiny, white satin cloth, which better reflected the colored lights and fluttered even more convincingly due to a carefully directed current of air. The effect literally became the fabric that bound Marc Davis's characters and Claude Coats's moody sets in the unbreakable ties of story.

TOP: Marc Davis's version of the Jail scene introduced the gag with the pirate inmates trying to coax the key from a good-natured "guard dog," one of the attraction's—and the feature film's—most memorable moments.

The JAIL

"Here, give us the keys, ya scrawny little beast."

"Can't ya reach any further, ya stub-winged bilge rat?"

GUESTS SAIL past the local jail, where undesirables are kept out of sight and out of mind in the catacombs beneath the town. With the pirate invasion well underway, it's a full house, and the prisoners are growing increasingly desperate to escape as the blaze creeps ever closer. A small dog holds the key to their freedom in his mouth, literally, and the pinched pirates make every attempt to lure him within snatching range. The dog is having none of it, however, cocking his head inquisitively and wagging his tail in response to their repeated calls for his prize.

Crackling Timbers

THE BATEAUX glide beneath a network of charred and burning timbers, part of a rickety wooden support structure that helps hold up the town. Tottering columns creak and moan as hungry flames continue to devour them. Smoldering crossbeams sway perilously back and forth on the verge of collapse, threatening to sink the bateaux passing beneath them at any moment.

This atmospheric passageway, which connects the Jail and Arsenal scenes, is actually a second transition tunnel through which guests make their return trip from the Pirates show building outside the berm. When the bateaux emerge in the Arsenal, guests are once again inside the basement that was once meant to hold the entire attraction.

The ARSENAL

THE ATTACK isn't over yet. Still more pirates have penetrated the town's subterranean arsenal, where they find themselves surrounded by a seemingly limitless supply of dynamite and black powder. Three kegs of explosives suspended from a boom hang over the canal, directly above guests' heads. Thinking the barrels contain rum rather than the clearly marked "EXPLOSIVOS," the buccaneers indulge in a little drunken target practice, taking aim at the powder kegs from opposite sides of the waterway as guests find themselves caught in the middle. Bullets ricochet all around the smoldering arsenal as the bateaux run a potentially explosive gauntlet. Oblivious to the danger, the trigger-happy hooligans laugh themselves silly as they continue to fire on the kegs and, as a result, everything and everyone else.

TOP: The drunken brigands in the Arsenal are unaware of the danger their target practice poses to passing guests—and to themselves. **ABOVE:** Marc Davis concept sketch. **LEFT:** Marc Davis sketch of the buccaneer X Atencio would christen "Mister Coote."

HIDDEN TREASURE

What's in a Name?

In a 1965 draft of the show script, X Atencio christened the Arsenal scene's two speaking characters with proper names, the only characters to receive such an honor, although the Magistrate's wife refers to her husband as Carlos and one drunken pirate invites some stray cats to have a drink with "old Bill." The pirate kneeling on a crate on the right side of the canal was referred to as Billie How, and the buccaneer sprawled across a cannon on the left was Mister Coote. The names stuck, at least with the original Imagineering team, even though they dropped out of subsequent drafts.

Billie How (right) and Mister Coote (below left, from Tokyo Disneyland) take aim at one another in the Arsenal scene. **BOTTOM:** Concept rendering for Disneyland Paris of the consequences of sailing into a burning arsenal. The resulting explosion sends bateaux plummeting into a network of haunted caverns.

Mister Coote:
"Avast there, Billie 'ow—Hic—Les see yer pop a 'ole in one o' them there rummmmm barrels—Hah, har!"

Billie How:
"Lor' love me, mate.
I'll do 'er with me eyes closed."

Disneyland Paris

Plunging into the Arsenal

At Disneyland Paris, the bateaux approach the entrance to a tunnel similar to the one leading to the Jail in the Anaheim show. It is dark inside except for a reddish glow and random flashes, heralding certain doom ahead. Guests enter the tunnel to hear the roar of an inferno, hot air blasting their faces. Signs warn of explosives as the bateaux continue into a burning arsenal.

Without warning, the bateaux drop into a dark abyss, streaking past a series of detonations, flaring flames, and blazing embers, the only source of light in the inky blackness. One last, cataclysmic explosion sends guests hurtling out of the arsenal and down a long, dark tunnel . . .

Time Travel

. . . where the concussive booms of the explosion turn into cracks of thunder as the bateaux sail into a misty vortex of space and time that brings guests back to the present day. A ghostly voice warns that "Dead men tell no tales," hinting at the ultimate fate of the pirates of the Caribbean, which guests are about to experience for themselves in a network of haunted caverns filled with the buccaneers' earthly remains.

Walt Disney World
The Treasure Room

In the Walt Disney World version of the show, the pirates do their Disneyland predecessors one better by stumbling across a treasure room hidden deep beneath the town. Two guards sit bound and gagged in the center of a room filled to the rafters with treasure chests, precious gems and jewels, priceless works of art, and other assorted valuables. Meanwhile, the giddy brigands in the foreground are falling all over themselves in a drunken reverie, taking target practice on anything that moves, including passing guests. Bullets ricochet in all directions as the bateaux make for the relative safety of a wooden dock up ahead.

All in the Family

Sharp-eyed guests will note that the coat of arms hanging above the entrance to the Treasure Room reads "Marco Daviso," an appropriately Spanish-inflected reference to the man whose artistic signature can be seen on so much of the Pirates experience. The family crests that decorate the walls of the Treasure Room are also based on those of Imagineers who worked on the attraction.

The Treasure Room provides a much-needed conclusion to Florida's abridged version of the Pirates story. In the Disneyland original, the cursed treasure lies hidden deep within the haunted caverns, never to be removed, if the grotto's skeletal inhabitants are any indication. Since that treasure makes no such appearance in Walt Disney World's much shorter grotto sequence, the Imagineers had to make it clear that the pirates were after *something*. The Treasure Room provides that narrative payoff at the very end of the story, showing that at least a few ne'er-do-well cads finally found what they came looking for, even if they're presently too drunk to make off with it. Florida's adaptation of Pirates was the first to stage the final outcome of the pirates' invasion at the end of the experience, a story trend that would later not only continue but expand in the Disneyland Paris version of the show.

ABOVE: Marc Davis rendering of The Treasure Room, a scene unique to Walt Disney World. **LEFT:** The scene pays off the pirates' search for the town's hidden treasure.

The UPRAMP

THE BATEAUX somehow make it safely through the arsenal and begin an impossible journey *up* a waterfall. Two hulking pirates struggle to make one last-ditch effort to escape with their prize, an enormous sack overflowing with all manner of loot, including a formal portrait of a famous, make that infamous, pirate captain. The strain is more than they can bear, however, and their escape has come to a standstill. As the bateaux continue up the waterfall, guests pass scattered remnants of the cursed treasure, along with the skeletal remains of still another buccaneer who has tried unsuccessfully to make off with it. The glowing eyes of bats and other night creatures blink at guests from distant caves and catacombs as the bateaux ascend forward in time and space, heading back to their "home port" of Laffite's Landing in New Orleans Square.

The Waterfall scene was another beneficiary of the major enhancements that Imagineers made to the show in 1997. The two pirates heaving and hoeing their treasure sack are veteran performers from Epcot's World of Motion. The painting protruding from the sack is not only a reference to a real pirate figure, Edward "Blackbeard" Teach, but also a major reference to a Disney film that was shot the same year as the attraction opened. It is a reproduction of a portrait of Peter Ustinov as the titular character in *Blackbeard's Ghost*, originally created by master matte painter and sometime Imagineer Peter Ellenshaw. The skeleton of a pirate that expired struggling to make it up the waterfall with his treasure intact was a significant narrative addition, bringing the story full circle to complement the "Dead men tell no tales" message of the Grotto sequence.

"I always felt like you sort of drifted out of the ride without making a complete statement there," Tony Baxter says of the addition. "So we had an opportunity there to, in an abbreviated way, complete the morality of the show."

"The whole point of that scene is to bookend the story," Bob Baranick told *Theme Park Adventure*. "It's the cursed treasure; you've been warned about it. You've been warned about it in the queue, you're

OPPOSITE AND RIGHT: The inclusion of several looters attempting to escape with the treasure, including a pair who clearly didn't make it, brings the pirates full circle. **BELOW:** Kirk Hanson concept sketch of the gag—designed to emulate the Marc Davis style. **BOTTOM:** The Talking Skull at Disneyland Paris.

warned about it before you go down the waterfall. The whole point of seeing the caverns, seeing the curse of the treasure, is that you've seen too much, you're not supposed to be here, and you may not get out of this. That's what the pirates are looking for all the way through the show. They're dunking the mayor trying to find the treasure, and so forth. So we thought we'd wrap the whole story up at the end, where they have found some of the treasure, and they're too greedy, if they were only trying to get one or two things out of there, they might succeed. But, they've grabbed their Jolly Roger flag, and they've wrapped up this huge bundle of treasure; there's no way that they're going to get out, there's no way they're going to succeed. So they're trapped down in this burning arsenal forever, which works with the cycle of the show; the fact that you see it over and over and over. Then, as a wonderful little thing at the end of that scene, we brought back more of the caverns, where the skeletons are, that from many years ago, have died trying to get the treasure out. That, with the audio over the top of it, 'Dead men tell no tales,' I think kind of wraps up the whole story."

Return to the Dock

"Please step out to your right."

THE BATEAUX reach the top of the waterfall and spill into a waterway that wraps around the sandbar guests observed as they entered the French manor house seemingly hundreds of years earlier. A parrot perched atop a treasure chest welcomes guests back to the "reality" (always a relative term at Disneyland) of New Orleans Square. The bateaux continue on to Laffite's Landing, where guests disembark and proceed down a path adjacent to the plantation house, which leads back to the winding streets of the old French Quarter.

Disneyland Paris
Talking Skull and Grotto

IN THE Paris show, the Grotto sequence ends with the same talking skull that marks the beginning of the original Disneyland adventure. But this time, instead of warning guests of the danger ahead, the skull prepares them to disembark using English and French laced with colorful pirate jargon. Guests leave their bateaux at the dock and make their way through a labyrinthine stone passageway back into the wilds of Adventureland.

Course Heading

The Movies

Return of the Swashbuckler

Curse of the Pirate Movie

In 1992, screenwriters Ted Elliott and Terry Rossio were hot off the success of their script for *Aladdin*, a blockbuster hit for The Walt Disney Studios that continued an animated movie winning streak begun with *The Little Mermaid* in 1989. Elliott and Rossio had their pick of projects, and could write just about any movie they wanted—or so they thought. What they wanted to write was a pirate movie in the grand swashbuckling tradition of *Captain Blood* and *The Crimson Pirate*, but with a fresh take on the genre that would reinvent the swashbuckler for a modern audience.

"I really love swashbucklers," Ted Elliott says, "but nobody was making sword-fighting movies anymore. We didn't believe the pirate genre was dead; it just needed something new for modern audiences. We realized that if we took the supernatural elements people associate with pirates and actually literalize them in a movie—not just *talk* about the curse on the treasure, but actually *have* the treasure be cursed, with special effects—then we could make something interesting. And then we were thinking about what Terry refers to as 'mental real estate.' What's already out there in the audience's mind that they'll associate with this?"

"If you're trying to get a studio to make a $150 million Western, it's better if you say, 'Oh, we have the rights to *The Lone Ranger*,'" Terry Rossio continues. "So for a pirate movie, you have *Blackbeard*, you have *Treasure Island*, but we said 'Pirates of the Caribbean'—people really know what that is."

"And then we realized that Pirates of the Caribbean actually had the supernatural elements in it that we were talking about," Ted adds. "We don't have to now make up a whole bunch. There's the cursed treasure and the moving skeletons, and we thought, 'Oh, my God, it's *Jason and the Argonauts*, it's pirates, it's everything you could possibly want.' So we said, 'That's it, Pirates of the Caribbean,' and we pitched it to Disney. But they weren't interested."

Unfortunately, this response made a certain degree of sense. Most pirate movies made in the early 1990s had failed miserably. Spooked studio executives felt the genre should stay buried, thinking nothing could pry the rusty nails out of the pirate movie coffin.

But *Pirates of the Caribbean* would not rest in peace. It would spend ten years in development. Not at The Walt Disney Studios, but in the strange, private development hell of Ted Elliott and Terry Rossio. In those ten years, however, a new executive team at The Walt Disney Studios would come to see the inherent cinematic value of the company's theme park properties, and Ted and Terry would finally get a shot at their swashbuckler.

Finding Treasure in Your Own Backyard

In the spring of 2000, Walt Disney Studios' executives Brigham Taylor, vice president production; Michael Haines, a creative executive; and Josh Harmon, a story department veteran, began to recognize the potential one of their theme park attractions had as a film property.

"This came out of weekly story sessions between myself, Michael, and Josh," Brigham explains. "We had a standing story meeting about movies we'd like

OPPOSITE: Industrial Light & Magic concept painting of a skeletal pirate. The cursed buccaneer has lit fuses woven into his beard, much like the real-life Blackbeard. A similar character appears in the finished film. **LEFT:** Screenwriters Ted Elliott (left) and Terry Rossio, on location in Rancho Palos Verdes, California. **PAGES 110-111:** Longtime Hollywood creature designer Mark "Crash" McCreery concept painting of a cursed pirate.

to see get made. It was in that meeting that we talked about the possibility of a pirate movie and the fact that we were the only ones who could call a pirate movie, *Pirates of the Caribbean*. We were jazzed about it, but a little sheepish at the same time, due to the possibility of getting laughed out of the room because it is the most failed movie genre of the modern era. But that was also a reason to pursue a pirate movie. No one has gotten it right, and we have the best title out there."

As a big-budget Hollywood film, however, it would still be considered a major risk, both creatively and financially. Brigham and his co-conspirators felt they should at least go into the pitch meeting properly armed. "We spent several months hatching a story in our spare time, and going over the pitfalls of the pirate genre and other movies that didn't quite get it right," Brigham recalls.

In July of that year, the executives emerged from that process with a rough treatment that broadly outlined the story of Will, a lowly prison guard who dreams of becoming a member of the Governor's elite guard. Will's hopes are dashed when Defoe, the Captain of the Guard, cruelly rejects him in front of the Governor himself and his daughter, Elizabeth. When Elizabeth boards a ship bound for the mainland, she is kidnapped by the notorious pirate, Blackheart, and held for an exorbitant ransom. The Governor dispatches Defoe with the payment, but the Captain of the Guard is secretly in league with Blackheart and plans to exploit the situation and unseat the Governor. It is up to Will to save Elizabeth, and he must form an uneasy alliance with the roguish Jack, a prisoner and a former member of Blackheart's bloody crew, to rescue her. In the end, Blackheart is vanquished, Defoe ends up in prison, and Will and Elizabeth end up together. And Jack, of course, is named the new Captain of the Guard, much to Will's dismay.

Brigham presented the idea and their treatment to Nina Jacobson, president, Buena Vista Motion Pictures Group. "They built a story with the bones of the movie we ultimately made," Nina recalls. "The basic underlying love triangle was there to some degree, but none of the attitude was in there and neither was the curse." The executive immediately saw the vast cinematic potential of Pirates of the Caribbean, however. "These attractions are deeply ingrained in our childhood memories," she states. "They also tell really wonderful stories; they're just great narratives."

Encouraged by her initial response to the general idea, Brigham and company polished their treatment and brought it back to the studio head for a second look. This time, Nina returned with the green light

TOP: Darek Gogol concept of the *Black Pearl* and its signature figurehead. **RIGHT:** Rendering by storyboard artist Simon Murton of a classic pirate movie swordfight high atop the *Dauntless*, a scene that did not appear in the film.

to find a writer to flesh out their rough treatment into a full-fledged script. Her approval made it unanimous: Pirates of the Caribbean was charting a course for the movies.

The search for a writer began. Ironically, Ted Elliott and Terry Rossio sat at the very top of the studio's list, but they were unavailable at the time and thus remained unaware of the fact that Disney had finally "caught up" to them. By the summer of 2001, the executives had instead turned to screenwriter Jay Wolpert, who wrote the similarly swashbuckling *Count of Monte Cristo* for Touchstone Pictures, to expand their original treatment into a first-draft screenplay. "Jay was passionately into this genre, and he got the ball rolling," Brigham says.

ABOVE: Simon Murton's ocean-floor view of the Graveyard of Lost Ships.

The executive team knew from the beginning that they couldn't just transcribe the attraction's script and shoot it. Much like adapting a novel, comic book, or TV show, they had to treat the attraction as source material and figure out a way to make it work on film. "We went to Walt Disney Imagineering and they arranged a walk-through of the attraction with Tony Baxter and X Atencio," Brigham recalls. "They walked Jay and me through the show before it was open. We didn't get a narrative from the ride, but we did get a backdrop, a milieu, from the ride. We wanted nods to the attraction in order to tie the two things together. It took a while to get things worked in there organically so it wouldn't feel like they were just thrown in."

Jay Wolpert's drafts made some definite progress from the executives' original story treatment, including cameo appearances by real-life pirate figures Captain Henry Morgan and Anne Bonny. The studio's next stop was Australian screenwriter Stuart Beattie (*Collateral*). Toward the end of 2001, Stuart took his first pass at a rewrite, contributing a number of new story elements along the way.

"In my draft, Commodore Norrington was in league with the bad guys," Stuart recalls. "His quest was for power. He wanted to rule the Caribbean, and he was first going to do that by marrying the Governor's daughter to gain power through marriage. When she turns him down in the first act, he goes into league with the bad pirate captain, whose plan, in my draft anyway, was to take control of the Caribbean, much like Henry Morgan did in the late 1600s."

Stuart changed some names from Jay Wolpert's draft—Captain Defoe became the equally treacherous Lieutenant Norrington; the vile Blackheart was dubbed Captain Wraith; and Elizabeth and Jack took on the avian-inspired surnames of Swann and Sparrow, respectively.

The executive team knew they were making progress and had a serious shot at breaking the pirate-movie curse in Hollywood. "Stuart's rewrite moved us a lot closer to our goal," Brigham says. "Dick [Cook, Chairman, The Walt Disney Studios] and Nina then knew they needed to find a producer, and they were pretty confident that they could do that off the Beattie draft."

Nina and Dick could see how far the project had come from Brigham's initial pitch. Nina had enough confidence in the script at that point to pass it along to a producer she had had in mind since the debut of his last blockbuster. "Dick and I were in Hawaii for the premiere of *Pearl Harbor*. We went for a walk and I told him that we should give *Pirates of the Caribbean* to Jerry Bruckheimer, and he said my favorite Dick saying, which is 'That's the best idea you've had all day!'"

With Dick's ringing endorsement, Nina sent the Beattie draft to the industry powerhouse. Jerry Bruckheimer had been a veritable hit factory since the early 1980s, when with his partner, the late Don Simpson, he produced a seemingly limitless string of blockbusters including *48 Hrs.*, *Flashdance*, *Beverly Hills Cop*, and *Top Gun*. In more recent years, Jerry

had been responsible for some of the biggest live-action hits in Disney history, including *The Rock*, *Armageddon*, *Remember the Titans*, and *Pearl Harbor*, and was the studio's first stop for almost every project of a certain caliber.

As it turned out, the notion of doing a pirate movie wasn't as outrageous to the prolific film and television producer as it might have seemed to the rest of the industry at the time. "Ironically, Jerry and his executive team Mike Stenson and Chad Oman were developing a Captain Kidd movie with the guys who wrote *The Rock* [David Weisberg and Douglas S. Cook], with Ridley Scott attached to direct," Brigham says.

"They sent the script over and we took a look at it," Jerry Bruckheimer recalls. "It was a straightforward pirate movie at the time, and not really something I'd want to go see, much less make. I also told them that as written it was going to be very expensive, around $275 million with all of the sea battles they had in there. So I asked them to let us think about how *we'd* make the movie and said we'd get back to them."

Jerry saw the potential of the Pirates of the Caribbean name and was intrigued by the idea of tackling a notoriously challenging genre with which he had grown up. "I loved watching pirate pictures as a kid," Jerry says. "*Treasure Island*, *Captain Blood*, and *The Black Pirate* were some of my favorites. Errol Flynn and Douglas Fairbanks were formidable, and although their movies are still exciting and very watchable today, I thought we could add some extra pizzazz to a popular theme."

The Bruckheimer team signed on. The script was still missing something that would make the movie a must-see—for both Jerry and audiences—but the producer was confident it could be found.

By that point, it seemed that everyone involved with the project instinctively knew that Ted Elliott and Terry Rossio were a perfect match for the material, and that confidence was well placed. Ted and Terry would soon contribute a story element that would single-handedly make *Pirates of the Caribbean* radically different from every swashbuckler that had come before it.

TOP: Miles Teves concept sketch of the *Black Pearl* and some uninvited guests. **ABOVE:** Producer Jerry Bruckheimer on the Fort Charles set in Rancho Palos Verdes, California.

"No Fear Have Ye o' Evil Curses, Says You? Properly Warned Ye Be, Says I."

In the ten years since *Aladdin* and their own ill-fated *Pirates of the Caribbean* pitch, Ted and Terry had gone on to co-write a similarly adventure-laden period piece, *The Mask of Zorro*, starring Anthony Hopkins and Antonio Banderas, and the computer-animated blockbuster, *Shrek*. Their supernatural spin on the pirate genre courtesy of a Disneyland classic had never entirely left their minds, however, and it all came flooding back with one phone call.

"Fast-forward ten years," Ted Elliott recalls. "We get a call from Mike Stenson and Chad Oman and they say, 'Look, we've got something . . . it's a little weird . . . and if you guys aren't interested, that's okay, but we're making this movie . . . you know the Disneyland ride, Pirates of the Caribbean?' And we said, 'Stop right there—Terry and I have an approach to this material. We'll come and we'll pitch it. If you like the approach, we will absolutely write this movie, but if you don't like the approach, then we'll have to find something else to work on together because this is the *only* approach we want to write.' And that approach was to literalize the supernatural, and then make a 'Golden Age of Hollywood'-movie that happens to have these supernatural and semi-Gothic elements in it."

"I began my studio career with Ted and Terry on an early version of *Princess of Mars*, " says Mike Stenson. "At Bruckheimer, Chad and I met with them three times to find a project together but nothing quite clicked. Finally, we approached them with *Pirates* and they said, 'My God, we've wanted to do that for ten years.'"

In Mike Stenson and Chad Oman, Jerry

ABOVE AND BELOW: Renderings by Simon Murton of Jack and Elizabeth walking the plank of the *Black Pearl*. The hammerhead sharks don't appear in the finished scene, although they do make a cameo in the Graveyard of Lost Ships.

Bruckheimer's top two executives, Ted and Terry finally found a receptive audience for their tale of a cursed treasure and the supernatural effect it has upon the pirates brazen enough to steal it. Not only did the notion of a *literal* curse differentiate their story from every other pirate film ever made, this key plot point was also firmly rooted in the theme park attraction that inspired it—and that was by design. Ted and Terry both felt it was important to remain true to the spirit of the Disneyland original, even if their script could never be a beat-by-beat adaptation of the ride. They knew the film's strength lay in the Pirates of the Caribbean name and the childhood memories people associated with it.

In the end, the attraction-inspired concept of pirates searching for a cursed treasure was what sold Ted and Terry's unique vision of the film. "We went in and said 'Here's the idea,' and they heard it and basically they heard 'pirates become skeletons in the moonlight' and they went 'wow,'" Ted recalls. "And then they pitched it to Jerry, and when he heard that he said, 'All right, that's a movie I want to see.' So it only took ten years for Disney to actually catch up with us, but there were regime changes and all that good stuff. It was just one of those weird things where a decade passes. So we can actually say we'd been working on *Pirates of the Caribbean* for ten years before Disney ever got involved!"

After four weeks of daily story meetings with Jerry, Chad, and Mike, Ted and Terry pitched the idea to Nina Jacobson. The screenwriters were happily surprised to find the current Disney studio executives equally receptive to their more fantastical take on the material. But the cinematic landscape had changed a great deal in ten years, both in terms of what filmmakers could pull off and what audiences would accept.

"I remember talking to Nina Jacobson and just flat out saying it'll be disaster if you don't include supernatural elements," Terry Rossio says. "Pirate films don't work; they haven't worked in fifty years, but with the advent of CGI [computer-generated imagery] there had been this emergent massive popularity for a number of fantasy-type films, because

ABOVE: Darek Gogol illustration of the attack on Port Royal. **RIGHT:** Concept art by Miles Teves depicting an imprisoned Jack Sparrow watching the *Black Pearl*'s attack on Port Royal.

CGI allows you to portray fantasy on-screen in a way that really hadn't quite been possible before. Now this may be a 'pirate movie,' but what the audience is going to respond to is the fact that they get to go into this fantasy world, and that fantasy world is what's going to give us access. Once you've hooked the audience by their interest in some of the genre conventions of horror or fantasy, they'll be perfectly willing to accept the conventions of a pirate movie or a romance or a thriller. That was the theory. I think it would have been very dangerous to try to make just a 'straight' pirate movie."

The Pirate Captain

Just as he had been waiting for the right opportunity to work with Ted Elliott and Terry Rossio, Jerry Bruckheimer also had his eye on up-and-coming director Gore Verbinski. "Gore has this artistic touch that I look for in directors," Jerry says. "It's hard to find that combination of humor and edge, because you usually get the ones that are really silly and have no edge, or you get the ones that are really edgy and have no sense of humor. He's got both."

Gore was a Clio Award-winning commercial director who made his film debut with *Mouse Hunt*, a family comedy starring Nathan Lane, before taking on the raw star power of *The Mexican*, an action-comedy headlined by Julia Roberts and Brad Pitt. At the time of Jerry's call in early 2002, Gore was directing *The Ring*, an American remake of a Japanese horror film that would go on to become a blockbuster hit.

Director Gore Verbinski on location.

"My agent called and said, 'How do you feel about a pirate movie?'" Gore recalls. "I mean, how often are you going to get that call?" He was instantly intrigued. "I used to love watching *Captain Blood*, *The Crimson Pirate*, all the old classics. There is something about piracy that speaks to the child within: it's rebellion distilled. Yet, if you look at cinema history, the pirate genre had its heyday and then vanished. I knew I was heading into dangerous waters, but when else would I get the chance?"

"We were lucky to sign Gore right before *The Ring* came out," Jerry adds. "This film is perfect for him because we encouraged him to use his wonderful sense of humor and his great storytelling skills. And because it has elements of the supernatural, Gore got to use lots of visual effects. His enthusiasm is like a little kid's. He loves to work with actors, and actors love him. We were fortunate, because he really was the perfect director for this project."

Gore met with Jerry and his team to hear their pitch. As Mike Stenson recalls, "We told Gore, the good news is, we have a great franchise, a great story, and great writers. The bad news is, you already have a start date, there is no script to read, and we need you to commit." To no one's surprise, it was the element of the curse in the story that appealed to Gore and, in his words, "was really an opportunity to turn the movie on its head and open it up as a genre."

"When I first heard the pitch, I liked that it was a terrific perversion of the classic tale," Gore says. "I came in asking, 'What is the standard plot structure? Is it a kidnapping? Is it buried treasure?' When actually, it has all of these qualities, yet the principal one is reversed. It is a film about finding the last piece of cursed treasure and putting it back. Only by doing this can the pirates get rid of the curse. I think that, beyond the ghost story, Ted and Terry's simple reverse in plot construct allowed us to create something unique."

"Gore proceeded without hesitation," says Chad Oman. "The very night he heard the pitch he started contacting his crew to put them on hold to do the movie."

In a not uncommon practice in Hollywood, Gore didn't wait for a revised script but immediately began prepping and storyboarding his film from Ted and Terry's outline. "It was no way to prep a movie: absolute chaos. But the storyboarding process gave birth to Jack's arrival on a sinking boat, the skeletal monkey, the pirate with a wooden eye, skeletons walking on the ocean floor, and so much more. In some way it was better not to have a shooting script because so much was born out of that primordial soup we were all swimming in together." Meanwhile, the screenwriters would attempt to corral some of that chaos in their first draft of the screenplay.

The Curse of the *Black Pearl*

TED ELLIOTT and Terry Rossio built on the foundation that the Disney executive team, Jay Wolpert, and Stuart Beattie had laid for them, as they wrote their first draft between March and May of 2002, weaving their cursed-treasure story line and its attendant supernatural elements into the existing love-triangle narrative. They considered all of the plot points and characterizations that were already embedded in previous scripts, dropping some and incorporating others into their new draft.

But it was the cursed Aztec gold that set everything into motion, driving every aspect of their story and linking all of the principal characters: the gold motivates Barbossa, the latest incarnation of the original Blackheart and his descendant, Captain Wraith, to lead a mutiny against Captain Jack Sparrow, maroon him on an island, and make off with his ship, the *Black Pearl*. It is the same gold that dooms Barbossa and his men to a hellish existence between life and death, launching their ten-year voyage to recover the forbidden treasure and repay the heathen gods, as well as Jack's ongoing mission to find them and reclaim his ship. It is a piece of the cursed gold—the last missing piece, as we'll come to find out—that brings Elizabeth Swann and Will Turner [Thornton in the Wolpert and Beattie drafts] together and unites them in a shared destiny. It's that same gold piece, which the governor's daughter has turned into a medallion, that brings Barbossa and his crew of the damned to Port Royal on a collision course with all the other characters in the first place, kidnapping Elizabeth for the medallion and her blood, which they think they need to lift the curse. But most significant of all, it is the cursed Aztec gold that causes the pirates to become skeletons in the moonlight, revealing them for what they really are: the hook that sold the movie.

ABOVE: Illustration of the cave's treasure room by Darek Gogol.
LEFT: Mark "Crash" McCreery illustration of the cursed Barbossa.

RIGHT: Darek Gogol illustration of Jack Sparrow and the cursed treasure. **BELOW:** Miles Teves concept rendering of the cursed crew of the *Black Pearl* "taking a walk" on the ocean floor.

"Ted and Terry are very sophisticated storytellers," says Mike Stenson. "They break the movie down to its constituent 'movements' and then put it up on index cards on a board. We had an opportunity to spend a number of sessions working with them as they outlined and re-outlined—frankly, it was a real education."

Ted and Terry saw plenty of opportunities to push the boundaries of fun and fantasy, from taking the characters' behavior to the extreme to completely overhauling major set pieces to adding several more references to the Disneyland attraction. "Stuart had keyed into a lot of the same ideas we had about what the romantic part of a pirate movie needed to be," Ted says. "And he also had that great notion of attempting to steal a big ship in order to steal a little ship. But in the second half of his script the pirates try to take over Port Royal, and it ended with an armada of British ships going after the pirates. There were none of the supernatural elements. There were a couple of little nods to the ride, but before we came on the idea of making it supernatural wasn't there, and there wasn't much of an effort to really *push* the Jack character."

In Ted and Terry's draft, each of the principal roles grew more finely delineated while even the supporting characters wound up with more to do; the pirates frequently manifested themselves as perpetually decaying corpses as a result of the curse; and much of the third act consisted of an epic hand-to-bone battle between the British Royal Navy and a horde of skeletal scoundrels. And as for the Jack character, "push" him they did.

Jerry and the Pirates

It's "Captain" Jack Sparrow

THE SEARCH for Captain Jack began while the screenwriters were still searching for a solid story. They had more of a notion of the movie they wanted to make than a script they were completely comfortable with, but it was enough to further pique the interest of an actor who had a notion to do a pirate movie.

"When we read the script," Jerry Bruckheimer recalls, "we thought carefully about casting the role of Jack Sparrow. The story is based on a theme park ride, so you have the potential to turn off teenagers who think that the movie will be for kids. I thought we needed to hire a brilliant actor who had an *edge*, to help us widen the audience and show how hip the film could be. The perfect actor in my mind was Johnny Depp. Johnny is something of an enigma in Hollywood; he doesn't follow the commercial Hollywood path. He only gets involved with projects he feels passionate about. So, often he can be found maintaining the rough edges on more difficult pieces of material such as *Blow* and *Fear and Loathing in Las Vegas*. He manages to open a small window of accessibility for moviegoers who might not otherwise give such challenging films a chance. I flew to France and talked to him about *Pirates of the Caribbean* because I knew he would bring a unique voice to the character and elevate it from what was on the page. Because he had one child at the time, and another on the way, he was interested in expanding the kind of movies he wanted to make. Dick Cook had a general meeting with Johnny and pitched him several movies on the Disney slate. So, when it came to Jack Sparrow, we were all in agreement."

Although Jerry pointed out that with Ted Elliott and Terry Rossio's supernatural take on the material they were going to re-invent the pirate genre, Johnny wasn't completely sold on the idea and said that he'd continue to think about it. For his part, Jerry knew he had found his Jack Sparrow. "The way you get an audience to really embrace a movie is to cast against the grain," Jerry says. "You find someone the audience would never expect to see in a Disney movie. I went after Johnny Depp. Johnny is an artist who's known to take on quirkier projects. He's a brilliant actor. He's not out to create a fan base for himself, or to simply select work based on salary; it's clear he needs to find a role that gives back to him artistically."

Once Gore Verbinski signed on to helm the movie, he too began lobbying Johnny to play Jack Sparrow, assuring the actor that he could take the role in as offbeat a direction as he liked. Based on the caliber of talent now involved with the project, his desire to make a movie for his kids, and the fact that the script was shaping up to be something quite "different"—a Depp specialty—Johnny signed on as captain of the pirates.

While Depp had never had a major blockbuster hit, at least not one he was credited with, and wasn't considered a bankable leading man, at least not in the traditional sense, it was clear he brought a more artistic and independent sensibility to even the most mainstream studio fare, and the executive team thought he could do the same for *Pirates of the Caribbean* and bring the project a bit more credibility and legitimacy at the same time. Industry players and pundits alike were already taking swipes at

ABOVE: Jerry Bruckheimer with his two heroes, Johnny Depp as Captain Jack Sparrow and Orlando Bloom as Will Turner. **OPPOSITE:** Johnny Depp standing tall as Captain Jack, in one of the most memorable—and ultimately misleading—entrances in movie history.

Disney for trying to turn a "kiddie ride" into a movie, and the studio knew that the actor's involvement would make them think twice about the project's artistic merit. "Jerry loves unexpected casting," says Chad Oman, "particularly casting an actor known for his serious artistry and putting him in a genre blockbuster that helps elevate the movie."

Johnny, meanwhile, was pleased with his decision to join the project, especially after he read a draft of Ted and Terry's script. "Isn't it every boy's dream to be a pirate and get away with basically everything?" Johnny asks rhetorically. "Who wouldn't want to play a pirate? The second I heard that Ted and Terry were writing the script, I knew we were in good shape. With Jerry's background and Gore's intense focus, I knew the film had strong shoulders to stand on. When I read Ted and Terry's screenplay, I was pleasantly surprised; they'd exceeded my expectations. They brought a great amount of humor to the story and created building blocks for the actors to elaborate, to really stretch the characters."

The character of Captain Jack Sparrow would wind up getting stretched almost beyond recognition, at least as far as he related to the rogue in the studio's original treatment. The studio had wanted Johnny Depp, but a very specific Johnny Depp, and it wasn't the quirkier Johnny of *Ed Wood* and *Benny & Joon*; they were hoping for the more traditional leading man who could be glimpsed intermittently throughout the actor's career. "He can be debonair and rakish, as in *Don Juan DeMarco* and *Chocolat*," Brigham says. "I think that's what we all had in our minds, even though we didn't discuss it. That perception ultimately had nothing to do with what he wound up doing with the role, of course."

TOP: Jack Sparrow offers a sly grin as he realizes that his plan to steal the *Interceptor* is working. **LEFT AND OPPOSITE:** Captain Jack Sparrow: crazy, or crazy like a fox?

But Jack Sparrow wouldn't be the square-jawed, two-fisted action hero the studio thought they wanted. The screenwriters were reluctant to deem Jack Sparrow a hero at all, preferring to think of him as an altogether different archetype—an anti-hero whose motives are in question every second he's on screen, and that was something Depp keyed into almost immediately. "He can't be a hero; he has to be a trickster," Ted says. "He has to be this absolutely amoral, self-interested character from beginning to end, someone you absolutely love because he is the cleverest and most fun person in the movie. Pirates need to be somewhat morally ambiguous to begin with, so we said let's go ahead and embrace that and make the guy absolutely amoral. Any morality that anybody ascribes to him is based on what they perceive of him as opposed to anything he's actually doing. Anything he does is completely in his own self-interest. And Barbossa is actually the dark side of that same idea. Believe it or not, there was actually some thought put into the whole thing."

"Jack Sparrow's the type of character that you enjoy watching steal money from a little old lady," Gore Verbinski adds. "He is basically a con man—he's lazy, he's a great pirate, but he's not going to fight if he doesn't have to. He's always going to take a shortcut. I think the big thing for Captain Jack Sparrow is his myth. He's kind of his own best agent—he markets himself very well."

Johnny had a long history of playing outsiders, and in his estimation, pirates were the ultimate outsiders—or worse, outcasts—largely because they were the undisputed rebels and bad boys of their day. "Pirates were the rock stars of their day," Johnny says. That conclusion led to an ingenious analogy: Jack Sparrow as one of the Rolling Stones, which would help Johnny create one of the most memorable characters in movie history.

"Johnny's known for creating his own characters," Jerry says. "He had a definite vision for Jack Sparrow that is completely unique, and he based it on a rock star. We just let him go, and he came up with this off-center, yet very shrewd, pirate. He can't quite hold his balance, his speech is a bit slurred, so you assume he's either drunk, seasick, or he's been on a ship too long. But it's all an act perpetrated for effect. And strange as it seems, it's also part of Captain Jack's charm."

"In Jack, I saw a guy who was able to run between the raindrops," Johnny explains. "He can walk across the DMZ, entertain a troop, and then sashay back to the other side and tell the enemy another story. He tries to stay on everyone's good side because he's wise enough to know he might need them in the future.

"No matter how bad things got, there was always this sort of bizarre optimism about him," the actor continues. "I also thought there was something beautiful and poignant about the idea of his objective. All he wants is to get his ship back, which represents nothing more than pure freedom to him. Of course he'll thieve and do whatever it takes, especially when the opportunity arises, but his main focus is just to get the *Black Pearl* back at whatever cost."

Ted Elliott put it best when he spoke of the symbiotic relationship between the generative act of screenwriting and the interpretative craft of acting: "I have the pride of authorship, but Johnny Depp has the pride of ownership."

LEFT: Commodore Norrington (Jack Davenport) and his men get the first of many drops on Sparrow, but Captain Jack quickly turns the tables on his captors (inset).

All Work and No Play Makes Jack a Dull Boy

Given Johnny's quirky reputation and permanent residence outside the mainstream, perhaps Disney should have been better prepared for a surprise or two when first viewing the actor's interpretation of the Jack Sparrow character. The studio executives figured they'd be getting something different in Johnny Depp; they just didn't realize *how* different. Johnny's unique brand of character development was kept between him and Gore Verbinski until a few weeks prior to filming.

"Day one," recalls Brigham Taylor. "Nina and I walked down to Stage Two, where they were shooting a hair and make-up test. That was the first thing we had to adjust to, [Johnny's] bohemian, gutter rat look. He had the hair, the dreads, the beard—the whole bit. And he had nearly every tooth capped in gold, by a real dentist. We asked ourselves, 'Can we get away with this?' He's not going to be the dashing, debonair Errol Flynn character wooing women; he's going to be this scraggly character.

"We thought maybe we could pull back on the braided beard and the teeth," Brigham continues. "There was a long process about what we were going to ask him to pull back on and who was going to make the phone call."

That person turned out to be Dick Cook. "Dick called Johnny," Brigham concludes, "and told him that we'd like to modify the look of the character so he would at least have a somewhat realistic smile. He said, 'Okay, I'll lose some teeth, but I'm keeping the beard.'"

The executives may have felt as if they made some progress on Johnny's unconventional appearance, but their anxiety level shot up again when principal photography began and they got their first good look at his performance. "Everyone was surprised because he hadn't rehearsed it that way," Brigham explains. "Johnny was very elusive during this period. He knew what was coming because studios had been second-guessing him for his whole career."

"Many people were incredibly nervous about how effeminate and drunken he was coming off in dailies," Nina recalls, "so I got to be memorialized as the nervous studio executive who called Johnny and asked what he was doing. But Jerry and Gore never tried to stop me from making that phone call, so I think it was something that was on everyone's mind, not just ours."

Nina asked Johnny if he could "dial it down" a bit, explaining that the film needed a traditional heroic character, even if Jack Sparrow was more of an antihero. He diplomatically pointed out that they were familiar with his work and the character choices he'd made. "I'd really appreciate it if you'd trust me on this," Johnny told Nina. "Come down here and I'll walk you through it because I have no interest in changing what I'm doing." The actor presumed that his résumé of unconventional characters was why they had hired him in the first place and didn't want them to contract a case of buyer's remorse now.

Dick Cook made the final call for Disney after Brigham showed him the dailies. "I keyed up what was probably the most palatable take," Brigham says. "And by that I mean the most audible and discernible take, and showed it to Dick. And to his credit he said, 'I'm okay with it.'"

A Pirate Crew

Once Johnny Depp slipped behind the wheel of the *Pirates* ship, the remaining principal roles and smaller supporting parts began to fill with performers of an unusually high caliber, giving the cast a distinguished pedigree that continued to alter some of the industry's preconceptions about the film. "We always try to populate our movies with great talent," Jerry Bruckheimer states. "And in this one we were lucky enough to combine respected, well-known veterans with several up-and-coming actors. Excellence begets excellence, and with every additional actor we signed, the bar just moved higher and higher."

Australian actor Geoffrey Rush, who won an Academy Award for his portrayal of pianist David Helfgott in *Shine*, signed on to play Jack Sparrow's cursed nemesis, the mutinous Barbossa. "We needed an equally accomplished actor to play Johnny's adversary," Jerry says. "Geoffrey Rush is enormously talented and is known for playing a vast array of characters. We were lucky that he had a break in his schedule and wanted to be part of this project. Geoffrey's Barbossa is the quintessential villain; it's a treat to watch him become the character."

In an effort to more fully inhabit his role, Geoffrey created a rich backstory for his character. "He achieved the position of captain by being a mutinous first mate and taking over the *Black Pearl* and claiming it as his own," he explains. "I thought, this guy has got to be a crack swordsman, and a very nasty, dirty fighter. He didn't go to finishing school with an épée; he probably had a sword on his belt from the time he was about thirteen, and he just knew how to hack off heads."

Timing was everything where the casting of Will Turner was concerned, with the production signing Orlando Bloom just as he began following in Depp's footsteps on his way to international stardom and bona fide teen-idol status. "When we first cast him in *Black Hawk Down*, I knew his time would come," Jerry says. "I just didn't know how lucky we'd be to grab him before all the frenzy started with the first two *Lord of the Rings* films. I actually talked to him about this role while we were on a promotional tour in Japan for *Black Hawk Down*, and he thought it sounded like a wonderful character."

Of his character, Orlando Bloom says that Will "really does develop" throughout the film, growing from a naive, straitlaced blacksmith into a bold

TOP: Academy Award-winner Geoffrey Rush as Captain Barbossa. **MIDDLE:** Orlando Bloom as Will Turner. **BOTTOM:** Jack and Will form an uneasy alliance to pursue their respective treasures: the *Black Pearl* and Elizabeth Swann.

RIGHT: Elizabeth gets Barbossa's attention by threatening to drop the Aztec medallion overboard. **BELOW:** Keira Knightley as Elizabeth Swann. **BOTTOM:** Jonathan Pryce as Elizabeth's father, Governor Weatherby Swann.

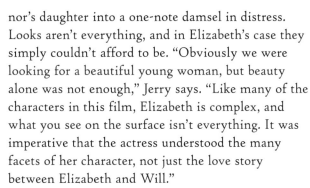

swashbuckler who can stand with the best and worst of them. "He's very earnest, very true blue. Then, without warning, he finds himself thrown into the middle of an exciting yet dangerous adventure. This is a coming of age story for Will."

And it's Jack Sparrow who turns into something of a surrogate father to Will Turner as he matures throughout the course of the story. "Will has grown up without a father figure," Orlando continues, "so he has to look to the role models around him, and in Port Royal, those are naval officers. When Will and Jack are thrown together, Jack opens Will's eyes to what it means to be a man. He teaches him that he can't just blindly follow nonsensical rules; a man has to make his own decisions, right or wrong, and go after what he wants in life."

As for Elizabeth Swann, who happens to *be* the very thing Will Turner wants in life, the role went to then seventeen-year-old Keira Knightley, who had appeared as one of Queen Amidala's handmaidens in *Star Wars: Episode One—The Phantom Menace* before starring in the international hit British comedy, *Bend It Like Beckham*.

The filmmakers had no intention of casting a pretty face that might turn the governor's daughter into a one-note damsel in distress. Looks aren't everything, and in Elizabeth's case they simply couldn't afford to be. "Obviously we were looking for a beautiful young woman, but beauty alone was not enough," Jerry says. "Like many of the characters in this film, Elizabeth is complex, and what you see on the surface isn't everything. It was imperative that the actress understood the many facets of her character, not just the love story between Elizabeth and Will."

"Elizabeth has a morbid curiosity about pirates," Gore adds. "She reads too many books on the subject, and she's become a sort of pirate groupie," continuing the rock star theme. "But instead of getting to meet the Jon Bon Jovi of pirates, she ends up with the Sid Vicious, and even though she thinks she knows a lot about pirates, she soon learns that all the rules she believes in are meant to be broken."

"She romanticizes the entire pirate thing," Keira says. "It's an obsession, really. So it's an interesting transition for Elizabeth to go from her romantic notions to the cutthroat, dirty reality of piracy. But she has a little pirate in herself. Don't we all?"

The Royal Shakespeare Company's Jonathan Pryce, also known as the star of *Brazil* and *Something Wicked This Way Comes* (and, in a strange bit of Rolling Stone synergy, played the role of "Jack" in *Jumping Jack Flash*) took the role of Governor Weatherby Swann, Elizabeth's father. BBC-TV star Jack Davenport (*Coupling*) filled the role of Commodore Norrington and another well-known U.K. actor, Kevin R. McNally (*Phantom of the Opera, De-Lovely*), was cast as Jack Sparrow's semitrusty lieutenant, Joshamee Gibbs. Film and television veterans Lee Arenberg and Mackenzie Crook, who costarred in the BBC's hit comedy "The Office," came aboard as Barbossa's dim-witted henchmen Pintel and Ragetti, two stooges in every sense of the word.

As the characters in Ted Elliott and Terry Rossio's script gradually assumed faces to go with their names, the physical world that they would inhabit began to form on sketch pads, soundstages, and backlots throughout Southern California, as well as on location in the Caribbean.

A Pirate's Look for Me

Even as Ted and Terry were expanding their rough outline into a first-draft script, Gore Verbinski and Jerry Bruckheimer began recruiting a team of artists and designers to transform their words into pictures for the first time. "I was able to do storyboards before many of the scenes were in place because a lot of the bones were already there," Gore says. "[Production designer] Brian Morris and I would start exploring ideas, we'd discuss them with the writers, and some of them would end up in the script."

Longtime creature designer Mark "Crash" McCreery, a veteran of such genre classics as *Terminator 2: Judgment Day*, *Jurassic Park*, and *The Hulk*, devised a range of proposed looks for Barbossa and his crew of the damned in various stages of decomposition, a process that would later continue in Northern California when the production recruited George Lucas's Industrial Light & Magic to supply the film's visual effects. The physical appearance of the undead buccaneers ran the gamut from skeletal warriors straight out of a Ray Harryhausen film to grisly amalgams of flesh and bone that would look more at home in a George Romero zombie movie. Visualizations of some of the film's main set pieces took shape in a series of moody renderings by conceptual designers Jim Byrkit and Miles Teves and storyboard artists Simon Murton and Darek Gogol.

Meanwhile, costume designer Penny Rose and her group began to establish the look of the film's mortal characters. As soon as an actor was cast in a role, an artist would begin sketching out what that performer might look like in period garb or full pirate regalia. Penny was a West End theater veteran who also designed costumes for big-budget Hollywood blockbusters such as *Mission: Impossible* and *Entrapment*, as well as the period pieces *Evita* and Lord Richard Attenborough's *In Love and War*. She had also worked on another interpretation of a Disney classic, the studio's 1998 remake of *The Parent Trap*.

Unlike the Golden Age films that inspired the original attraction, Gore Verbinski's vision didn't

TOP: BBC-TV star Jack Davenport as Commodore Norrington.
RIGHT: Early concept sketch of Barbossa costume

Costume concepts for Elizabeth Swann and Jack Sparrow. Thanks to Johnny Depp, Captain Jack would wind up looking nothing like the original designs.

include many of the traditional trappings of a pirate movie. "I didn't want these pirates to look similar to what we've all seen before," Gore says. "No hooks for hands or eye patches everywhere. I didn't want to see trick-or-treat belts or striped shirts. In reading about that period, it's clear that people didn't live very long; they were essentially rotting away. Ships leaked, there was nothing in the way of medical attention, and not a lot of personal hygiene. Things were pretty disgusting. Strange as it may seem, it was fun finding that disgusting quality and texture as we began casting extras and creating the looks of all the pirates. Some of the extras were so dedicated, you could smell it!"

A number of the film's signature costume pieces included full shirts with big sleeves, recalling the classic Errol Flynn look of Hollywood's Golden Age without being slavish to it. Penny wanted to see a lot of movement in the costumes, knowing it would only enhance the many action sequences called for in the script. "The coats all had six or eight pleats in the back," she says. "You see them during film fighting, and they've got a lot of movement." She was also concerned about the heat during filming in the Caribbean. "Everything was made out of silk or linen or cotton, so nobody had anything scratchy or heavy on."

An actor's wardrobe is one of the most useful instruments in their toolbox, and for many performers, a character cannot truly come to life until they are in full costume. For Johnny Depp, the character of Jack Sparrow finally came together for him during the extensive costume fittings and hair and makeup tests that took place in the weeks leading up the commencement of principal photography. "The first day I was in full makeup and wardrobe, seeing the guy for the first time, I was very pleased because I knew it was Captain Jack," Johnny recalls. "Gore came in, looked and said, 'Yeah, that's it.' He got it immediately; he knew where I was going with the character. He supported it; he understood it and he got the humor. It was the beginning of a great relationship."

The World of *Pirates of the Caribbean*

Setting to Sea

The physical world of *Pirates of the Caribbean* began to form under production designer Brian Morris, whose credits include *Sabrina*, *The Insider*, and *Unfaithful*. "The scale of Gore's moviemaking was very attractive and appropriate to this piece," Brian says. "Gore is incredibly visual. Even in his personal environment, you can tell immediately that he's got style and taste. He gave me a feeling that he trusted me to handle the job, which is always great."

The story was a study in contrasts, in many ways a visual representation of the pirates' contrasting appearance in daylight and moonlight. This gave Brian and his design team a wealth of thematic material with which to create the film's physical environments. On one hand, the curse and an overall sense of evil and villainy were the most prevailing themes. On the opposite end of the spectrum was the spit-and-polish order of the prim-and-proper, upper-crust British colonists. The stark differences between the opposing forces would be reflected in the worlds they inhabited.

Dariusz Wolski, with whom Gore had collaborated on *The Mexican*, reprised his role as director of cinematography on *Pirates of the Caribbean*. "He was the perfect choice," Gore says of his cinematographer. "I've worked with him before but in a completely different way. *The Mexican* was about the absence of style; *Pirates* is about creating a definite style and design."

While Brian Morris pored over paintings from the period and beyond, including the influential pirate art of N.C. Wyeth and Howard Pyle—the same imagery that had once influenced Marc Davis—Gore and Dariusz spent as much time as possible screening old pirate movies and examining story elements and visual components of great adventure films. They decided to take their pirate movie in an even more majestic and embellished direction than its predecessors from Hollywood's Golden Age, a creative choice that would be reflected in the film's sumptuous production design.

The most obvious example of this extravagance is the treasure cave on Isle de Muerta, where Barbossa and his crew have stashed the spoils of piracy, the centerpiece of the many sets constructed at the Walt Disney Studios in Burbank. The cave was constructed within the largest soundstage on the Disney lot, Stage #2, the same space the studio had redesigned in 1997 to accommodate Bruckheimer's gargantuan asteroid set for *Armageddon*. The recently enlarged stage was the ideal location for Brian and his team to build their lavishly adorned cavern complete with a labyrinth of winding waterways, hidden grottoes, and treacherous rocky passageways. It was Claude Coats's haunted grotto writ large, a big idea that dwarfed that small basement in Anaheim just as surely as the attraction itself had.

"We were trying to take a little bit of the Disney feel of the cave in the ride at Disneyland," says Derek R. Hill, the film's supervising art director, "so we came up with the concept that the Aztec gold is

Captain Barbossa and the cursed crew of the *Black Pearl*.

ABOVE AND LEFT: The massive treasure cave set was constructed on Stage #2 at the Walt Disney Studios, which Jerry Bruckheimer had previously used to build the asteroid set for *Armageddon*.

hidden in this volcanic cave in the mountains. It was fun to go back and do this kind of stuff because now you're creating a ride that someone's going to take in the film."

"The cave set is one of the largest sets built on a stage in Hollywood," says executive producer Bruce Hendricks. "It took about five months to build, with over a hundred craftsmen working on it. It was partly sculpted out of Styrofoam and partly built with wood frame and plaster." The set was then filled with 300,000 gallons of water, or a little over four feet, a process that took three to four days, and dressed over a period of three weeks.

Gore Verbinski wanted gold everywhere, and repeated his mantra to the art department every chance he got: pirates are not art collectors—they're in it for the money. "Gore would remind us that pirates are only interested in the face value of any given item," set decorator Larry Dias explains. "We painted hundreds of cubic feet of rock to look like gold nuggets and collected hundreds of yards of fake pearls and beads. We found a mass of odd objects that would have been looted by pirates. It was tricky; we tried to get a certain texture going without becoming too ridiculous. We were very careful in creating disorder and making the cave look haphazard, as though the pirates had taken boatloads of their loot and just dumped it in heaps wherever they found space."

The original attraction's other primary location, the unnamed seaport ransacked by pirates in search of cursed treasure, became Port Royal in the film. The production design team created the town proper by redressing the facades of European Street on the Universal Studios backlot, the same network of quaint streets and village squares prowled by the Universal classic monsters in the 1930s and 1940s. The creaky wooden dock where Jack Sparrow puts in—barely—was built on location in the Caribbean, and the bayfront area where the pirates come ashore was actually situated north of Los Angeles in Rancho Palos Verdes, close to the Fort Charles set. Both locations were designed to match the European Street sets on the Universal backlot.

Just a few steps away from European Street was the backlot's legendary Court of Miracles set, best known as the scene of Quasimodo's ultimate humiliation in the 1923 version of *The Hunchback of Notre Dame*, starring Lon Chaney, which was dressed up as part of the pirate's paradise of Tortuga. The rest of Tortuga was fashioned on a converted Mexican Street, a short distance away on the Universal backlot. Tortuga was the setting for a number of references to the attraction, including the infamous "bride" auction,

the dunking of the mayor, cut from the film but included among the deleted scenes on the DVD, the inebriated pirates balancing on kegs of rum, and a drunken buccaneer sleeping it off in a pigsty.

Port Royal's Fort Charles was constructed on the former site of the Marineland theme park in Rancho Palos Verdes, California, high atop a three-acre bluff that offered camera-ready, 180-degree views of the ocean. That was no small achievement considering that Southern California's massive suburban sprawl has made it almost impossible for film crews to find undeveloped land with panoramic backdrops that would be so close to Los Angeles suitable for any historical period. There were no electrical wires, no skyscrapers blotting out the horizon, and no visible roadways, making it the perfect place to double for an eighteenth-century military base in the Caribbean.

The immense faux fortress complex also included the Commodore's office, a dank prison cell block—the setting for a humorous scene straight out of the attraction—and, in the fort's center courtyard, the gallows that would host Captain Jack Sparrow at the end of the film.

The sprawling Rancho Palos Verdes location was also home to several other key sets, including interiors and exteriors of the Governor's mansion, the Bay of Port Royal, and a space to accommodate the background blue-screen work that would lend an appropriately Caribbean backdrop to select scenes.

Additional mansion interiors were shot on a soundstage, considering that few owners of historic landmarks would be willing to let even make-believe pirates loose in their homes. "We couldn't go shoot an existing house because the pirates rampage, set it on fire, and swing on the chandeliers," Derek says. "It's all built from scratch. We built the interior location at the Raleigh Studios in Manhattan Beach. Then we built the exterior facade at Marineland. And then we built a miniature model to do a CG composite in the location on a hillside on the island." In the finished film, the transitions between real-world locations and interior and exterior sets and live-action and computer-generated imagery feel completely natural, creating one seamless image of Port Royal in the minds of moviegoers.

TOP AND ABOVE: In reality, "Port Royal" existed in no less than three places: Rancho Palos Verdes, California; the Universal Studios backlot; and the island of St. Vincent in the Caribbean. On film, the transitions between set and location are seamless.

Ports of Call

"It's called Pirates of the *Caribbean*, so you don't want to shoot it in Long Beach," Jerry Bruckheimer says. "You want to shoot it in the Caribbean."

While that may sound like a foregone conclusion, an expensive Caribbean-location shoot is far from a given in cost-conscious Hollywood, even for a movie called *Pirates of the Caribbean*. On the other hand, the days in which a studio water tank could successfully pass for the entire Pacific Ocean are long gone, so the filmmakers knew they were going to have to find a real sea, but which of the proverbial seven would best suit their needs and budget? They initially considered trying to save a considerable amount of time and money by shooting on Catalina Island off the coast of nearby Long Beach, but quickly realized that what they wanted and what the film demanded was a backdrop with a much more realistic look and feel.

"We could have considered looking at Australia and Thailand," executive producer Bruce Hendricks adds. "But it would have looked like what it is—the South China Sea. We really wanted to maintain the look of the Caribbean, similar to the way we made *Pearl Harbor*: you have to go to Pearl Harbor. We always want to be faithful and accurate to the subject matter because it shows on-screen."

The quest for reality considerably narrowed their choices and confirmed what they had suspected all along. This was one film that would have to be shot on location—literally. If the filmmakers had tried any geographical sleight of hand, the audience would have known they were faking. "There's a quality to the water, sand, and palm trees in the Caribbean, so we knew we wanted to go there," Gore describes. "We ended up searching around the entire Caribbean for months. I'm sure we looked at a minimum of twenty different islands."

Even with the entire Caribbean suddenly at their disposal, casting a suitable location wasn't as easy as it may have first appeared. "It's amazing when you scout a film like this how quickly you realize that the world is insanely overpopulated," the director continues. "You go out looking for a lush, deepwater, cul-de-sac-shaped bay, one that doesn't have a hotel sitting right in the middle of your shot. There aren't any unpopulated islands out there anymore. They just don't exist."

After a lengthy but surely not unpleasant survey of the region, the filmmakers finally found what they were looking for in a small southeastern corner of the Caribbean between St. Lucia and Grenada. "We picked St. Vincent because it didn't have much," Derek Hill says. "It had a few piers in the water. We extended one pier and built a couple other new piers. Then we augmented a couple of the existing buildings and we added to the town so we could make it look like the Universal backlot."

St. Vincent was an obvious choice for the production's base of operations thanks to its geographical features, including Gore's horseshoe-shaped cove, which the filmmakers found in the island's

TOP: The desert island on which Jack is marooned—twice—was actually located in the Grenadines. **RIGHT:** The sea conditions in this photograph illustrate the challenges of shooting on the open sea.

RIGHT: Keira Knightley and crew shooting on the desert island location in the Caribbean. **BELOW:** Orlando Bloom shoots a scene aboard the *Lady Washington*, the real world sailing ship that portrayed the *Interceptor* in the film.

Wallilabou Bay. And while St. Vincent may not have the white-sand beaches one might expect of a Caribbean isle, the filmmakers were able to go to nearby Petite Tabac and the Grenadines to achieve that look for select scenes. The outer islands of the Grenadines worked particularly well for the proverbial desert island where Barbossa maroons Jack (for a second time) and Elizabeth.

The tranquillity of the location did not, however, make the prospect of filming a movie that takes place primarily in, on, and around water any less daunting. Since the Caribbean sets were spread over essentially thirty-six miles of open sea, boats were not only used for filming, diving, and working, but for transportation.

For one particular two-week stretch, the company put out to sea like the actual pirates of the Caribbean hundreds of years before them. They filmed on the open waters eight to thirteen miles off the shores of Wallilabou Bay, where the art department had re-created Port Royal's harbor as well as a base camp for the crew. Up to four hundred people a day made the hour and a half, round-trip trek to Wallilabou and the surrounding inlets by boat. With waves swelling six to eight feet, most of the cast and crew were constantly popping seasickness pills.

From dawn to dusk, with no land in sight, even the most basic aspects of life became a major source of aggravation and a serious obstacle to production. "It's all true what they say about shooting in water," Gore says. "Everything that can go wrong will go wrong, that's just the way it works. Just feeding the crew, for example. You start shooting in the morning, and you're four miles out by the afternoon.

Suddenly you've got this armada behind you trying to catch up, chasing you with sandwiches."

At least they weren't trying to film the catering crew. The sea saved its most formidable challenges for when the cameras were rolling. "As soon as you get a boat in position, the wind changes," the director adds. "Even if you anchor things down, everything is moving, relationships are moving. The camera is here, and we frame a shot of the actor, everything is drifting away, so either the wind is right to fill the sails, but then, the sun is in the wrong direction and if you want a good backlight, then the sails are negative . . . " and on it goes.

In addition to losing valuable shooting time to an uncooperative sun and unruly wind and waves, the filmmakers' single biggest headache was maintaining continuity from one scene to the next, from the conditions of the sea to the color of the sky. You can't have a clear blue sky and a flat surface in one shot and storm clouds and six-foot swells in the next. "The hardest part from a director of photography's point of view was when we shot day exteriors," Dariusz Wolski says. "Normally when you shoot day exteriors, you know where the sun travels and you turn yourself around accordingly to maintain some continuity in lighting throughout the day. Now you're adding another element, which is a boat. And a boat is only going to go a certain way. It's going to go the way the wind blows."

Even setting the considerable technical issues aside, shooting on the water wreaked havoc on the actors, who had to be ready to give their performances on command as soon as weather or sea conditions were just right. "You would be waiting to do a really substantial, meaty, dialogue-driven scene on the deck," Geoffrey Rush explains, "and then the wind would change and the smoke would blow in the wrong direction. You would have to wait for seven boats to come around. It was painstaking . . . as it needs to be."

Chilling Effects

Skulls & Crossbones

Cutting-edge visual effects are a key component of any modern Hollywood blockbuster, but in the case of *Pirates of the Caribbean*, the film couldn't even have been made prior to the movie industry's fairly recent digital revolution. "Historically, Hollywood used to make these movies a lot, and then they just got too expensive," Gore Verbinski says. "With the advances in digital animation, you start to see all of these films coming back. You're basically taking what we've been doing in cel animation and making it photo real."

An epic pirate period film by itself would have been one thing, but the filmmakers were also making a ghost story at the same time. "We have an added ingredient in the film," says Jerry Bruckheimer. "And that's the supernatural aspect of the story. It lends itself to incredible visual effects, so we went to ILM (Industrial Light & Magic) because they've done a great job for us in the past."

"The visual effects on this picture fall into three categories," says John Knoll, visual effects supervisor. "There are the matte paintings used to establish environments, the ships at sea [since the filmmakers didn't have complete ships for the *Dauntless* and the *Black Pearl* like they did for the *Interceptor*], and the skeletal pirates." And ILM had to be ready to handle all of the varied cinematic illusions called for in the script, from putting the finishing digital touches on Port Royal and Tortuga to long shots of the *Dauntless* and the *Black Pearl* at sea to the full computer animation of Barbossa and his crew of the damned.

The ILM team had had a lot of experience creating entire alien worlds and veritable fleets of land and space vehicles in the *Star Wars* prequels. Using digital matte paintings to simulate an eighteenth-century British colony and the lawless port town of Tortuga, and sophisticated computer models to sail convincing tall ships were all in a day's work. But walking, talking, working, and fighting undead pirates were another matter. In some scenes, characters would go from living, breathing human actors to complicated live-action–computer animated hybrids and back again. Other scenes would be devoid of human actors; the effects artists would be responsible for building and animating dozens of digital performers.

The filmmakers looked at their computer-animated skeletal pirates as the twenty-first-century equivalent of Walt Disney's Audio-Animatronics performers. "Seeing the barking dog and the talking skeletons [in the attraction] made you question whether or not it was real," Gore says. "But today's audiences are savvier because of effects. We are using computer-generated animation to achieve that same reality for today's audience."

Like the Imagineers thirty-five years before them, John Knoll and his visual-effects team were responsible for creating the illusion of life in their animated performers. John and animation supervisor Hal Hickel began the process with sketches and an animatronic sample. "We started off by doing a lot of

ABOVE: Aaron McBride rendering of the "costume decay" for scenes featuring the cursed Barbossa. **OPPOSITE:** ILM study of the cursed Barbossa in a state of "extreme decay."

these early concept paintings of pirates in their skeletal cursed form," says visual-effects art director Aaron McBride.

John then spent countless hours with Gore and Jerry discussing just how to go about illustrating the pirates to find the perfect balance between living yet slowly decomposing at the same time. "A lot of effort went into designing what the pirates look like when they're skeletons, so that they would all have recognizable features," John says.

Visual effects were used not only when the actors are seen transforming into skeletons before the audience's eyes, but also when each character becomes a fully animated skeleton. The filmmakers did not want to use traditional stop-motion animation, á la Ray Harryhausen, or other comparable techniques used so frequently in mythical stories. "John Knoll and his team came up with some unique images that really impressed us," Jerry says. "The time constraints ILM had to work under were unspeakable. It's amazing the detail and care that's been taken."

The process of designing the skeleton pirate characters began with taking photographs of the

actors in full costume and makeup. "Then Aaron McBride spent time painting a version of each of them in skeletal form," John explains. "We went through a couple of revisions until we got approval from Gore on what these characters should look like."

Once Gore signed off on the look of the characters, the effects team took 3-D scans of all the actors. "So for each of the actors we've got a full-body scan, and we have a more detailed head scan," John adds. "We built one very detailed skeleton that has all the right bones in it. Since everyone's skeleton is a little bit different from everyone else's, the first step is to take the skeleton and kind of fit it properly inside the particular person's envelope, or 3-D scan. There's a lot of scaling and smushing to get it to fit."

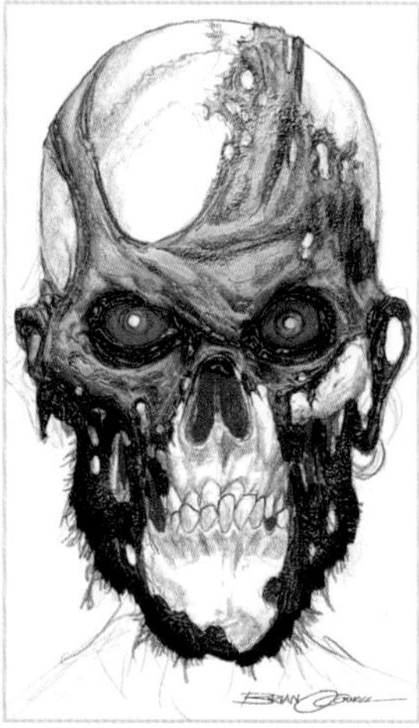

The designers built a few layers of skin by scanning turkey jerky into the computer to help them replicate what Aaron McBride calls "the dried and desiccated meat look" of the skeletal pirates' flesh. The team then painted the skin with different textures and transparencies to create a more complex look. "We have side-by-side comparisons to head shots that we got of the actors who were cast to play Barbossa's crew," Aaron explains. "We started by playing around with how much meat-to-bone ratio we wanted. For the character of Pintel, we actually took digital photos of turkey jerky and graphed in sort of this 'turkey-jerky' texture on top of a skull that we had taken a digital photo of as well. And then we added little flakes of skin coming off the chin and matted hair to give each one of the pirates their own unique pattern of decay."

TOP: ILM's Brian O'Connell created this concept painting of skeletal pirates. **MIDDLE:** Brian O'Connell rendering of the cursed Bosun. **LEFT:** Aaron McBride concept art of the cursed monkey, "Jack."

"It essentially starts with a modeling supervisor and the modeling staff building the exterior skin," says cloth-simulation supervisor James Tooley. "That'll go to what we call the view painters, and they make sure that it's got the proper color, that you get the right kind of microscopic bumps and detail."

LEFT: Early study by Sang Jun Lee of cursed Jack Sparrow. **BELOW:** Geoffrey Rush begins his digital makeover into the skeletal Barbossa.

In addition to their grisly amalgam of skin and bone, the characters all possessed different combinations of hair, clothing, and props. "The wardrobe is multilayered, and so we needed to simulate that so it all folds properly and interacts with all their props," John Knoll says. "A lot of them have sashes and muskets and swords and necklaces and all sorts of things that the cloth has to properly behave around."

The creation of these computer-generated costumes was an art unto itself, and the artists had to ensure that their digital "fabrics" worked with and not against the skin, muscles, and bones that had already been built into the characters. "The envelopers made sure that the skin the modelers generated followed the articulations of the bones that we'd put into the skeletal system," James Tooley adds. "Then we could continue to take other elements of their high-resolution geometry, such as the clothing, and start designing that so that if a creature spins around, the clothing sort of moves out a little bit or collides properly against the body.

"Ultimately, all of those different elements come into a hub of what we call the TDs, or technical directors," James finishes. "They took all that information and on each frame made sure that it had proper lighting and rendered it to make it look as photo real as we could get it."

Since the pirates would be seen in both their mortal and cursed forms throughout the film, a lot of work went into designing the individual characters to make them recognizable in both live-action and as computer-animated skeletons. "Some of them have particular bits of wardrobe or particular facial features that we carry through," John Knoll says. "Ragetti's got a wooden eye and he's skinny with bags under his eyes. Pintel has long hair and he's bald on top. Koehler has these really interesting dreadlocks; when he moves they sway all around. Twigg has a beard, and a knit cap with a big hole exposing skull through it. Jacoby has a very long beard, kind of in the form of dreadlocks, with fuses woven into it. When he's fighting they're lit, so they are smoking."

The results were convincing enough for the film's director, whose foremost concern was maintaining an actor's performance whenever their character took a digital form. "When you see the

characters as skeletons, you know immediately which pirate is which," Gore elaborates. "Even when they're one hundred percent computer generated and their clothing is in shreds, you'll know. Not just from the actor's voice, but from every nuance, which is why we shot entire scenes only as reference."

"One of the big challenges on this movie is the detail with which we have to mimic the actors' performances," says ILM animator Andrew Doucette. "That way we have something that's already been approved by the director and producer. It's a performance that they're happy with, and it's also a performance that's done by the actor who we're trying to emulate in the shots."

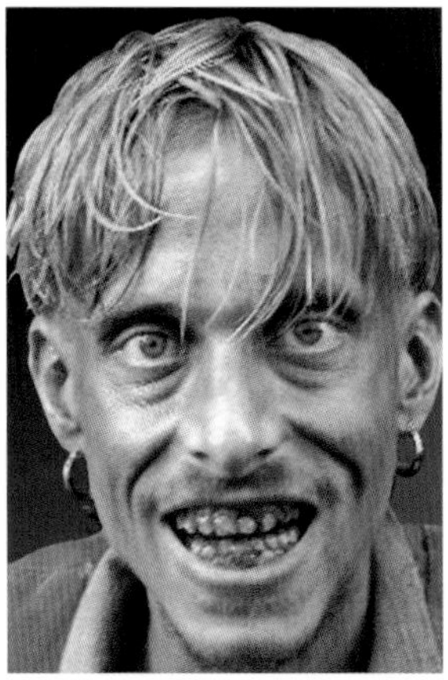

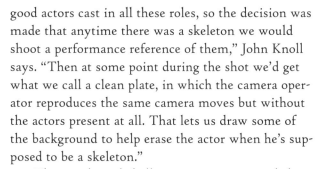

That meant the actors portraying the crew of the *Black Pearl* shot every scene in which their characters appeared, even the ones in which they would be completely replaced by their digital counterparts. The resulting reference footage gave the ILM team something to match when they went to reproduce the actors' performances in their computers. This process was the only way to preserve as much of the actors' original intent as possible and was the best defense against turning the pirates into "cartoons," even though that's technically what they were, albeit very sophisticated ones. "We have really good actors cast in all these roles, so the decision was made that anytime there was a skeleton we would shoot a performance reference of them," John Knoll says. "Then at some point during the shot we'd get what we call a clean plate, in which the camera operator reproduces the same camera moves but without the actors present at all. That lets us draw some of the background to help erase the actor when he's supposed to be a skeleton."

These technical challenges were compounded considerably in the many fight sequences in which the computer animated pirates interact with the human actors portraying the British sailors, forcing Gore and director of photography Dariusz Wolski to rely on a combination of skill and guesswork. "It wasn't only difficult for us, it was equally demanding for our stuntmen, our stunt coordinator, and ultimately, our cameramen," Gore states. "I wanted a lot of handheld composition during the swordplay. First we'd photograph the British navy and the pirates fighting as reference. Then we would have to shoot the British navy fighting alone in order to add the CGI skeletons. The guys are essentially fighting air,

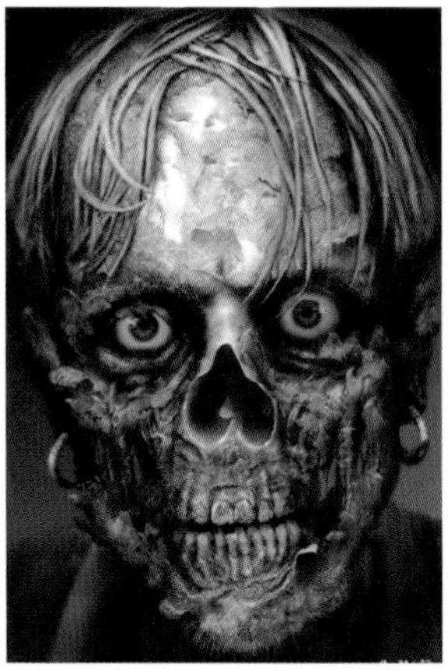

TOP: Barbossa mid-transformation. **ABOVE:** Mackenzie Crook as the dim-witted Ragetti, seen in sunlight (left) and moonlight (right).

which looks pretty silly by itself, and the cameramen would need to try to repeat every aspect of the previous take. We would photograph an actor fighting and then pan over to a skeleton that wasn't there, say his line of dialogue, and then pan to another bit of action. We had a lot of technical discussions on set about how to pull focus to a fictional point of reference while still keeping the excitement of a combat scene. I really didn't want to get into motion control or static compositions. John Knoll and the team at ILM let me keep it loose and intuitive. That's what gives those scenes their energy."

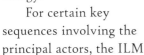

For certain key sequences involving the principal actors, the ILM team went beyond reference footage and turned to motion capture, a technique in which a computer literally captures an actor's movements through sensors strategically placed all over his body. Such was the case for the scene in which Jack Sparrow snatches a cursed coin in order to make himself temporarily immortal for his climactic duel with Barbossa. "One day I had to go in and put on this weird kind of track suit with tiny little Ping-Pong balls [sensors] on it and go through my actions," Johnny Depp recalls. "It's like when Geoffrey stabs me, I back up into the moonlight, so I had to basically redo the scene, but by myself wearing this bizarre uniform."

Once the digital animators had Johnny's physical performance captured in their computers, they could begin their established process of transforming him into a decaying corpse, just as they had with Barbossa and his crew. The key difference in this case was that the audience would see Johnny Depp's performance for themselves as opposed to an animator's interpretation of it culled from reference footage.

The filmmaker's unique vision of *Pirates of the Caribbean* was largely predicated on their story's supernatural component and the ghostly effects the "curse of the *Black Pearl*" has on Barbossa and his crew. There was no way they could have pulled it off without state-of-the-art visual effects that would enable audiences to accept the central conceit of pirates who transform from humans into skeletons and back again as they dart in and out of the moonlight.

ABOVE: Johnny Depp, "before" and "after" ILM got through with him. **BELOW:** Barbossa's metamorphosis is complete.

The Pirates Cast Off

The Curse is Lifted

The film wrapped production in March 2003 and spent a scant fourteen weeks in post production, an extremely aggressive schedule for an effects-laden film of its scope. In that time, Gore Verbinski and editor Craig Wood, along with editors Steve Rivkin and Arthur Schmidt, turned hundreds of hours of raw footage into a swashbuckling 143-minute adventure to rival the best of Hollywood's Golden Age. Meanwhile, up in Northern California, ILM worked their special brand of visual-effects magic, putting the finishing digital touches on hundreds of shots and adding the film's many computer-generated thespians. And composer Klaus Badelt (*K-19: The Widowmaker*, *The Time Machine*) contributed a sweeping and appropriately nautical score, lending an irresistible sense of mystery and suspense to the story's supernatural elements and driving the many action sequences home with its own pulse-pounding rhythm. The film was completed at a final cost of around $180 million (including $40 million to market), making it one of the biggest productions in Disney history.

The filmmakers and studio executives first suspected they had something special on their hands after the initial test screening. "The first preview was spectacular," Nina Jacobson recalls. "That's when we knew, when we went to that first screening. The second they saw the dog in the cell and started laughing—that's when we knew it was going to be more than a movie. It was going to be a cultural phenomenon." All that was left was for the film to sail into theaters.

Pirates of the Caribbean: The Curse of the Black Pearl premiered on June 28, 2003, at the place where it all began, Disneyland, and it was the Park's first movie premiere. The crowd roared its approval as stars Johnny Depp, Orlando Bloom, and Keira Knightley joined producer Jerry Bruckheimer and director Gore Verbinski for a procession down a red-carpeted Main Street, an unlikely sight that rivaled the wildest Hollywood opening. The film was shown on a floating movie screen in the middle of the Rivers of America, not far from the infamous bend in the river where the pirates were launched on their journey decades earlier.

The film opened in theaters across North America one week later, on July 9, 2003, and throughout the world in the following months. A film that the industry initially derided as a flimsy popcorn-movie rip-off of an amusement park kiddie ride earned $46 million during its opening weekend before going on to take in $305 million domestically, making it the third highest-grossing film of 2003, and $348 million internationally. The film's success was especially welcome considering that Dick Cook and Nina Jacobson had been championing the project from the moment Brigham Taylor and his team first pitched it in their page-and-a-half memo. "Dick and I really believed in it from the beginning," Nina says. "We

The epic, and expensive, ship-to-ship battle, shot on location in the Caribbean.

believed it would do over $200 million. We had faith. Now, we may have been completely out of our minds, but we thought it would work."

Even more important to the storytellers, the film won millions of fans around the globe, accelerating both Orlando Bloom and Keira Knightley's rise to superstardom, and making a bankable leading man out of the long artistically respected Johnny Depp. Since audiences and critics alike attributed a good part of the film's success to Johnny and his decidedly original take on Captain Jack Sparrow, Nina had no problem giving credit where credit was due on behalf of all the initial nonbelievers at the studio. "I sent Johnny a letter telling him that he was right in asking us to trust him," Nina says. "It was a learning experience for me, and I told him so." After the overwhelmingly positive response to his performance, Johnny Depp was not likely to encounter any such trust issues anytime soon.

Perhaps the ultimate vindication came in January, 2004, when Johnny's portrayal of Captain Jack Sparrow earned him an Academy Award nomination for Best Actor, in addition to earning a Golden Globe nomination for Best Actor and winning the Screen Actors Guild and MTV Movie Awards for Best Actor.

Pirates of the Caribbean: The Curse of the Black Pearl ultimately became the highest grossing live-action film in the history of Walt Disney Pictures. Not only did it become a bona fide cultural phenomenon that granted the studio its first live-action movie franchise, it did so utilizing a property with its feet firmly planted in Disney's storied past, which could not have been more fitting, according to Nina Jacobson. "Up until now, we haven't gotten to sit at the table with a live-action franchise like a *Harry Potter*, a *Lord of the Rings*, or a *Spider-Man*. To think that we'd finally get there with one of our own rides is incredibly thrilling. *Pirates of the Caribbean* is something that started with Walt Disney and still had the cultural relevance to become a phenomenon. This film is based on something that came directly from Walt's brain, and that's incredibly cool."

TOP: Ever the trickster, Jack Sparrow cheats death—with a little help from his friends at ILM.
RIGHT: Elizabeth Swann ponders her choices.

Charting a Course for the Future

And so, a pirate movie based on a theme park attraction inspired by classic pirate films brought Pirates of the Caribbean full circle, celebrating all it had been while illuminating everything it could be. At the movies, *Pirates of the Caribbean: The Curse of the Black Pearl* reinvented the pirate film and reestablished it as a viable genre. At Magic Kingdoms around the world, the film also introduced a whole new generation of fans to the attraction on which it is based, something that would have profound implications for both The Walt Disney Studios and Walt Disney Imagineering in the years following its release.

With no intention of losing its seat at the table, The Walt Disney Studios gave producer Jerry Bruckheimer and director Gore Verbinski the green light for not one but two sequels, to create a trilogy of films that tell one epic story. In the fall of 2004, Ted Elliott and Terry Rossio returned to the keyboard to chronicle the further adventures of Captain Jack Sparrow, Will Turner, and Elizabeth Swann, reuniting them with old friends and pitting them against old foes, along with enemies that have yet to reveal themselves. The two films went into production in February 2005, and were shot back-to-back. *Pirates of the Caribbean: Dead Man's Chest* is set for release in the summer of 2006, with the third installment slated to follow in the summer of 2007.

Meanwhile, back in the Magic Kingdom, guests can discover, or rediscover, the adventure that started it all, experiencing the original Disney magic and delighting in the indelible connections between attraction and film. At the same time, Imagineers are now at work making changes that will allow Captain Jack and his crew to sail into three dimensions at the Disney parks. There are now and will be entire generations of guests whose first experience with Pirates of the Caribbean might very well take place in a movie theater, creating a very different set of expectations that they will bring with them when they visit the Magic Kingdom. And so it is likely only a matter of time before the world sees an attraction based on a film adapted from another attraction inspired by still other films, taking Pirates of the Caribbean from the Magic Kingdom to the movies—and back again.

Of the future, only one thing is certain and perhaps Captain Jack himself put it best: "Bring me that horizon."

ABOVE: This Chris Turner attraction poster concept suggests that some familiar Pirates of the Caribbean will soon make a voyage from the movies to the Magic Kingdom. **BELOW LEFT AND RIGHT:** Concept art by Crash McCreery of Davey Jones, captain of *The Flying Dutchman*, and a candlelight vigil in the bayou, from *Pirates of the Caribbean: Dead Man's Chest.*